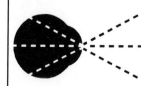

This Large Print Book carries the
Seal of Approval of N.A.V.H.

UNCONDITIONALLY SINGLE

Unconditionally Single

Mary B. Morrison

THORNDIKE PRESS

A part of Gale, Cengage Learning

 GALE
CENGAGE Learning™

Detroit • New York • San Francisco • New Haven, Conn • Waterville, Maine • London

GALE
CENGAGE Learning™

LIBRARY OF CONGRESS CATALOGING-IN-PUBLICATION DATA

Morrison, Mary B.
   Unconditionally single / by Mary B. Morrison.
      p. cm. — (Honey diaries series ; 3) (Thorndike Press large print African-American)
   ISBN-13: 978-1-4104-2090-9 (alk. paper)
   ISBN-10: 1-4104-2090-6 (alk. paper)
   1. African American women—Fiction. 2. Ex-prostitutes—Fiction. 3. Large type books. I. Title.
PS3563.O87477U53 2009
813'.54—dc22   2009034558

Published in 2009 by arrangement with Dafina Books, an imprint of Kensington Publishing Corp.

To Selena James, my wonderful editor

every second
of every day
singles have
the right of way

WHY I'M UNCONDITIONALLY SINGLE

Date:

Given to:

Given by:

Personal message:

ADVISORY

If you have not read the Honey Diaries, please note that *Unconditionally Single* is the third book in a trilogy. *Sweeter than Honey* is book 1 and *Who's Loving You* is book 2. I strongly advise reading the series in order. Enjoy!

PURPOSE OF BEING UNCONDITIONALLY SINGLE

PART I

unconditionally single — a person who understands his/her relationship needs, communicates effectively, willingly compromises, and refuses to settle

Before reading *Unconditionally Single,* I'd like for you to take a moment to identify your relationship needs. These are the things you must have in order to cultivate a healthy union with the person you'd like to marry or consider your life partner.

After identifying your needs, list your desires. These are the hobbies or things you enjoy and would love to do with or without your mate.

Next, let your imagination explore your deepest childhood and sexual fantasies. Take a moment to do this now.

Some of you already know; others wonder, What is my passion? You absolutely positively *must* permit yourself personal time to discover your passion. What drives you? Excites you? Exhilarates you? Your primary passion usually stems from a greater humanitarian purpose. For me, I love my son unconditionally and I live to write. I write to live. I write to make a positive difference in somebody's life. I pray that person is you.

I find that most individuals cannot *readily* identify their personal or relationship needs. Nor do they discuss being in a relationship with a prospective mate. They kind of meet a person they're attracted to, then they stumble into "like," trip into love, then slip into hate or resentment — never having asked the other person, "What are your relationship needs?" Or "What do you need from me in order for us to have a healthy relationship?"

Somewhere along the way, perhaps months, maybe years after meeting, they get to know one another for real. They tire of being possessed or possessive. Qualities once admired become annoying. Some find out that money and material acquisitions — the house, the car, the clothes — are more important to their mate than love. The one with the most money feels entitled to control the other person. Sex once a day, once a week, once a month, or in some cases once a year is either too much or not enough. In creeps emotional and physical infidelity. "If my woman or my man refuses to fulfill my needs, *I have the right* to get my sexual needs met elsewhere." The person who makes this decision becomes upset if he or she discovers the mate cheating. In creep disrespect, misery, and relationship disaster.

When a woman or teenage girl gets pregnant, she automatically expects the man to do all the right things for her and their child. Most women hope the man will marry her because she's carrying his baby. Instead, the man feels trapped. He stands on the fifty-yard line for nine months like he's watching a football game — drinking beer, chilling with his boys, bragging about his other woman, what he did to and with her last night. All the while he's waiting for the fourth quarter to end, waiting for her third trimester to conclude, and praying there is a flag on the play, that his request for a review of the play — a DNA test — will reveal he is not the father, mainly so he doesn't have to pay child support. But he'd flip a coin on the child's paternity, not caring if he gets heads or tails as long as she'll let him fuck her again.

Clueless about how much day care, diapers, and the daily cost of providing for a child is, she gives birth, barely closing her legs before her six-week checkup and he's back. Clueless that one night of pleasure could bring her a lifetime of emotional and financial hardships, she ends up pregnant again. So goes the story.

The natural progression of blind love and lust eventually leads to resentment for both partners. Thus begins the battle of the sexes to see who can emotionally and physically destroy the other person first. These relationship tragedies can be avoided or minimized through effective communication and safe sex; more importantly, both individuals must enter the relationship knowing their needs.

Unconditionally single does not mean you don't desire marriage. I'm encouraging you to know yourself, know what you need and desire before getting married or becoming involved with someone. The majority of people do not know what wedding vows they are committing to on the day they marry. Please, if you're getting married, I strongly advise you to write your own vows. Do not stand at the altar reciting commitments you've never read.

Unless you are 100 percent sure you want to be a parent, do not get pregnant. Share what's important to you with your potential mate. I urge all men and women to read The Honey Diaries series and *Single Husbands* before getting married.

On my way from the 2008 Antigua & Barbuda Literary Festival, I boarded the plane in Antigua to Miami, settled in my window seat. A newly married couple sat next to me, the wife to my immediate right, her husband next to her. The seemingly happy, giddy, constantly kissing couple couldn't keep their hands off each other. He lived in Canada. They were headed to Los Angeles to pack her belongings, then drive to their new residence in Canada. Halfway through the flight the husband pulls out two sandwiches, looks at his wife, and asks, "Do you like rye? I wasn't sure. Or would you prefer the other sandwich?"

My eyebrows raised as I continued reading — Eric Jerome Dickey's *Sleeping with Strangers* — thinking, *They barely know one another.* Obviously he liked rye, he'd purchased the sandwiches, and he didn't ask what she wanted. How well should a couple know one another before marrying? Too many marriages end in divorce because people not only sleep with strangers, they marry strangers. Oh well. That couple are probably of the majority who wander in and out of love, life, and relationships wondering why they keep choosing the wrong mates.

I hear some of you asking, "What are Mary B. Morrison's needs, since she has all the answers?"

Honestly, I don't have all the answers but I am a thinking woman and I do know my passions, talents, what excites me, and I understand my needs. Like you, as I continue to grow emotionally, my needs change. My basic needs are always clear. I'll share what's important to me in the Purpose of Being Unconditionally Single Part II at the end of this novel.

How can we avoid marrying virtual strangers? We can start by talking to them more often. Ladies, one of the things I do often because I seldom cook is dine at nice restaurants. If I'm eating alone, I never request a table. I sit at the bar . . . strategically next to a great-looking man whenever possible. I'll also talk to whoever's seated next to me. I've met lots of wonderful women and couples of all races that way. And I frequently engage the bartender in conversation. Genuine compliments are perfect icebreakers. My topics are improvised, but if you're shy, develop a few questions you're comfortable asking. Here are a few tips:

- I smile and introduce myself.
- I ask the bartender and the man next to me, "Can you recommend a succulent appetizer?" I ask in such a way to determine if his attention is on the menu or me. I stay focused on the menu.
- I offer to share my appetizer. I love oysters and calamari.
- I find out if he's local or visiting. If he's local, I ask, "Where was the last place you vacationed?" If he's visiting, "So where do you live?" If I haven't been to his city/state/country, I ask him questions about his town.
- Eventually I engage him in relationship talk. "I'm trying to understand men more. What's most important to you and why?"

If he's interested on a personal level, he'll express his likes. A clear sign that a man is not interested is when he mentions his girlfriend, wife, kids, or family first. That's the perfect time to pick his brain about relationships because he's already in one. Once I tell a man I write erotica, married or not he tells me his deepest secrets and fantasies. Then he wants to know more about me. The most common questions I get are: Do you write from experience? Have you been with a woman? Have you had a ménage à trois? Seriously, this happens to me all the time.

Men love to talk openly about relationships, but not with their mates because they have to censor their thoughts. Men love to feel they are educating us. I believe that in reality women are smarter; however conversations work best when ladies are friendly but allow men to take the lead. Women have to follow through with intelligent, intriguing responses. You can ask, "Are you saying that you prefer a woman who cooks or are you saying you have to have a woman who cooks? What if she loves cooking but the food sucks?" Make him laugh.

I'm not reserving or preserving myself or praying for God to send me Mr. Right. Waiting for one good man to call all mine is a waste of my time. I enjoy each man to the extent that I'm interested in him.

To get a glimpse into my outlook on life, read my favorite book in the Bible, Ecclesiastes. After reading the book of Ecclesiastes, you will better understand my definition of *Unconditionally Single* and the significance of your consciously determining what is meaningful to you and why.

PROLOGUE:
HONEY

Sometimes a woman had to kill herself to survive.

My mother hated me. My father disowned me. Stepfather molested me. Johns used me. My ex-husbands abused me. I had scars on my heart. Blood on my thirty-year-old hands. Despite my hardships, I held my head high. I'd learned that bad things happened to good people. My life was bad. My heart was good.

I hadn't overcome countless trials and tribulations to exhale my last breath without dignity. The one man who truly loved me for me, I'd pushed away. If I died, right here, right now, I'd regret not telling Grant, "Baby, I love you. Forgive me." Determined to get my man back, stand at the altar, repeat after the minister, "I, Honey Thomas, take you, Grant Hill, to be my lawfully wedded husband . . ." and give birth to our children, I had to escape.

21

As I stared down the barrel of his .22-caliber pistol, my ex-man Benito pointed at the one place I was sure he would like to blast all of his bullets — my mouth. Eradicate his troubles, his jealousy, his insecurities, his love, his hate, his pain by shutting my — scintillating, candid, sharp, sarcastic, independent — ass up for good.

I stared into Benito's eyes. Women living in fear died at the hands of heartless men who were never worthy of their love. Good pussy made men do strange things. Isolate women. Stalk women. Kill women. Benito didn't want me; his ego didn't want another man to have me.

"What are you waiting for?" I asked Benito, pointing my gun at him. "Shoot me or let me go."

Too many women who were emotionally buried alive suffered in silence. Compromising their children, bartering their bodies, sacrificing their souls, surrendering their sanity in exchange for having a man, in many cases a man who didn't love, appreciate, respect, or deserve them.

Benito pleaded, "Lace, please don't make me do this. Put the gun down."

No way in hell was I going to die, not like this. Held hostage in a parking lot, a deserted guard shack in the distance. Abandoned brick buildings with broken windows created an eerie backdrop. The wind howled like a pack of hungry wolves preparing to feast on me. If my kidnappers killed me, then tossed my body inside one of those buildings, who'd think to search there for my remains?

I panic. They panic. Didn't want to die from freaking them out.

Valentino said to me, "I never imagined you'd cross me. Bitch, I am the one who got you off your back and you fucking steal my money." Then he spoke into his cell phone. "Onyx, if you want to see Lace alive, the ransom is non-negotiable — fifty million dollars."

The muscle in my calf cramped — horrible timing for the onset of a charley horse. I flexed my toes, inched toward the edge of the SUV. There was enough space between the two men for me to get out of the trunk. Benito stood to my left, Valentino to my right.

The chain-link metal fence surrounding the lot stood ten feet high. If I got a good running start, I could climb the fence, but the rusted barbed wire at the top made me change my mind. A bent STOP sign partially blocked the lot's exit, its pole rested horizontal to the ground. I could hurdle it praying my heels didn't get caught on the hem of my pants. Didn't want to be the chick in the scary movie who'd escape, run, trip, fall, and be killed.

Flexing my toes far back as I could, I kept quiet while Valentino barked out his demands to Onyx. Onyx had become my number-one escort after my favorite escort, Sunny, was killed. The one year I worked as Valentino's madam was my worst year in the business. Sunny Day was a gorgeous twenty-year-old girl who should've never started prostituting. Her parents loved her. Her twin sister adored her. The day I'd planned to send Sunny home to her family, Valentino refused to let her go. He'd shot Sunny in the head. A part of my spirit died that day. The six hundred thousand dollars Valentino paid me for those twelve months wasn't worth Sunny dying.

I tried calming myself with *there's nothing to fear but fear itself.* The words sounded great but with a gun a few feet from my face, I felt only one emotion: fear. Terror. They didn't know that was my truth. My reality was fear. Perspiration slicked my palms, making it difficult to hold my gun. Toes curled back, I alternated wiping my hands on my pants.

Valentino frowned, told Benito, "Nigga,

don't watch me. Keep your eyes on that bitch." He bit his bottom lip, then said, "Onyx, you used to work for me. I know how you think. Don't fucking insult my intelligence. Make it happen today or else I'm coming after you."

Less than a block from us a few cars traveled east and west on University Avenue. Hotlanta commuters were too far away to notice the SUV I was trapped inside. Were they preoccupied with the declining economy, saving their homes from foreclosure, or worried about how the 11.1 million unemployed would impact them? Maybe they were en route to a Waffle House for breakfast. I had no idea where those people were going. What I did know was that none of them noticed me.

Summer visited winter. Sweat covered my breasts, arms, stomach, and back, causing my silk shirt to stick to my skin, irritating me more. Thoughts of not seeing Grant again motivated me to do whatever it took to get out of this situation. Dying was not an option.

Silently I prayed, *Dear God, please don't let me become a statistic.* I tried bartering with God. *God, do not, please hear me, do not let me die without fulfilling my purpose to help save the women who've given up on get-*

ting out of unhealthy relationships. Don't I get some credit for using Valentino's money to retire the remaining eleven girls? Answer my prayer and I promise You I'll help a victim every day of my life. If that wasn't what He wanted to hear, I said, *God, You gave me a brain, courage, and a heart. Tell me which one to use first before I kill both of these fools.*

Benito stood there tilting his head side to side. "V, can you make arrangements for us to meet with Onyx? You're burning up my minutes, man."

During the time we dated, Benito accepted, though he seldom acknowledged, women were smarter than men. I was smarter than him. He hated my constant reminders that I was the one who'd paid the bills the three years he lived in my house. Didn't need him for much outside of sex. Proved it to him often. The day I'd tied him up, shoved a gun up his ass, left him in my bed in Las Vegas, I'd hoped was — the same as with my first and second husbands — the last time I'd see him.

I saw Benito again on Thanksgiving Day when I arrived at Grant's parents' place in Washington, D.C. He was seated at the dinner table. Benito was worse than a bad penny, making my world smaller than I desired in a bad luck kind of way. One step away from him, two back.

I kept staring at Benito. I should've remained his number-one fan instead of dating him. His wide shoulders aligned with his waist. His thick body, solid not fat, was the same as when I'd met him. Flat abs. Full lips. Muscular thighs. He'd gained a few pounds. Though his career was over, his football physique was intact. Benito was an excellent lover. His face had changed, though not his warm brown eyes or smooth toffee skin. It was the wild hairy beard I hadn't seen before.

I prayed silently again, *Lord, please don't let this man be my destiny.*

Our breakup made me realize I barely knew Benito. When we were together, Benito seldom talked about his family. Gave me no indication he had a half brother. Whenever he mentioned his childhood, he blamed his adoptive white mother for screwing up his life. College scholarships, multiple multimillion-dollar football contracts, and Benito was the same as O. J. — broke. No one took Benito's money; he'd given it away before we met. Pretended he still had it going on. Lied his way into my heart and my house. Communication between us had gotten so bad, I didn't bother putting him out. I left. According to him, nothing was ever his fault.

I asked Benito, "Haven't I given you enough?"

Valentino answered, "I don't give a fuck what you gave him. Bitch, you stole my money, not his."

"Why do you think I have fifty million?"

"Bitch, I've got eyes in the back of my head. I can tell you every time you take a piss."

Here we go. I was tired of men trying to scare women into submission. Who'd betrayed me? Who'd told Valentino where I live? It had to be one of the girls.

Valentino could charm or intimidate other women, not me. His hair was slicked into a luxurious ponytail that hung between his shoulder blades. His black hair was as long as mine. My black hair was dyed blond to match my golden complexion and highlight my natural green eyes. His blemish-free cocoa face was chiseled, strong, defined, and hairless with the exception of his full brows, long lashes, and trimmed mustache. His voice was seductive when soft, harsh when deepened. The two both stood about six feet two inches. Difference was Valentino was slim, not thick like Benito.

"I just want alimony," Benito said, shuffling his feet.

28

What? I never married that fool. His nervous energy bothered me. Was he imitating a boxer or preparing to swing at me? I wished he would. Put down his gun and I'd bust him in his head with mine.

Valentino told Benito, "Nigga, you mean palimony. That's not a bad idea."

I became enraged at them, more at Benito's pathetic behind. Wanted to shove my gun up his ass again. Tired, frustrated, angry, I found courage to pull the trigger. "Take this," I said, firing my .45, not knowing, not giving a fuck whose head I'd put a bullet in first.

CHAPTER 1
HONEY

Pow! Pow! Pow! Pow!

As I fired the pistol, my body hammered against the mat, forcing me back a few inches deeper inside the SUV. Four gold bullet shells lay in front of me. I had nine rounds left plus one in the chamber. I prayed I'd make it out of this situation alive. The sound of police sirens blaring close by, then fading in the distance gave little hope of my being rescued. My only option — escape. I squinted at the beaming sunshine, searching for an answer to my prayer.

Brain? Courage? Heart?

I should've put each bullet in Benito's forehead. I couldn't. I once loved him. How did we get here? How does any couple go from love to hate, a hate so deep they could kill one another? I was still in love with Benito's brother but this was not the time to have compassion for my enemies. Grant's abandonment of my heart made him my enemy too. He should've been man enough to stay with me.

"Ah!" Benito screamed soprano when the shots were fired, ducked, covered his face, peeped at me between his parted fingers. His .22 fell, clacked three times on the pavement, spun, stopped in front of his feet.

I flexed my toes. The charley horse had subsided. Pressing my lips together, I swallowed my chuckle. Benito's reaction reassured me I'd done right getting rid of him. Former pro-quarterback champion punking out in a shoot-out, intentionally grounding his weapon, terrified of being defeated by a female. If I were a referee, I'd throw a flag on the play, give Benito a fifty-yard penalty, and restrain him from coming near me again. Why was I still protecting Benito? Kill Benito, kill all my chances of getting back with Grant.

Lying knees to chin in the trunk, messing up my red designer pantsuit, inhaling exhaust fumes along with the new car scent oozing from the mat, I aimed my gun at Valentino's head. My target. The same place I'd shot and killed his bodyguard, Reynolds Ramsey, between the eyes. I wouldn't miss, if my brain prevailed.

Aw, damn. My cellular was partially exposed. Rolling onto my side, I hid my cell phone. The only person I'd phoned repeatedly in transit to this deserted location was the woman who'd given me Valentino's money and the one woman who could track down any man in America and wouldn't hesitate to kill him. Sapphire Bleu. Called her repeatedly, something they didn't need to know. Left her one message not to call me back. I'd call her again when it was safe.

"What the fuck is your problem, Valentino?" I said. "Onyx is not going to listen to you. Hand me your goddamn phone," keeping my gun and eyes fixed on him, with Benito in my peripheral vision.

"Benito, if you bend over to pick up that gun, I'll slap you upside your head, then shoot you in your ass."

Standing, Benito brushed his dingy black slacks, squinted, stared over his shoulder as though trying to figure out how I'd shoot him in the ass while he faced me. Maybe I should ask God to give him a brain.

"Nigga, I knew I shouldn't have trusted you with the gun," Valentino spat out. "Fuck what she say. Pick up the gun and shoot that bitch."

The last time I'd seen Valentino was the day Sapphire arrested him at his mansion in Las Vegas. Sapphire gave me a way out of the business without my having to figure out how to exit alive. What if she'd given him a way out too? Would Valentino have had a reason to kidnap me? I had what Valentino desperately needed. Kill me and he'd never get what he'd come for.

Why were these low-down dirty bastards agitating me to the point of wanting to blow their brains out? I could kill them both. Splatter the cells God intended as two male masterpieces against the scorching asphalt beneath their insidious souls. No one would know. But I didn't want to go to jail or go insane without Grant in my life.

Curling into the fetal position, I pulled the trigger to scare Valentino. Waited a few seconds, pulled it again. Valentino dodged my first bullet, escaped the second. He moved in the right direction both times.

"Slowly toss me the damn phone before I kill your ass for real!" I growled.

Valentino tossed his cellular inside the trunk. "Shoot her ass, nigga," he said to Benito. "Don't just stand there! You want her to kill me?"

I wanted to laugh. One toy gun between the two of them and it was on the ground next to Benito's worn black shoes that curled at the toes.

Valentino tightened his fingers into fists. "Bitch, you gon' give me my money before

I bash your face in."

This time I had to do it. "Ha-ha, ha-ha-ha," I belted from my belly, keeping my gun aimed at Valentino. "Benito, get the gun. Give it to me." I pressed the speaker button on Valentino's phone, hoping Onyx was still on the line. I laid the phone on the mat, kept my gun aimed at him.

Money was the root of evil for the person who didn't have any. The cash was mine, a gift from Sapphire. I didn't owe Valentino shit. Neither did she. Easy come, easy go. "You didn't bust one nut for that money."

"The one I bust inside your pussy don't count?" Valentino asked.

I hated to admit. Valentino and I were more alike than we were different. I'd fucked him once and it wasn't bad. If we'd met under more amicable circumstances, would we be friends?

My assistant Onyx shouted, "Honey, tell us where you are."

"McDaniel and University."

"At the university?"

Benito frowned at Valentino, eased toward me, kicked the gun closer to Valentino. Shifting my aim from Benito, I quickly pointed the gun back between Valentino's eyes. Coldly stared at him. Eased back the trigger.

"One wrong move and you're dead. I intentionally missed the first time. You're bad. Go on. Try me."

Benito sadly asked, "You fucked my girl, V?"

"Pussy can't come between us, nigga. Let's go. That bitch is crazy."

Sometimes a woman had to be a bitch to get a man's attention. But I wasn't crazy. I was a woman who didn't take shit off abusive men. Not any more. Dealing with two life-threatening marriages and these two fools here, I should be crazy, but I wasn't. The only people I was crazy about were Grant and my deceased sister, Honey.

I'd killed myself on paper, buried my birth name, *Lace St. Thomas,* then resurrected my sister's name, *Honey,* dropped the *St.* and kept the *Thomas.* Maybe if I were more like Honey, my past life of prostitution, being a madam and a murderess would perish and never return to haunt me.

"Onyx, I got this. Don't hang up. Stay with me."

"What? You're naked? I think we have a bad connection."

Valentino stooped to the ground, crawled alongside the car. "Lock that bitch in the trunk and let's go! I'ma personally put a bullet to the back of her head!"

Always smarter than Valentino's wannabe pimp ass, I'd organized and ran his escort service, Immaculate Perception. Managed his twelve escorts for a year. Now they were my girls, all except the one he'd killed. Losing Sunny made me retire the survivors from their pain and suffering, give them restitution, and let them live with me. I was proud of them and myself. They were no longer prostitutes and I was no longer a madam. Whoever said "Money doesn't matter" had enough of it.

Valentino had sufficient time to do whatever he'd intended. Instead he ran like a bitch. Valentino wasn't a coward — he was outgunned. He'd be back. I'd be prepared for his return. Next time I wouldn't have a heart. No talking. I'd shoot to kill.

I pointed my gun at Benito. He hadn't moved.

"Lace." His eyes softened. "Please give Valentino back his money. He'll give me half. Forget paying me alimony. I'll take care of you. You deserve that much from me. I met you first. My brother doesn't love you the way I do. I know you better than Grant ever will."

"Nigga, this ain't *Deal or No Deal,*" Valentino said from the driver's seat. "And it's *palimony,* not *alimony,* nigga. Lock that smart-ass bitch in the fucking trunk and let's go."

Benito whispered, "Give us the money, Lace. I could never hurt you. Can't you see I'm still in love with you? I'd die before I'd kill you."

With no gun, he was right. Aim. Click. Turn. *Pow, pow! Pow, pow!* I shattered the front windshield, reminding those fools if they drove off with me in the trunk, that was their death sentence.

Benito reached for my ankles. I reached for Valentino's cellular. Two inches too far, I couldn't grab the phone. Benito pulled me out of the trunk. I stumbled to my feet watching him scramble into the passenger's seat as Valentino sped over the STOP sign and out the gate. With the rear door in midair, the SUV disappeared north down McDaniel Street.

Damn, their gun was on the ground and Valentino's cell phone and mine were in the trunk of their SUV. "Fuck. Now what?" I was certain that SUV belonged to Valentino's baby mama, Summer. Some women really were insane. How could Summer love Valentino after he'd killed her twin sister, Sunny? I couldn't figure that out. Maybe Summer was plotting revenge for her sister.

No money. No phone. No transportation.

But two guns. I stood in the middle of the deserted parking lot, placed my gun back in the holster under my arm. Tucked their gun inside my pants behind my back, exhaled, then said, "It's too early and too hot for this bullshit."

Red stilettos clicking against the black sweltering asphalt, sweat dripping from my head, soaking my hair, rolling behind my ears, down my neck, I was too exhausted to cross the street to the paved sidewalk. I trampled on the grass instead. Bypassing a hair salon, a restaurant, I walked up University Avenue through the heat wave toward the interstate.

I was too weak to drag my aching body and throbbing feet underneath the freeway to the north entrance of I-75/85 and hitchhike home to Buckhead. I leaned against a pole with a black and white sign that read 54-S and held up my thumb.

CHAPTER 2
RED VELVET

If the women took care of the women, the world would be a better place.

I'd come to Honey's office to invite my girl to lunch. Pop champagne and celebrate my exciting news. Thanks in part to Honey, I was on my way to Hollywood to star in my first feature film, *Something on the Side*. My juicy booty and big titties wore my leopard hip-hugging dress that stopped right above my knees. My mani and pedi were the new hot color all the celebs were sporting since Obama was elected, black. My long brown hair swayed across my back. My juicy red lips and dramatic eyelashes commanded attention. Honey told me it was better for a woman to command attention by the way she presented herself. Stripping for a few years at Stilettos, the switch in my hips made men beg to lick my clit.

Posing with my hand on my hip, I was not prepared to hear Onyx tell me, "Honey has been kidnapped." Honey didn't adhere to the law, she lived by her own rules. I had to admit her methods were unorthodox but highly effective. I prayed Honey was okay.

Kneeling on the plush gray carpet, I buried my face in my hands and screamed, "Noooo," then held tight to Onyx's smooth-shaven leg. Clawing my way up her skirt, I held her curvy hips, gripped her waist, then clamped her biceps. Her muscles were firm, her stance was weak as mine. My trembling hands slowly slid down her silky jet black skin to her long slender fingers. I interlocked my fingers with hers, then squeezed real tight before letting go. Two inches from her face, I cupped my wet cheeks, crying between sniffles. "Where is Honey? Please tell me where she's at. Is she all right? What are we waiting for? Let's go get her."

Onyx held up her hand. "Red Velvet, please stop. You're not helping."

I backed away from Onyx. She wasn't aware of my feelings for Honey. I was Honey's first pro bono client. Honey had tracked down my son's father, Alphonso, blackmailed him, got me seventy-two grand in back child support from the creep, a sleazebag who'd raped and impregnated me, then threatened me not to call him ever again 'cause he didn't want his wife to know

41

he'd fathered our son, Ronnie.

Onyx and I were alone in the office. Onyx came to me, held the phone behind my back, hugged me, pulled my nose to hers, then whispered, "I'm scared too. Before you walked in, I heard gunshots."

"Huh . . . gun?" I cried. "God, no. Don't take Honey." I was four years younger than Honey. An only child with a child, I'd felt like Honey's baby sister when she'd come to my aid.

Onyx slapped her palm to my mouth, smearing my red lipstick. Her large brown irises swept hard against her eyelids, loosening the edge of her lash. "If he hurts Honey, I swear, I'ma kill him. No questions asked."

Could I kill? For my son, definitely. My mother, absolutely. Honey, maybe. Honey believed in my dreams of becoming an actor. She'd accompanied me to Los Angeles to meet with my agent and took us to Alphonso's house unannounced so that Ronnie could meet his father for the first time. When Honey boldly invited herself, my mother, and Ronnie in, I stayed in the car. While questioning Alphonso and his wife about Ronnie, Honey discovered Alphonso was Sapphire's stepfather and later learned from Sapphire that the scumbag had repeatedly raped Sapphire when she was sixteen.

42

The triangle of triumphs uniting Honey, Sapphire, and me was no coincidence. Scared to tell her mother, Sapphire became a runaway or as the system had labeled her, voluntarily missing. At the age of sixteen, Honey had been kicked out of her house. I'd never met Honey's mother but any woman who'd put her child out was mean.

My mom would never put me out. Not much to say about my dad. No man I'd ever met had put me first, including my dad. Not the way Mr. President treated our First Lady. I saw the love in President Obama's eyes for his wife, Michelle, his daughters, Sasha and Malia. I wanted a man to feel that way about me. The possibility existed. I knew it did the moment I saw how Grant looked through me (without speaking a word) and saw Honey. I felt his love for her was ingrained in his eyes, his heart, his pores, his spirit, and his delicate touch. Grant and Mr. President showed me that if a man didn't look into my eyes with passion and compassion, that meant he was reserving that special part of himself for someone else.

It was too quiet in the office. Onyx's face was expressionless as she held the phone to her ear. "What are they saying?" I asked her.

"Nothing. I'm pissed at Valentino. He

didn't earn the money. We did." Onyx mumbled, "Men ain't shit."

I'd lost faith in men when my father abandoned me, left my mother to bear the burden of raising me alone. Had my father forgotten I was alive? He'd taken the initiative to get my mom pregnant, but did he expect me to take the initiative to contact him? There was a part of me that maintained hope that all men were not selfish like Valentino and my father. So far, I'd been wrong. I refused to give up my dream of believing good single men existed. Had to maintain that sparkle in my eyes so my son wouldn't become the type of man his father was. And so my childbearing hips could spit out a baby for my future husband. Whoever he was.

No pity party for Velvet Waters. I was blessed. Thanks to my mother, I knew love and I knew how to love. I was grateful to have a mother who sacrificed treating herself like a queen in order to make me her princess. Couldn't imagine life without my mother. Other than my mom, Honey was the only woman who had shown me love. I had to help find Honey but had no idea where to go.

Onyx wiped her tears. "Before you came in, Valentino demanded his money back.

Wants me to get it to him. I'll gladly give him the million dollars Honey gave me. I'm sure the other girls would do the same, but he wants fifty million, not eleven. If I don't get him what he wants, I don't know what he'll do. . . . He might . . ." Onyx drew me closer to her.

What was I getting into? Scared, I cried harder, praying my life wasn't endangered over money I didn't have or have access to. Onyx spoke about millions of dollars as though it was no big deal. Honey was a megamillionaire? I stared at the dangling black diamonds in Onyx's ears, the Rolex watch, and the large square emerald surrounded by diamonds. The ring fit comfortably on her middle finger. Onyx was rich for real? The other girls were too? They seemed so ordinary, down to earth. I was more diva-ish than Onyx. With so much going on, I hadn't dwelled on the fact that thanks to Honey, I too would become a millionaire once I made it to Hollywood and picked up my check from my agent.

Pulling away from Onyx, I matched the intensity of her hatred for a man I hadn't met. "You sure you heard gunshots?" I was outraged. A real man would never take money from a woman. Before she answered, my voice escalated. "Who the fuck does

Valentino think he is? Where is he? I'ma kick his ass." I was cute but I'd fight if I had to. Kicking his ass was better than killing him.

Onyx pressed the mute button on the phone, then raised the phone to her ear. "This isn't Hollywood, Red Velvet. Stop acting. This shit is real. Valentino might try to kill all of us." Her large breasts repeatedly rose and fell. I suffocated, forgot to breathe. This nightmare had to end.

CHAPTER 3
RED VELVET

Standing in Honey's office of Sweeter than Honey, I told myself, "Think, Velvet." I noticed the place was immaculate. How much had she paid for the chocolate desk with platinum trimming facing the door? The plush wall-to-wall carpet? On the opposite side of the room, beyond the ceiling-to-floor glass window, was a chocolate round table covered with a custom mirror, surrounded by six white leather chairs. Surveillance cameras inside black domes were mounted on the ceiling. How much could we get for the office and the furniture?

A tall, thin woman about six feet tall stormed into the office, interrupting my thoughts. "Help me, please! My husband is threatening to kill me if I leave him. He's crazy! He'll do it. He's following me. I have to hide."

Reacting as though she was accustomed to the woman's type of behavior, Onyx firmly told her, "Get behind my desk and be quiet. I'm in the middle of a crisis." Onyx retrieved a key from her bra, opened one of the lower desk drawers, removed a .45, all while she continued holding the phone to her ear with her other hand.

Bam! The office door swung open. I jumped aside. A madman approached me. "Where's my woman?"

Click. Onyx pointed the gun at his face. "Get the fuck out of here and don't come back unless you want a bullet in your head. She doesn't want you."

His flaming red eyes scanned the conference room. "I saw her come in here. I'm not leaving without my woman," he grunted.

Onyx calmly sat the phone on her desk, pointed the gun at his head. "You've got three seconds to leave. One . . . two . . ."

"Don't shoot him!" the woman yelled, coming from behind the desk. "Please don't kill my husband."

Click. Onyx pointed the gun at the woman, told her, "Get out of my office."

"No, no. It's okay. Shoot *him*," the woman said, backing away from Onyx. Her eyes moved in different directions but she hadn't looked at her man. "I can't take him beating me. Help me, please."

Help her? I had to rescue Honey first.

"You're going to regret this day," the man said, backing up toward the door. "You've got to come home eventually and when you do, I'ma beat your ass so bad you'll wish you were dead." He shot her a menacing glare before leaving.

"Get her an intake form. Put her in the conference room. I'll help her later," Onyx said, putting the gun in the drawer. She locked the drawer, placed the key in her bra.

I escorted the woman to the conference room. "Have a seat, fill this out, and stay here. I'll be back," I said, closing the glass door, returning to Onyx.

Onyx's eyes closed. Tears streamed over her cheeks, staining her sleeveless gold silk blouse. Her mouth opened. Blackberry lips parted, exposing chocolate gums that complimented white teeth. Circling her long black ponytail in her palm, she jammed the phone to her ear, squinted. She was taking too long to say something. I snatched the phone from her hand.

Onyx waved at me. "I was listening. Waiting. Do not hang up. Honey said, 'Don't hang up.' Things got quiet but I think she's still on the other end. Oh, God, help us, please." rubbing her palms on her skirt, Onyx paced the floor, circled her desk.

I pressed the phone to my ear, heard lots

of static.

Onyx cried. "He's serious. He killed Sunny and he'll kill Honey. Valentino is crazy. He's going to kill her if he doesn't get his money back. I know he will."

Killed Sunny? His money back? Honey had stolen his money? I had to find my replacement for my acting gig. "I'ma call Grant. He'll straighten this out. Grant is a real man and he'll kick Valentino's ass." I scrolled my electronic phonebook.

I'd saved Grant's number in my phone when my ex-boss, Trevor Williams, owner of Stilettos, arranged for me to pleasure Grant. I'd sexed Grant so Grant would partner with Trevor on a real estate development deal. I didn't know the details of their deal. All I knew was I'd gotten paid one grand to fuck a fine ass man that I would've sexed for free. The business deal collapsed when Grant declined Trevor's offer. The encounter with Grant happened before I'd met Honey but Honey sensed our energy. At first she was mad at me. Then she was upset with Grant. None of that mattered now that her life was endangered.

Onyx shook her head. "I talked to him before you got here. He's on his way."

"That's whatz up." Plan B. "I'll call

Sapphire then." I pressed the letter S on my phone.

I'd met Sapphire at a bar in Las Vegas. Honey and Grant were upstairs in their hotel room having make-up sex. I didn't want to stay alone in my room so I went to the bar. Sat next to this sexy stranger. The more we talked, introduced ourselves, I found out Sapphire knew Honey and Alphonso. What I didn't know that night was Sapphire also knew Grant. Our separation was less than six degrees.

"She's on her way too," Onyx said.

Relieved that we had serious backup on the way, I yelled into the cordless, "Hey! Valentino! Answer this damn phone. This is Red Velvet, motherfucker."

The constant static in the phone stopped. Silence crept into my ear. Chills crawled up my spine, tensing my neck when I heard a man's voice, "Who the hell is this?"

"This is Red Velvet and I'm going to personally beat your ass if you harm Honey." I stood in the doorway. The outskirts of downtown Atlanta were close to the hood. Convenience must've been Honey's motive for choosing this location on Peachtree. "Punk. Where is Honey?"

Calmly he said, "I thought this call had

dropped. Put Onyx on the phone, Red Velvet."

"I'm running this show. You gon' talk to me."

"Okay, Red Velvet. Is red your favorite color?" he asked.

"Yours?" I countered. "Stop wasting my time, you motherfucking coward. Where in the hell is Honey?"

"Honey is dead."

Speechless, I prayed the fool was bluffing. He wasn't that stupid. If Honey was dead, why would he be talking to me?

"You mean Lace. If I don't get my money, she's going to die," he said. "I'm a generous motherfucker so I'll personally drop her dead ass off on Blackland in front of her house, and trust me you won't be able to identify her body. Or I'll take her to a mortuary after I cut off her arms and legs. Save the coroner a trip. Since you're in charge, you decide. You can give me my money in exchange for your precious Lace St. Thomas. Or I'ma put your ass on your back, spread your legs wide open until *you* fuck enough johns to earn me my money, bitch. All of it!"

Lace St. Thomas? Honey must've given Valentino a fake name.

Memories of Alphonso Allen raping me

on Venice Beach haunted me. Valentino's words took me back to a place I hated going. In my mind I could feel the sand in my hair, Alphonso's dick trying to dig out my insides. I blamed myself for trusting a man I didn't know. The more I cried, the harder he fucked me, until he came, until he emptied his seeds inside of me, then left me alone to give birth to his son. I wanted to abort his baby but I couldn't kill my child. *Fuck Valentino.* He couldn't put me on a stroll. Could he? I had to sort this out quick. I gestured at Onyx. She took the phone.

"Valentino, give me forty-eight hours," Onyx pleaded. "I'll find a way to wire you the money. I can't withdraw funds from Honey's account but I think I can arrange a wire."

"What? Are you crazy?" I snatched the phone from Onyx. "We ain't giving your ass shit, you hear me. No Honey, no money. You wanna talk? Meet us tonight at Stilettos Strip Club at eight o'clock and don't be late. I want to meet your retarded ass in person."

"You're a hothead. Liable to get yourself killed tonight. I'll be there. Eight o'clock. But your forty-eight hours start right now," Valentino said, ending the call.

"Hello? Hello?" I looked at Onyx, then

said, "He's gone."

Onyx sat behind her desk.

I sat on top of her desk. "Now what?"

Onyx pointed at the leather-cushioned seat beside her desk. I eased into it.

"I want you to come to our house, meet the other women, but keep this between us for now. I can't trust any of them, especially Girl Six," said Onyx, picking up her cell phone. She touched her keypad several times, placed her cell phone back on the desk.

Who was Girl Six? If I had to meet them, I had to look right. I got my lipstick and compact mirror, then said, "We need Sapphire Bleu." I stroked on a fresh coat of red. "She'll take care of Valentino."

Our triangle had the law to protect us. Sapphire was a cop, Honey's friend, and my new friend. But I didn't know Sapphire or Onyx the way I thought I knew Honey.

Onyx held my hand, then said, "I owe Honey my life. We all do. The other eleven girls too."

"Where they at? The other girls you keep talkin' 'bout. Shouldn't they be here? They could help us." More like take over for me so I wouldn't miss my flight to LA. My relocation was in a few days but no one knew how long Honey would be missing.

"They're all out working, trying to convince prostitutes to stop selling their bodies. Red Velvet, we were all escorts in Vegas. High paid escorts. Honey was our madam. Honey started this business in Atlanta to help women get off their backs. Now she's the one who needs our help. Let's go," said Onyx. She picked up her purse. "I just texted Girl Six and she hasn't hit me back."

I followed Onyx to the door, stood outside and waited for her to lock up. I was beginning to understand that Honey was like the drug dealer who'd built a community center for neighborhood kids. Her money was dirty but her intentions were pure. What if Valentino didn't bring Honey to Stilettos? What if he didn't show up? What if Trevor was still upset with me for quitting?

Trying to reassure myself more than Onyx, I said, "We'll find Honey. Believe that. This car is straight sexy." I settled into her sweet ass black-on-black Lexus LX with tinted windows, the kind of car men envied a woman having. This was not the car Onyx was in when she dropped Honey and me off at Hartsfield when Honey took me to Las Vegas and Los Angeles.

Onyx kept her focus on our surroundings as she drove past the Fox Theatre. I had to ask, "What was it like? Being an escort. You know, lots of females have sex for free, let men used them. Must be better getting paid. How much did you make?"

A cold, hard expression appeared on her face. Onyx stopped at the red light at Seventeenth, then stared at me. "A woman would be better off auctioning her soul to the devil than letting a different man stick his dick in her mouth . . . pussy . . . asshole every night. Sometimes two, three, four men a night. Back-to-back-to-back. Two grand a night isn't worth it when you end up shot in the head like my best friend, Sunny. One day before her twenty-first birthday, that bastard Valentino killed my best friend."

Onyx wiped her tears. We passed the King Tut exhibit on our right, the Margaret Mitchell Museum to our left. I prayed Honey's spirit hadn't gone with the wind. Honey was a survivor. Onyx made an illegal U-turn, doubled back to Seventeenth, turned left, headed toward Atlantic Station. That was near my house.

"Don't take me home. Best if I stay out while my mom has my son."

"I'm not taking you home," she said. "Just driving around to see where the girls are. See if I spot Honey or Valentino."

Gently, I placed my hand on Onyx's thigh. "I'm so sorry to hear about your friend."

Onyx's leg trembled. She spoke as though she hadn't heard me. "Honey could've left us in Vegas but she didn't. She gave us airline tickets. All of us came right away, except Girl Six." Onyx's eyes widened. She picked up her cell, placed a call, then said, "Girl Six, get your ass to the house. Now."

Eyes shifting to Onyx, bottom lip tucked between my teeth, I asked, "You think Girl Six set Honey up?"

"Don't know. The prostitution business made us hard-core. You're a bad bitch yourself the way you stumped your spiked heel into that man's wife's pussy," she said, giving me props.

Tolliver's wife came to Stilettos the night Honey and Onyx were there. My mom had asked Honey to show up at Stilettos to convince me to quit stripping. Tolliver's wife wanted him to stop fucking me. She had the right idea, wrong approach. When his wife tried to stab me in my back with a knife during my on-stage performance, Honey grabbed her. Onyx hit Tolliver in the head with her stiletto. And I stomped Tolliver's wife in her clit with my spiked heel.

"Self-preservation," I said, glad I'd given up stripping. "You ever been married?"

"I am married."

"Were you married while you were an

escort?"

"Yes," she said, driving by Victoria's Secret at Atlantic Station. "He was abusive. Either I left or I was going to kill him. He lucked out. Me too. I love my life now." Onyx picked up her cellular. "Girl Six didn't answer her phone. But I'm definitely going to find out if she's involved in Honey's disappearance. If she is, she's dead. No questions asked."

Onyx and Honey had my back that night but did that make me obligated to both of them? I had my son and my mother to protect. "On second thought, take me home."

"I need you to stay with me until we find Honey," she said, heading back toward downtown. "And you've got to pay attention to details. You forgot about the client you took into the conference room. I intentionally locked her in the office so she wouldn't go home. We have to go back to the office, then to the house."

"I didn't forget. I assumed you wanted her to stay there," I lied.

Onyx slammed on her breaks. "Stop lying! This situation is serious!"

Could she get charged with vehicular manslaughter if she had caused my neck to break? Thank God I had on my seat belt. At

the peak of my career, I questioned my existence.

CHAPTER 4
GRANT

Meanwhile . . . in Washington, D.C.
An honorable man sacrificed for family, for success, for love.

The second Onyx phoned and told me Honey was in trouble, I was on my way. I never got out of my car in front my parents' home in D.C. I backed out of their driveway and headed to the nearest airport with the most direct flights to Hartsfield.

"Yes! Finally, I have a legitimate reason to go get my baby back." I hadn't called Honey since we'd parted in Vegas. The possibility of her rejection bothered me. No way was I going to call Honey and confess, "Baby, I love you. I want you to be my lady," and give her the chance to tell me, "Grant, you're not man enough for me."

Two women in my life were worth dying for, my mother and Honey. My mother knew how much I loved her; Honey had no idea. My mom loved me unconditionally.

Mom made loving her easy. Made being myself comfortable, acceptable. Mom consistently wanted the best for me. My wife didn't have to be my mom, but she had to have my mother's qualities. Mom supported my indoor grasshopper farm when I was six, my riding dirt bikes when I was twelve, and my decision to sell the house my dad bought me for graduation to invest in my first apartment complex when I was eighteen.

I turned up WPGC, jammed right with Michel Wright. Early afternoon traffic on the GW Parkway was congested. Michel made my commute fun. She was a radio personality, writer, producer, and more than a pretty face with a knockout body. Michel was the type of ambitious woman that successful men like me were attracted to.

I merged into the creeping fast lane, got back over into the slow lane, which moved a little faster. Alternated until I hit the Dulles Airport access road. Drove the speed limit to avoid being pulled over. Getting a ticket would set me back in time and money. My stomach churned. What if I risked my life, rescued Honey, and she rejected me? I'd feel like a fool. Maybe I should go home. But what if I could've saved her life and didn't try?

"I'm doing the right thing," I said to

61

convince myself.

Emotional support was free but women acted as though it cost a fortune. Would Honey come to my aid if I were endangered? I believed she would, but Honey didn't love me the way my mother did. Honey loved me conditionally.

My ego ripped me from Honey's arms when she'd given me an ultimatum to commit or quit. Fear of marriage encouraged me to leave that hotel room in Las Vegas (after having the best sex of my life with Honey) without telling her good-bye. We'd argued because she wanted a relationship that I was unsure of.

When I'd said, "Let's do it," she'd said, "You don't know what you want," convincing me she didn't know what she wanted. I waited for her to call or text me like she'd always done after our emotional breakups. She didn't. Constantly, I replayed memories of her in my mind. Tired of waiting on her to make the first call, I'd sexed a few women — held on to the hope that Honey would come back to me. I came inside a condom, pulled my dick out of each woman pretending they were Honey. Honey didn't deserve to endure more suffering; she'd had more than her share of hardships. She'd told me parts of her rough upbringing. Empathy was all I could offer.

Born with a silver spoon, the moment I opened my eyes I wanted for nothing. I grew up in a luxurious house with loving parents, had my first car at fifteen. My parents loved and treated my brother and me the same.

Arriving at Washington Dulles International, I parked in short-term not caring how long my car would stay there. No luggage in tow, I zigzagged across three lanes of congested airport traffic, slapped the hood of a car that almost sideswiped me. The startled driver looked up, frowned at me, then honked her horn. "Inconsiderate woman better keep her attention on the road before she hurt somebody," I muttered.

Benito was self-centered and unappreciative. He totaled his first and second cars, sold his house, then pissed away the money impressing his so-called college friends on the football team. Never would've gotten that four-year scholarship if it weren't for my mother adopting him before she'd met my dad. Benito claimed he made it to the pros on his own. He was an outstanding athlete but Benito talked a better game than he'd played. Women would throw their panties at Benito while he was on the football field. Honey had shared her house, Jaguars, money, heart, and the key to her soul with Benito. All of that wasn't enough. Benito was a leech and leeches sucked blood until they drained their life support system; then they'd move on to a fresh victim.

I ran through the automatic sliding doors, up to the ticket counter, pulled out my credit card and ID. I'd never met a woman with so much fire, enthusiasm, drive, determination, brains, beauty, sex appeal, bedroom skills, bodacious booty, business sense, and money. Didn't need or want her money, had my own, but she'd ruined me for other women. Life without my Honey wasn't happening.

CHAPTER 5
GRANT

The ticket agent smiled and greeted me with, "How may I —" Before she said, "help," I handed her my driver's license and my Grant Hill and Associates business credit card.

"I have a life or death emergency. You've got to put me on your next direct flight to Atlanta. I don't mean your next available, let me make myself clear. I must be on your next flight leaving for Atlanta."

Her smile vanished. "Hmmph. Give me a minute . . . Mr. Hill." Her acrylic nails swiftly skated across the keyboard.

"I might not have a minute. Hurry up."

Her head stayed bowed, jaws suctioned, lips tightened. Her eyes lifted toward me, then narrowed with disgust as she slowed her pace to pecks.

"Listen, lady, I apologize. Please, help me. The woman I want to marry is missing and I have got to find her before it's too late."

She looked up as if seeing me for the first time. Her smile returned. She typed faster. "Sign here," she said, handing me a first-class boarding pass along with my ID and credit card. "Wish we had more men like you. Your flight departs in twenty minutes. You have got to hurry up," she said, pointing to her right.

For this trip I didn't care if I was in the last row with a nonreclining seat as long as I got on the plane. "Thanks!" I said, running to a security checkpoint. My jacket flapped under my arms like a bird taking flight before a natural disaster.

Sure hope I have the fortitude to deal with this Valentino guy. What if he had a gun? Fighting was barbaric. Shooting a man was criminal. I hadn't done either.

I removed my belt, emptied the contents of my pockets — wallet, cell phone, keys — in a white bowl, held on to my boarding pass. Just as I placed the bowl on the conveyor, my phone revved with my motorcycle ring tone: *varooom.* I snatched the tray.

"Excuse me, sir, you can't reach into the X-ray machine. Put the bowl back," a man in a TSA uniform said.

Best to ignore him, avoid misdirecting my anger, risk getting detained, or charged with some hidden post 9-11 felony for cursing him. I hadn't checked my caller ID before anxiously answering, "Hurry, I've got two minutes. Give me some good news." I stepped aside allowing other passengers to go ahead of me, praying Honey was rescued and all I had to do was comfort my baby.

"Hey, bro. Won't take but a minute," my brother said. "I need some more money. The five hundred you gave me back in Vegas is long gone, man, and I haven't found a job yet."

Benito was incredible. What would Mom want me to do? I responded the way my dad would have. "You've got to look for a job to find one. Where are you?"

"Gotta have money to look. I'm hanging out in Atlanta for a few days. So, can you help me out or what?"

"Atlanta, huh?"

"Yeah, I'm in the ATL, bro. You know me. I'm a transient. Atlanta, Vegas, D.C., never know where I'll show up. If you go to Wal-Mart, the wire is cheaper," he said.

Wal-What? I felt my blood pressure rising. Wanted to curse him out, then question him about Honey. Didn't want to give him time to make up lies if he knew the truth.

"I'll call you back at this number in three hours." I ended the call.

Placing the bowl on the conveyor, along

with my shoes and jacket, I hurried through the metal detector. I had to get a security clear card. Should've been at my gate by now. I ran to the shuttle, stood the entire ride. First off the shuttle, I ran to my gate barely beating the last call for my flight.

I doubted I could avoid being arrested if the door was closed and I'd fallen on the floor kicking and screaming for three minutes like that woman who was on every major news channel. "Wait! Wait! Please don't close the door!" I yelled, running toward the door and waving my boarding pass.

Breathing heavily, I settled into 1B, then told the attendant, "Let me have an OJ with ice please." I was in the same seat I'd sat in when I'd met my Honey for the first time, except a different woman was seated at the window.

Her black skin glistened. Long hair flowed over her shoulders. Skirt rose a few inches above her knees, exposing her bare legs. No wedding band. Open-toe shoes revealed her impeccable pedicure — black stripes with diamonds across the tip of toenails. Elegant. Her fragrance, sweet like candy, the kind of scent that would ordinarily draw me real close to a woman, make me introduce myself. Not today. Regardless of how sweet she may have been, she wasn't sweeter than Honey. No woman was.

"Here's your juice," the attendant said.

The cabin door closed. I fastened my seat belt, gulped the juice, then shut my eyes. Wanted to cry. What good would that do? Wondered how much Benito knew about Honey's disappearance. Adrenaline did strange things to people. Gave men the strength to move mountains. If my brother was involved in Honey's disappearance, our parents couldn't save his ass from the worst beat-down of his life. I hated having to communicate with him but for now Benito was my only lead until I'd speak with Sapphire.

Sapphire, with her resources, could find Honey. But would she? I'd made the mistake of letting Sapphire seduce me when I'd flown to Las Vegas. Sapphire Bleu, born with the name Tiffany Davis, promised to give me background information on Honey. I'd hoped the results would be useful in my making an educated decision about whether to stay with Honey.

I'd first met Tiffany at a hotel when we were only sixteen. Her cheerleading squad was in Vegas for a competition. I'd heard in the hallways that Tiffany was easy and she gave great head. Had to find out. Fifteen years later, I'd confirmed that Tiffany aka

Sapphire still gave great head. But Sapphire sucking my dick wasn't motivation enough to leave Honey.

I felt the lightest touch on my shoulder, opened my eyes.

"I don't mean to bother you but you seem like a man who enjoys sports," the woman next to me said.

I exhaled, nodded, and closed my eyes again.

She tapped my shoulder again, then said, "I'd like to offer you two box suite tickets to see my son play in Atlanta tomorrow night."

Answering her without opening my eyes, I asked, "What's your son's name?"

Softly, she said, "Darius Jones."

I'd heard Darius Jones's story on the news a while back when he'd entered the draft. He'd changed his last name from Jones to Williams when his paternity test proved Darryl Williams was his biological father.

I sat up, looked at her. "You mean Darius Williams who publicly announced he'd changed his last name to Williams has now changed his name back to Jones?"

Her lips parted. Her smile captivated me. I took a deep breath, inhaling her perfume. She seemed nice.

She nodded. "Long story. Short version,

70

my son changed his name back to Jones after my husband, Wellington Jones, died."

"Why'd he change his name back to Jones?" I asked her.

"My husband was a good father to Darius but when Darius learned Wellington wasn't his biological father, he became upset. Changed his name to Williams. My son's biological father is —"

"Darryl Williams, ex-pro-basketball player." I smiled back her. She'd lied to her husband. I could see why a man wouldn't want to let her go. "You are incredibly gorgeous, stunning." But lying about paternity was justifiable termination for any relationship.

"Thanks. My name is Jada Diamond Tanner," she said, handing me her card.

"This cannot be happening." I shook my head. "Black Diamonds. So you are the mastermind behind the scintillating marketing of hundreds of companies and the multimillion dollar endorsements for your son. No offense, but I didn't know the owner was a . . . a . . ."

"Woman?"

"Yeah." I dug in my jacket pocket, handed her my card. "I'd love to meet with you in a professional setting to discuss the possibilities of your representing my company. With

71

this unpredictable economy, I could use a boost. I mean my company could use a boost. I split my time between D.C. and Atlanta."

She touched my hand. "I live in Roswell. What are you doing for dinner? Perhaps I can get you off to a good start tonight."

Didn't want to be rude and move my hand, so I left it there and replied, "I'm going to Atlanta on an emergency. Rain check?"

Her smile shrunk. "Sure. What's your emergency?'

"The woman I want to marry is missing. I have to find her. I love her."

Jada moved her hand. Her eyes filled with tears.

"I'm sorry. I didn't mean to upset you. Was it something I said?"

"No, no, don't apologize. It's just that my husband felt that way about me before he died. My Wellington wasn't a perfect man but the one thing I knew for sure was my husband loved me with all his heart. Doubt I'll ever love like that again but I haven't given up. There are a few good men like you, somewhere out there." She released a long sigh. "Listen to me. Going on about myself when I should be listening to you.

"I've got people. If there's anything I can

do to help you find your future fiancée, you have my number."

"I appreciate your offer," I said, touching her hand.

Jada could be my backup if Sapphire wasn't dedicated to finding Honey. I wrote Honey's names, birth location, and what little information I had on Valentino and Immaculate Perception.

I had no idea what compelled her but Jada leaned my head on her shoulder, held my hand, and comforted me until our flight arrived in Atlanta. Maybe I was the one comforting her.

Chapter 6
Sapphire

Meanwhile . . . in Los Angeles

Molestation.

If there were a survivors' club, thirty-nine million Americans, both men and women, would be members. How did so many individuals get away with sexually abusing children when 95 percent of the incidents were preventable? I knew why, knew all too well how some parents reacted. My mother looked at me but she didn't see me. She never saw the fear in my eyes whenever he entered my bedroom. I felt so ashamed, I ran away from home when I was sixteen and didn't return until fifteen years later.

Honey was the one who'd reunited me with my mother. She'd given me a flyer she'd gotten from my mom. On the flyer was a photo of me with MISSING across the top and my name, age at that time, last seen at with the name of my high school, and a contact number to call if anyone had seen me. If Alphonso hadn't fathered Red Velvet's son, if Honey hadn't decided to help Red Velvet find Alphonso, I wouldn't be sitting in Mother's living room.

My reunion with my mother was bittersweet. Today I'd returned to my mother's house, less than an hour later I had to leave. Told my mom I'd visit her after she settled in to the house I'd bought her. The house she was living in, the same house that Alphonso once lived in with her, with us, I wanted to tear it down with my hands. Beat him over the head with each plank.

"Bye, Mom," I said, kissing her forehead. "I've got to go."

"I know baby. I understand. I love you, Tiffany," she said, following me with her eyes to the door.

I left my mother sitting in that living room. Got in my car. Not wanting to interrupt my brief overdue heart-to-heart talk with my mother, I'd left my cell phone in my car. Big mistake. Twenty-six missed calls from Honey were registered on my caller ID, one voice mail saying she'd been kidnapped and for me not to call.

Immediately, I was in motion. Drove in the carpool lane, then switched to the emergency lane along the 405. Merging across four lanes, I took the Century Boulevard exit to the Los Angeles International Airport.

Reflecting on my childhood, I cried. "Mama, why? Why didn't you stop the abuse?" I wanted to question her. I'd get my chance to ask her to her face when I returned to Los Angeles.

Was it my mother's fault that Alphonso Allen repeatedly molested me? What pleasure had my stepfather derived from making me suck his dick, then taking his dick out of my mouth and painfully forcing his erection into my virgin vagina that was too tight, too small, and too young? Being an undercover cop, I realized that very few molesters reformed, but if my mother had filed charges against him, maybe he wouldn't have raped Velvet Waters.

I exhaled, parked in a garage at LAX, grabbed my purse, and speed-dialed my former boss in Las Vegas. Marching to ticketing, I stomped toward the lady suited in a white hat, white dress, neutral stockings, and white shoes, holding a bucket soliciting for money. Hoping her cause was dedicated to helping women, I donated five dollars.

Molesters became husbands who harbored their secrets from their wives. Molesters became rapists, sexually abusive boyfriends, or husbands who'd beat their wives into submission, threatening their lives if they called the police. Celebrities were no exception. Not enough of the women who married rapists and molesters confronted their men. It was easier to ignore the abuse. Maybe my mother feared he'd kill us if she reported him.

To suppress my emotions, I married my job. Attached myself to causes that kept my mind occupied. Had to stay busy, keep moving. When I'd heard Honey's message, I was rejuvenated. I had a new mission.

My ex-boss answered, "Bleu, less than a week into retirement and you're calling me already?"

I had to have his permission to do this job. I should've warned Honey that Valentino's wife had bailed him out of a Nevada prison. Should've warned Honey I'd seen Benito at the Las Vegas airport a few weeks ago, but I hadn't been concerned about Valentino or Benito.

The day I'd seen Benito, I'd gone to LAS to meet Grant Hill at baggage claim. I'd met Grant for the first time in Las Vegas when I was an out-of-control sixteen-year-old cheerleader. Hadn't heard from him again until I called Honey and he'd answered her cell phone. I felt my reunion with Grant was meant to be. Desperately I wanted to make that man mine.

"With or without your permission, boss, I'm going on special assignment to Atlanta. I have my badge in my purse."

Any woman who'd met Grant Hill would feel the same. I lured Grant to my bedroom by dangling information on Honey's wild and wicked past in front of him. Compromised my womanhood hoping my underutilized good tight pussy and the fact that I'd fucked him first would qualify me as his first lady. I'd sucked peanut butter and jelly off his dick fifteen years before he'd met Honey.

"That's my badge, Bleu. Not yours."

"Mine until I give it back to you, boss."

Grant had rejected my advances emphatically, saying, "I'm in love with Honey."

He'd pissed me off. Hurt my feelings. Made me angry. With him. With Honey. With myself. Ultimately Grant made me get real; the man wasn't interested in me. I had to be honest with my desire to have my own man, one who would adore me the way Grant worshipped Honey. Grant restored my confidence that good men were out there somewhere. He awakened me to my new reality: Sapphire Bleu was forever unconditionally single. Next time, I'd let the man pursue me. Prove to me he was the right one for me. Let him fall in love first. Let him propose. My new single attitude was to treat a worthy man like my king by being his queen.

I told myself, "Do not make sexual advances toward Grant. You're going to Atlanta to help him find Honey."

"Bleu, once you've made up your mind, woman, there's nothing I can do to change it. We both know that." He paused for a moment, then asked, "What now, Bleu? One minute you quit, now you want me to expedite special orders for you to go get involved in what? And why in the world Atlanta? Don't bullshit me, Bleu. Give it to me straight. Is this business or a personal vendetta?"

"A little bit of both, Bossman. Valentino James violated his parole. Left Nevada. He's in Atlanta, trying to kill someone close to me."

"What? You stay out of it. I'll put Hunter on this right away."

"Oh, hell no. Not Hunter."

Hunter was tall, bald, and blue black. Whenever that man spoke, he made my pussy quiver. We'd worked on lots of assignments together. Hated fucking my counterparts, but I had to fuck him once. No regrets, he was good, but as fine as Hunter was, he had too much baggage — an estranged wife who made him pay her two thousand dollars a month, two boys ages four and six, and a gambling addiction that altered his personality based on whether he'd won or lost.

Rumor was Hunter was indebted for several million. Went in big on a lead for a boxing match, came out financially bruised, having bet more than he could pay. There were too many issues in his head for me to fuck him again or take him seriously. I could bail him out but he'd gamble again. Or I could assist his debtors with arranging an inside hit if Hunter didn't pay up soon. If it were just Hunter, I would have done the job myself. But agreeing to kill his wife and kids, I'd refused. Let the mafia hire one of our counterparts to do their dirt.

"Bleu, I'm hearing a lot of money came up missing on this Valentino bust — lots. Let Hunter handle this one. Walk away while you can. Too many dead heroes out there. You're too close, Bleu. Let it go."

For the first time boss had let me know he knew what I'd done. What I hoped he didn't know was I'd kept half and given Honey half. That way if I ever took the fall, I had at least one person with enough money to bail me out.

Women had to stick together. She deserved it. Earned it. Honey and I had a lot in common. I could've busted her along with Valentino but I had a soft spot in my heart for madams. Plus, Sunny Day was our mutual friend. My first run-in with Honey was at a Vegas casino bar. That night, I'd insisted Sunny decide if she wanted to work for Honey. Honey showed me the gun in her garter. I showed her the one sandwiched between my triple Ds. Neither of us backed away from Sunny. Sunny decided to go to work that night. Her decision turned fatal. I couldn't blame Honey. Sometimes a woman had to live or die by her decisions.

I told my boss, "You can send Hunter but Honey is my friend — I have to go. I'll bring Valentino back to Nevada. Put him away forever. With or with —"

He exhaled, "I know, Bleu, without my permission. You've got thirty days, Bleu. Then I want your badge in my hand forever. Find yourself a man to marry and stop sleeping with your job."

Bossman, as I called him, was my biggest supporter. He believed in me. Gave me the opportunity to prove I could handle sting operations. I'd dress hot and sexy, lure in men, married and single, offering to pay for sex. I'd take them to a hotel room. Until

81

prostitution was legalized, men had to accept that soliciting for sex in the city of Las Vegas was illegal. Once the money was exchanged, my job was done. Hunter took over and the solicitor was on his way to jail. Disguising as a prostitute was fun but killing pimps was awesome. I loved arresting men more than having sex with them.

Bored after one week of not working, I refused to make the mistake of retiring early. "Won't need but three days to deliver Valentino back, possibly in a body bag. Thanks." I stepped to the counter. "A one-way ticket on the next flight to Atlanta," I said, handing the agent my badge and credit card. "Boss?"

"Yeah, I'm here."

"I'll take you up on your thirty-day offer. I have some unfinished business in Los Angeles when I'm done in Atlanta." Boss was not getting my badge in thirty, sixty, or ninety days.

"Bleu?"

"Yes, Bossman."

His voice was stern. "Cover my ass first, will you?"

I crossed my fingers, then told him, "You got it. I'll call you when I get to Atlanta." I'd do my best, but in my line of work there were no guarantees.

CHAPTER 7
SAPPHIRE

I'd make sure Honey was safe, then return to Los Angeles for the unfinished business of killing Alphonso. Bastard probably thought I'd forgotten about him. All the better for me. I'd blow his brains out when he'd least expect it.

I had an hour to spare before boarding, so I headed to Karl Strauss for an extra spicy Bloody Mary. One seat left at the bar and it was mine. I sat between a man and woman chatting. "Excuse me." I arched my back, ordered my drink.

The woman gave my breasts a frown, the man smiled. "We were talking," she hissed, pushing back her stool.

"It's okay," he said. "You'd better get going. Your flight is leaving shortly."

"Bitch," she muttered at me between her teeth, then smiled at him. "Nice meeting you, Santonio."

Bitch? A better attitude or a friendly

request — "Would you mind exchanging seats?" — would've worked. She was no diva and definitely not from LA. LA women had perfected false flattery. Like a scorpion preparing to deliver the sting of death, the more an LA woman despised a person, the friendlier she'd become. Irrespective of intent, image was everything.

Easing my celery stick in and out my mouth, I smiled at him. "Santonio, hi. I'm Sapphire Bleu. And" — I touched his ring — "you are a Mason. Nice. And you have very nice hands."

He blushed. "Yes, I am. Let me buy your drink."

The woman next to me bumped my leg, waved at the bartender. "Check."

I pivoted in her direction while Santonio ordered an Amber Lager, then paid our tab. I placed my badge on the counter and opened my purse for her to see my gun. "Be careful, sweetheart. Real careful. Check your damn attitude. And do *not* touch me again."

Santonio touched my arm. "Everything okay?"

I picked up my badge, nodded, turned my back to her, faced him. "Where're you headed?"

"Carolina for business, but I live there

too," he said, and took a big swig of his beer. "Travel a lot for my job."

Gulping, swallowing, anything except sipping. I did not like men who sipped pussy or alcohol. "North or south?" I asked.

"North, Charlotte to be exact. And you?"

"I'm headed to Atlanta," I said, looking over my shoulder. The woman stood behind her chair waiting for her tab. The bartender was on the other side of the bar mixing a drink. Some people were constantly ignored because they didn't respect others.

Santonio handed me his business card: "Santonio Ferrari, Chief of Police." "If it's okay with you, I'd like to take you out to dinner."

"She said she's going to Atlanta, not Charlotte," the woman commented.

I refused to respond to the nosy bitch suffering from an overdose of rejection.

"Go ahead. Get mad. I don't care if you are a cop. You can't arrest me. I haven't broken any laws. You need to cover your titties up. I'm going to report you."

What was her problem? I remained silent.

Santonio said, "I'm talking to a lady, not to you. And she has beautiful . . . breasts."

Yes! He said breasts! Santonio might just be my kind of man. "I'd love to join you for dinner," I said, writing my cell number on a napkin. "I'll wait for you to call me."

The woman tossed twenty dollars on the bar and left.

Santonio smiled, shook his head. "I knew there was something I liked about you the moment you sat next to me. Sapphire Bleu, you are one classy woman."

CHAPTER 8
VALENTINO

Back in Atlanta . . .

All females were confused bitches in heat or heated about some dumb shit.

Shit lingered in a bitch's subconscious waiting for an innocent or ignorant nigga to show up. Fuck me on the first date. Treat me like a lady. Pay for our meals. I got it, baby. Don't come over to my house ever again. Here's a key. I wanna have your baby. I wouldn't have your child if my life depended on it. I don't want a relationship. Marry me. Let me suck your dick. Your sorry ass ain't shit. Get the fuck out! Baby, don't go.

Pimping was therapeutic. A nigga couldn't win no fight with a woman.

Women were forensic fucking scientists searching for clues and shit to argue about, roaming though a nigga's pockets, cell phone, car, wallet, and computer history to make a nigga more miserable than her ass.

Very few women were happy with themselves but they wanted men to make them happy.

Why didn't you take out the trash, send me flowers, call me back, or invite me out? Why did you look at her? Is she prettier? Does she have bigger breasts, a better ass? Do you want her? "No." Yes you do. "No I don't." Go be with her then. "Who are you talking about?" Her!

Women were born fucked up in the head. If they weren't self-taught how to dog men, they eventually learned from haters. Women turned good men bad, bad men worse. Blame it on PMS: "I'm cramping." Premenopause: "I forgot." Menopause: "I'm hot." Postmenopause: "I'm all dried up." Always imbalanced and, shit, women were forever straight trippin'.

Red Velvet didn't know me but the sick trick threatened me not to hurt Lace. Onyx professed she was trying to meet my monetary demand to save Lace's life. I knew damn well Onyx couldn't come up with fifty million without Lace's approval. Bitch was stalling.

I had to keep shit moving. Find Lace. Get paid. Blaze the fuck up outta the ATL. Pause. Backtrack. Retrack. The ATL could do me righteous. Whores, strippers, and freaks were plentiful. I could open a new Immaculate Perception. Do it up Vegas style like my original spot with theme rooms and shit. Fuck. Lace arranged all that shit. Maybe I should apologize, talk her into coming back to work for a nigga. One thing at time. I had to stay focused.

Back to Lace. Her ass was too fucking brilliant to go home after we left her in the parking lot. And I wasn't crazy enough to show up at her house again. Driving sixty, the light freeway traffic was decent. The hot wind blasted my face, making it hard to breathe. Covering my nose, I inhaled short breaths.

"Valentino James is nobody's fool, B."

Tricks told me to meet them at Stilettos, their turf, their time. Did they believe I was that stupid? Lace might show up. They'd probably called Sapphire's ass. Bitch wasn't going to arrest me twice. But all that shit had me thinking. If I were missing, who'd search for me? Who'd give a damn?

Benito's tongue lapped out his mouth. That nigga was breathing with ease.

"Man, I'm taking time to enjoy the view. This ride is better than being at Six Flags over in Georgia. You know what, V?"

"What now, nigga? What? What?" Pointing at the shattered windshield, I yelled at his dumb ass, "This is not an amusement park thrill."

Shaking his head, he slumped in the passenger seat.

Smack!

I hit his ass on the back of his neck. "You fucked up . . . again. Now we drivin' around in a SUV with no fucking windshield. I should slam on my brakes. Send your silly ass straight to the moon."

"Do I get a spaceship?"

Smack!

Benito massaged the nape of his neck. "I had a plan, V. I almost had her. I could tell by the way she stared at me. She couldn't shoot me. She loves me. You gotta trust me on this. Lace got away but when my brother calls me back, he'll lead us straight to her."

Hurling a fist full of bullets through the missing windshield, I said, "Fuck that nigga Grant. He's on her team, not ours. We can't shoot his ass. We have ammunition and no fucking gun. How did you fuck that part up?"

"Past tense. Had ammunition. Had . . . Wasn't my fault. The gun was too small for my hands," he said, spreading his fingers. "Besides, I've never killed or shot anyone. I'm not going to jail like you. You already have pimping, pandering, and murder charges, man. You could possibly get . . ." Nigga counted on his fingers like a kindergartener. "You should've kept the gun. Yeah, you so hard. Why didn't *you* shoot her?"

Nigga had me trippin' and shit. I wanted him to man the fuck up. Kill Lace's ass. I couldn't shoot her. If it weren't for my money, I'd have no beef at all with Lace. She was cool. The one time that she gave me some of that good pussy, I wanted more. More of her. Knew she wasn't interested in me. My ego was huge and fragile, hated rejection. I'd rather not pursue a bitch than to have her ass turn me down, especially in public, and definitely not in front of Benito's ass.

"It's because you fucked my girl, V. None of us can hurt her. She whipped it on you, on Grant, and on me. Got all of us acting stupid."

"You ain't acting, nigga."

Only punk-ass niggas chased women. Had to give those bitches Lace and Sapphire credit. I was on top of my motherfuckin' game, earned my first notch to becoming a billionaire, and in one fuckin' bust my ass was dead broke. Bitches.

Hadn't realized I'd said, "I can't stand Lace's ass. That bitch outsmarted me," until Benito replied, "Me too."

91

"Nigga, that toe-tapping, adding, multiplying, and dividing dog Suze that was on Oprah could outsmart your dumb ass. Nigga, we need another car quick, before we get stopped by the police."

CHAPTER 9
HONEY

A woman's strength was determined by how much she loved herself.

Could she forsake all others to live her life the way she wanted? Could she learn to embrace happiness even if it meant losing the only man she'd ever loved?

Determined to hear Grant say my name, touch my breasts, fall asleep in my arms, I had to get home. I yearned to lay my head between his legs, kiss and sniff his balls. I craved to wake up exhausted from making love. Delirious from standing more than two hours in the heat, I fantasized to forget, if only for a minute, all the gruesome things that had happened to me.

My immediate agenda was to get home, to notify my banker to freeze all account activity not originated by me, and to take a long hot bath — in that order. Onyx was the only person authorized to access my money. I knew she'd do anything to save my life, but I prayed she hadn't given away my money. I had to check on my girls, my business, speak with Sapphire, ask her to track down Valentino and Benito. Better to have Sapphire kill Valentino and Benito than for me to do it.

Toot-toot. A handsome man in a burgundy Benz waved, kept going.

"Don't honk at me, give me a ride! Why won't anyone give me a ride?" I yelled, resenting the hundreds of drivers that had zoomed by me. My feet were numb, I couldn't feel my toes, but it was too hot to take off my shoes. Too hot to sit. Too hot to walk. Too hot to stand much longer. Weary, I was on the verge of passing out. Fidgeting, I scratched my neck, pulled my hair, then massaged my left breast. What if I had a heart attack, fell to the ground? Would a stranger stop to help me?

What if Valentino or Benito had killed me in that parking lot? My millions of dollars would matter the most to those who deserved it the least. I had no will. No husband. No kids. No burial instructions. No next of kin that I'd acknowledged, including my parents. The state of Georgia would claim my assets. What had the government done for me except take, take, take? I wasn't dying without a notarized last will and testament.

My body swayed; I stumbled. "That's it," I said. "Somebody is going to give me a ride." I used my left arm to support my right arm. Holding up my thumb, I leaned against the pole. More cars zipped by. I cried. "Damn, does everybody in Atlanta have hitchhiker phobia? Where are all those church members of Reverend Dollar's ministry?" Couldn't blame them for not stopping. Strangers begging for a ride were usually running from something or someone. The recession made people leery of strangers. Giving up on holding my thumb in the air, I started crisscrossing, flagging, flopping, and wailing my arms at each driver like I was a kid.

Yes, there is a god. My arms collapsed to my sides. Finally, a white commercial van with two windows on the driver and passenger sides and no rear windows parked a short distance ahead of me. Lowering her passenger window, the stranger tooted her horn.

Staggering to the van, I stared at her license plate, memorizing the number as I approached the passenger window. I rested my arms on the door, leaned my head inside the van. A cool air-conditioned breeze, a friendly smile, warm round dark brown eyes accented with crow's feet and long dark lashes greeted me.

She appeared about thirty-five, forty maybe, depending on how well she'd taken care of herself. Approximately five foot ten inches, two hundred pounds, give or take five. Black shoulder length hair matched her nail polish. Large breasts protruded under a plain black long-sleeved T-shirt. Faded black denim jeans loosely tapered her thighs and black tennis shoes covered her feet. There was a cell phone in the cup holder closer to her, a brown paper coffee cup with a white lid in the other. The caged metal barrier behind the seats separated her from what was back there.

"I'm not a crazy woman," I said, observing every detail I could inside her van. Not much else to see.

In a deep sweet raspy voice, she said, "You're too classy to be one of them kind, suga'. But you do look worn. Hop in." She turned off her engine. "These gas prices are killing my pockets."

Was she serious? Gas prices had dropped significantly.

"I'm headed north. Off of Piedmont and Roswell. I've had an unbelievably rough day. Mind if I see what's in the back of your van

96

before I get in?"

Her smile vanished. "Geez, sweetie. Are you an undercover cop or something? I'm the one trying to help you out here."

"No, I'm not a cop. Mind?"

She leaned over, pushed open the passenger door. I glanced behind the seats. The barrier blocked my view. I braced my hands on the gray vinyl seat. Placed one foot on the mat, left the other on the ground. It bothered me that I couldn't see back there.

Being a former prostitute, I'd learned women who were too trusting sometimes got gang-raped because they didn't check out the backseats and trunks of johns' cars. At times, I hated the part of me that couldn't let go of my past. Everyone was suspect.

Looking at her clear glossy lips, I asked, "Don't mean to sound pushy but can you get out and open the back doors? I can't see back there."

"You want a ride or not, baby? Get in or get out. I'm trying to help you. Make up your mind. I've got to go," she said, starting her engine.

A voice whispered in my ear, "Don't do it, Madam." Sounded like Sunny. Imagine that. Sunny protecting me from heaven and I couldn't protect her on earth. I shook my head, silenced the voice inside it. How long would I have to wait for another ride if I refused this one? I was tired. I had to get home. "I do need a ride. I'll pay you a hundred dollars when we get to my house."

"Then you are heading my way," she said. Her friendly smile returned.

Against my better judgment, I closed my door.

CHAPTER 10
HONEY

Entering I-75 South, the woman driving the van merged into traffic at fifty miles per hour. Merged over again doing sixty.

Calmly, I said, "We need to go north. You're driving south." I glanced at my swollen feet, lifted my pants. My ankles were the size and color of eggplants.

"Some of us do have to work, lovely. I've got to make this delivery first. Won't take but a few minutes. I'm late," she said, plunging her accelerator to the maximum speed limit, seventy miles an hour, swerving into the fast lane.

I prayed the delivery wasn't me. Deepening my tone, I said, "You're heading in the wrong direction. Stop the car and let me out."

"Geez, you so-called smart women are so stupid. So you thought I was just giving you a free ride? That I'd just pick you up on the side of the road and be your complimentary chauffeur?" she asked, pushing eighty.

Lord, is this some sort of joke? I am not laughing. Is this a test? You cannot be serious. Please don't tell me I went from being kidnapped to being picked up by a deranged woman.

Bypassing the airport exit, she took the Virginia Avenue ramp and turned left at the light. The city of East Point's gazebo landmark was to our left. Across the street from the gazebo was a Waffle House. Six blocks down another Waffle House. She pulled into the parking lot of Johnny's Pizza and Subs, made a U-turn, then said, "You got me all twisted up here. I was headed in the wrong direction."

"Got that right," I replied. If my feet, legs, and ass weren't aching so bad, I would have jump out and walk back to the freeway. This time I'd stop at the northbound entrance. "Fuck it," I said, tugging on the door handle. I banged the window with my arm.

"Suga' plum, you gon' mess around and dislocate your shoulder. I put the safety lock on for your protection. I'll take it off when we get to where I'm going. Then if you want to get out, you can get out safely."

Backtracking, we bypassed the gazebo, continued on Virginia Avenue to the opposite side of the freeway. Passed another

Waffle House, KFC. She took a left into the cemetery, drove toward the pole that waved an American flag. My mounting frustrations made me want to choke her ass.

She steered off the paved road toward a secluded area. Dirt and rocks crunched under slow-rolling tires. Flowers, vases, and grass were mashed beneath the black rubber treads as she drove on top of graves.

Not many trees around us. That was good. Not many people either. That could be good or bad. People three blocks away placing flowers on graves probably assumed we were doing the same. I had to question why bad things kept happening to me. I saw a housing development in the distance. Again I was too far away for anyone to hear me if I had to call out for help. Not my day. Should've prayed in bed instead of getting on my knees. That way Valentino and Benito couldn't have crept up behind me in my house, tied a bag over my head, bound my wrists and ankles, then stuffed me in the back of their SUV. Amateurs. They'd used Scotch tape, not duct tape. I was out of bondage before they'd stopped the car.

She was an amateur too, but she'd done this shit before.

She was bold. Certifiably insane. Possibly capable of murder. I couldn't underestimate her next move. She turned off the engine. I was not going to be her victim.

"Now you can make this easy on yourself, darlin'," she said, unzipping her pants. "I want you to give me some of that good pussy you got right there, then I'll take you wherever you want to go, sweetheart. Fair exchange is no robbery. I don't want your money."

I sat still. Stared at a big dick stacked on top of his balls. This motherfucker got me good. No way in hell did I ever suspect he was impersonating a woman. I was too close to him to shoot the bastard. Needed more space. Needed his van to get back to my house.

He stared back. Reached into his pocket, pulled out a knife, pressed the button. A stainless-steel blade ejected. He twirled the switchblade handle between his fingers with ease. "Don't wanna mess up that pretty face of yours. You any good at sucking a big dick? With those sexy soft pretty lips, of course you are. Come here, suga' plum."

I sat still. Stared at his hair, his lips, his lashes, at *him?* He was absolutely gorgeous, like he was born in the wrong body. I kept my eyes on the chameleon that appeared helpful minutes ago. Should've followed my instincts. Had no idea what was in the back of his van. By the time I'd get to either of my guns, he could stab me. He was too close. We were too close.

This time he yelled, "I don't want to hurt you! You can make this easy. Give me a blow job. Or I can kill you first, then take that sweet pussy from you before your dead body turns cold. Leave you here where you belong."

My body was already cold, stiff, but far from being dead. Fog crept up the windows, obstructed my view.

"By the time anybody finds your body, I'll be —"

"Dead," I said. My eyes fixed on his. I had no idea where Valentino and Benito were, but I'd find them after I dealt with this confused fool, whoever he was. He was wasting my time.

Slap! His laugh was hearty, like he was a comedian laughing at his own joke as his backhand landed against my cheek. He pressed the knife under my chin. The tip pricked my skin. I felt blood trickle down my neck, which felt weird, like a bug crawling on me. I wanted to knock that motherfucker upside his head with my gun, but he was too close.

Lifting my chin away from the knife, seductively, I paced my words. "You remind me of a love I once knew. Would you like me to suck your dick first, then ride you real good?"

He paused, smiled. His raspy voice was deeper than before. "That's what I want to hear. I done lucked up and found me a whore. Call me Ken."

If Ken was schizophrenic, he could snap. Kill me without realizing what he'd done. I licked my lips. Leaned over his lap. "Ken baby," I whispered like I was back at the brothel talking to one of my johns, "let mama suck your big juicy dick. And you can drop those balls in my mouth too, daddy. You can cum as many times as you'd like." Leaning toward him, I moaned, deep, long, then exhaled into his mouth.

Ken dropped his knife on the floor between his leg and the door. Both hands on the side of his pants, anxiously Ken wiggled out of his jeans with anticipation, eased his pants and boxers down to his knees. His dick was hard, gigantic like a twelve-inch dildo.

"Oo-wee! I'm ready when you are," he said, chuckling.

Why was this motherfucker wasting my damn time? How many women had he taken advantage of? In three seconds, I released the child protective lock, put my hand on the passenger latch, opened my door, got out the car, then . . . *slam!* I closed the door.

Ken scrambled to pull up his boxers and pants.

I had to get to him before he got out of the van. Racing to the driver's side, I drew my .45. Arms straight. Both hands on my piece. I pointed between his long dark lashes. I had six bullets left. Wouldn't need but one.

"Bat your eyes, motherfucker, and you're dead."

His eyes widened. His head rattled.

"Yeah, you don't seem so bad right now. Get out the car, motherfucker. Get out!"

Ken held up his pants as he scrambled from the car. "You are a cop. You lied to me. Don't shoot me. I'm on the list. I'm unarmed," Ken said, holding up his hands. His pants and boxers fell, stopping at his calves. "I wasn't going to hurt you. I just wanted to have a little fun. That's all. I really am pre-op. I'm on the list for a sex change operation." He looked at his dick and continued, "This old thing here is harmless. I just wanted to give him a farewell blow job."

"Liar. Shut the fuck up. You are a disgrace to women, men, transsexuals, your mama, everybody. Turn around, bend over, and hold your ankles."

He didn't move. Ken stared at me like I'd done to him earlier.

Click! I eased back the trigger.

Ken jumped backward. "That's what I get for trying to help you. Bitch, walk home."

Softly, I said, "Ken, call me a bitch again. I dare you. Let's see how crazy you really are." I paused, then said, "I'ma tell you one last time. Turn around, bend over, and hold your ankles."

Ken's ass and legs had long deep scratches. His upside down face turned red, and his large dark brown eyes stared up at me. His wig fell on top of a flat tombstone revealing his bald head, now flushed too. His dangling nuts were my target.

"How does it feel, Ken?"

"What are you going to do to me? I told you I'd give you a ride and I will. Forget sucking my dick. How about I just drop you off for free, suga?"

That wasn't funny but definitely reminded me of something Benito would say. "I asked you a question. How does it feel raping women?" I didn't care how insane Ken was, what he'd attempted to do to me was inhumane.

Ken's face turned maroon. "Fish. I hate

fish. Women are fishy. I hate women."

I wondered if Ken had any sex slaves held hostage in his house, his basement, outdoors in a shed. "You hate black women, white women, all women?"

He released his ankles. Raised his back.

"Put your hands back on your fucking ankles," I shouted, staring at his asshole, "and answer my damn question."

"All women," he mumbled.

"Including your mother?"

"Especially my mother."

"Well, we've got something in common, Ken. I hate my mother too. But I don't go taking out my childhood frustrations on women and men because I don't like either of my parents."

That wasn't completely true. Ken made me think. Was I the culprit or the victim? I had beaten Girl Six because she had a pimple on her ass, killed Reynolds because he'd plotted with Valentino to kill me, and I truly hated my mother because she loved my sister but she never loved me. I didn't know enough about my father to say I hated him, but I definitely did not like Jean St. Thomas.

"Ken."

"Please don't kill me. I swear I won't eat any more fish."

"Don't play crazy with me. How many women have you raped, Ken?"

"Lost count. Eighteen, I think. I'm sick. I need help. Help me. Don't kill me. Please, don't kill me. I have a wife and two beautiful children."

I didn't doubt him. Some women were so fucking gullible a man could lie and say he was a business owner, he was a former pro-ball player, he'd just lost a lucrative job or contract but was negotiating a better deal, and without conducting a background check or questioning him, women believed men. Some women thought whatever a man had would validate their existence, eventually upgrade their lifestyle. She'd support him until he was able to support her. She'd marry him, then years later she'd realize he was a con artist. Then he'd divorce her and take half of all her possessions, including her heart. That would never happen to me.

"Okay, Ken, I won't kill you."

Pow!

Holding his balls, Ken screamed, "Ahhhh-hhhhhh!" His dick dangled between his legs as he fell headfirst into a tombstone that read, "I died long before I was buried."

The bullet lodged into the dirt. I intentionally missed but the blood he'd imagined was spilling from his nuts could scare him to death. "Spineless bastard. So you thought I was just going to give you a free ride. Geez, you men are so stupid," I told him. "Killing you would give you an easy way out of your sins. I hope you suffer a slow and excruciating painful death. That would serve you right for raping women."

Ken had chosen his graveyard. I hadn't. Even if he knew he wasn't shot, I was sure he'd stay on the ground until well after I was gone.

I shot the license plates from Ken's van, tossed them on the passenger seat, hopped in. Before closing the door, I got out. Placed my hand on the lever, tugged, opened the back door. Looked inside.

Oh . . . my . . . God.

CHAPTER 11
VALENTINO

There was so much that had gone wrong this morning, a nigga had to figure shit out before sundown. Rolling up on Onyx and Red Velvet at Lace's office was no guarantee I'd get more than what was in their purses. Neither one of them was worth holding hostage. Who'd pay more than a grand for the two of them combined? And both might have a gun.

"I'm getting off the freeway here. We gon' park this bitch in the woods, then walk back to that upscale restaurant right there off the Chattahoochee River," I said, pointing. "Our timing is perfect. It's too late for lunch and too early for dinner and I know they're open."

Benito shook his head. "I'm not hungry, V. Last time we ate at a fancy restaurant you treated me like I'd ordered from the fucking side of the menu."

"You did, nigga," I said, smiling.

"I'll wait in the car, V."

Smack!

"Damn, cut that shit out," Benito complained.

"Get out the car before I slap your ig'nant ass again," I said, turning off the engine. "We have what, a few more minutes or so before your brother calls you? Let's go get new transpo before we meet up with Grant."

Atlanta had hundreds of wooded areas. I wondered how many tricks were left for dead but hoped like hell we didn't discover any stiff bitches on our way out. Tramping out of the woods, we made it to the service road. Had about the equivalence of a block to walk.

"B, you ever think about finding your real parents?"

Benito was quiet.

I respected his silence. What if Summer's dad hadn't kept my seed away from me? What kind of dad would I have been to Anthony? Sunny would be alive. They'd be my new family and we'd be happy. One person's fucked up decision could ruin another person's life.

"B, what will you do with your life, nigga, after I break you off?"

"Get back with Lace," he said. "She'll take me back. But you've gotta promise not to fuck my girl again."

Nigga was in denial. Some niggas could get rejected a thousand times by a woman and ask to be with her again. That was straight dumb shit. Tell me once, I'm out for good. But given the opportunity, I'd fuck Lace again.

Making our way into the restaurant's parking lot, I motioned for Benito to stay beside me. I stood next to a parked silver Mercedes. "Talk to me, nigga, like this is my car and we're getting ready to leave or something." Our timing was perfect. Two cars entered the lot, both drove to the valet stand, waited for the one attendant who was doing it all — parking and fetching cars. The recession had rich motherfuckers cutting back on staff, filing bankruptcy and shit.

I observed the valet attendant getting out of the car he'd parked, watched him race back to the stand. We waited until he handed the woman a ticket. He handed the man dressed in beige slacks with a lavender shirt a ticket too, took his key, placed it on the podium.

I told Benito, "Let's move closer, nigga. This is our chance."

We waited until the man and woman walked inside the restaurant. The valet hopped inside the car, then drove toward the side lot.

"Follow his ass in that car, wait for him to park, then cut him off on his way back. Start a conversation —"

"About what?"

"I don't care, nigga. Get him to turn his back toward me, then you keep talking until I get in the car. When I drive toward the exit, he's going to panic. I'ma keep driving. When he runs inside the restaurant for help, you run to the car, nigga, and get your ass in. Can you handle that part without fucking it up?"

"You know me, I do my best work under pressure," Benito said.

"Like when your remedial ass took Sunny's dead body back to her apartment?" I got mad all over again. I felt like punching that clown in his nose. Benito was the reason I had been falsely charged with Sunny's death. I'd swear on my parents' graves that I did not shoot Sunny. I placed the gun to her head. She pulled the trigger. Maybe I should move out of the country. Go to Paris. Travel the world. Find me some international bitches. My best chance of getting the charges dropped was to marry Sunny's twin sister, Summer, and have Summer testify on my behalf. That was if the law caught up to me.

I waited for Benito to distract the valet, then rushed to the podium, picked up the keys, hopped my ass in the red convertible, and made my way toward the exit.

The valet looked at the car I was in, looked back at the podium, then yelled, "Hey, stop the car!"

Benito surprised the shit outta me. When dude turned to run toward the restaurant, Benito punched his ass in the back of the head so hard he fell on the ground and stayed there. Benito bent over.

No, nigga, no. What the fuck are you doing?

Benito shoved something in his pocket, then raced to the car, got in. I closed the top and we drove the fuck off.

There was a reason I gravitated to Benito. A reason bigger than the fact that we were friends while he played college football, that he was my only friend, that both of my parents were deceased, and although I had a son and twins on the way by Summer, a nigga felt empty inside when I was with her. How could I have no feelings for my wife, my seeds? I think it was because the few days I'd lived with Summer after she'd bailed me out of prison, I witnessed my son Anthony was a fucking mama's boy. He needed to man the fuck up but his mommy kept babying his ass. Made my son soft and shit, like he was a bitch. "Yes, mommy. No, mommy. Mommy, mommy, mommy, mommy." I hated that shit. Benito was all I had.

Now that my whores were no longer loyal to me, Benito made me feel not so alone in this fucked up world. He gave me someone I could control. I'd come to the realization that after my mother died, a part of me hated every woman except Lace. What I didn't know was why I hated women so much. Maybe I was attracted to Lace because that bitch was the epitome of womanhood but exemplified the strength of a man.

My mother wasn't hard but she was a good mom, a loving and nurturing mom. I thought she'd live to see my kids, see me walk the stage in high school and get my diploma and shit. Why'd she have to die so soon? My dad, he was cool with me but he wasn't a man. Not a real G. He'd done whatever my mother told him to do. When she died, he died until I buried him beside my mom. I had to get off this sob shit that was making a nigga soft.

Benito reached into his pocket, pulled out a lot of ones and fives. "Yeah, boyie."

"You done good, nigga, count that shit. See if it's enough to get us a cheap motel room. We need to take these tags off this bitch-ass car and lay low until Grant calls."

"One hundred and thirty-seven dollars and sixty-two cents," Benito said.

"Good job, my nigga. You keep the sixty-two cents," I said, taking the dollar bills from him while driving down Piedmont Avenue.

We passed the botanical gardens. I tried to see that fuckin' area where that bridge had collapsed and killed a worker. What a fucked up way to die, on the job. I kept going, stopped at the light at Monroe Drive, made a left, made my way into the Ansley Mall parking lot.

"Where we going, V?"

"Publix, nigga. Where we're staying, there won't be no room service." I parked in the middle of a long lane near Pier 1 Imports. We got out of the only red fucking convertible in the entire lot. "Check the remaining minutes on this prepaid bitch." I handed the phone to B. I should've gone to Ansley Wine Merchants and loaded up on alcohol but we were so fucking broke, we couldn't afford it.

"We have twelve minutes left on the phone. Let me have a ten," Benito said, holding open his hand. "I'ma go to Starbucks and get me one of those ice cold frappuccinos."

I grabbed his shirt. "No, nigga, no. You need to stay with me." I couldn't risk letting that nigga out of my sight for one second.

CHAPTER 12
HONEY

Was I my sister's keeper?

The last time I'd been that close to a dead body was at my sister's funeral. The woman in the back of the van was naked. Stiff. Eyes wide open. Mouth taped shut. What was her story? Every woman had one. Some didn't live long enough to say. Others lived a century but refused to tell. Did men make women mutes? Beside her precious body, a muddy shovel, a slate tombstone, artificial red roses with long green plastic stems in a white plastic vase.

Two for one? A package deal? Was Ken planning to bury us together? Make me dig my own grave? Why should I care about her? Too late to save her. Maybe she was better off. Who was I to say? Didn't want to get involved. Have the cops questioning me, considering me a suspect. Best to keep quiet. I had my own plethora of problems.

"Ken, who the hell is that in your van?" I

asked, slamming the door. My stomach churned. I almost puked. I swallowed bile, focused on Ken.

He stayed on the ground. "What difference does it make? She should've shut her mouth. Crazy chick kept screaming, so I shut her up. She deserved to die."

Crazy men like Ken could on the surface appear normal. A wolf in sheep's clothing so to speak. Men who didn't value women weren't always easy to spot. Men who'd murder women like that man in California who shot his wife and five kids in the head because he and his wife were laid off their jobs. He didn't want anyone else to take care of his. So he killed them?

"You're not God, Ken." Neither was that man in California. "You can't decide when other people deserve to die," I said, pointing my gun at Ken's dick.

Killing Reynolds was self-defense. What I was getting ready to do to Ken was considered an eye for an eye. Too often women were too generous, too forgiving at inappropriate times.

Ken covered his genitals with both hands, pleading, "No, don't. I didn't mean to kill her. It was an accident."

"So you think you deserve to live?" I asked him, staring at his wig on the ground beside him. "You go around disguising yourself as a woman to deceive women, then you rape and kill them."

"If it helps, I didn't rape her," he pleaded.

"You only killed her. Yeah, I can see how that was a better alternative." I stood over Ken, aimed closer to his hands.

"I swear it was an accident." His hands clamped tighter together.

Was his ass crying? Yes, indeed. "Well, Ken, this is no accident. This is intentional," I said, pulling the trigger.

Ken screamed as the bullet penetrated his hands.

I was beginning to hate the woman men had made me become. There was satisfaction in shooting Ken but no joy. Somebody's daughter was in the back of his van. She could've been a mother, or a wife, an honor student, or a teacher, a community activist, or a first lady of a church. Tears streamed down my cheeks. I kicked Ken in his ass. "Bastard!"

Reaching inside his van — not that Ken was going anywhere but to make sure — I took his keys, his cell phone. Opened his wallet. His name really was Ken. Ken Draper. I removed the cash, a hundred-dollar bill, then headed on foot back toward Virginia Avenue.

I stopped at a fast food restaurant, ordered a chicken wrap. "Can you spare a roll of quarters, please?" I asked the cashier, who looked barely sixteen. "Thanks," I said, taking the roll from her hand along with four twenties and a five.

"Miss, your food?"

"Keep it." I left her holding the bag. I wasn't hungry for fast food. I needed the change. Change to make a phone call. Change for a taxi. Change to ride MARTA. I stood in a secluded space on the asphalt beside the restaurant, thankful the temperature had dropped at least ten degrees.

Ken's phone rang. *Mommy Dearest* appeared on his caller ID. His mother would find out if her son was dead or alive but not from me. I declined the call. Make a call, risk having the number traced, risk being associated with the murder of a woman I didn't know. Have Ken lie, if he survived to testify, that he was innocent. Hear him tell a judge I was the one who'd shot him, killed her. Should've left his useless phone in his van.

I walked back inside the restaurant, entered the women's restroom. Went into the stall, dropped Ken's phone into the toilet, covered it with toilet tissue, then flushed. Who'd think or want to surf through a sewer of shit for a phone? I washed my face, tucked my blouse, straightened my hair, then left.

Made my way to the nearest corner in search of a pay phone. No luck. Went inside an office building. Held twenty dollars in front of the receptionist, then asked, "Is there a phone where I can make a call in private?"

She looked at the money, looked at me. "Sure, follow me."

A short distance from her desk was a small conference room. I closed the door, dialed Sapphire's number.

"Hello."

"Hey, Sapphire. It's Honey."

"Honey, oh my lord! Thank God you're alive! Where are you?"

I couldn't lie. The relief in her voice warmed my cold heart. "I'm safe. Where are you?" I asked, right before hearing a boarding announcement for a flight to New Orleans. Maybe that's where I'd go and chill for a moment. Get away from the madness. At some junction, I had to stop running from life. I was a one-woman show, chasing, never catching myself.

"Just arrived at Hartsfield. Getting ready to pick up a rental, then I'm coming to wherever you are," she said.

Happy and sad at the same time, I smiled a half smile. That was a good idea. I didn't have to take the MARTA train or a taxi. Finally someone I could trust was coming to get me. How did my life go from great to tragic in less than one day? Sapphire would navigate my safe landing. I told her to meet me at the fast food restaurant, then asked, "Have you spoken with" — I paused, wanting to say Grant, but asked — "Onyx?"

"Yes. We're meeting Valentino and Benito at Stilettos tonight at eight. I don't want you there. Can you believe those fools are trying to convince us they still have you held hostage? I'm ready to wrap this case up. Put Valentino and Benito on a plane in handcuffs and shackles, send both of them straight to the Nevada pen."

Unless Benito had prior charges in Nevada, he'd have to be tried in Georgia. Benito could survive without Valentino. I doubted Valentino could make it without Benito.

"Yeah, let everybody believe that I'm missing. Let them believe I'm missing until I know for sure Valentino and Benito are behind bars." How long would it take Sapphire to find them? I thought about Grant. I missed him so much it hurt. Did he miss me the same? Did he know what

I'd been through? Did he care?

"Including Grant?" Sapphire asked as though reading my mind. "He's here too. Got in a few hours before me."

Tears flowed down my face. I cried and laughed in the phone. "Including Grant?" Had to hear her say his name again.

Sapphire reiterated, "Yes, baby. Including Grant. He came right away. He loves you, Honey. Don't mess it up this time. Promise?"

"Promise," I said, ending our call. I hugged myself. Cried aloud, then shouted to heaven, "Somebody loves me."

The receptionist opened the door. "Miss, are you all right?"

"Yes, I'm better than all right. I'm blessed." I left her office, made my way back to the fast food restaurant, sat inside and waited for Sapphire.

Brain? Courage? Heart? Heart. For the first time in my life, I was sure even if my parents didn't, people truly loved me.

CHAPTER 13
GRANT

The raw essence of a woman could captivate a man when he least expected it.

A blank canvas. A beautiful woman, a model image. Abstract. Concrete. An attentive artist. One brush. Four basic colors. I'd start with the soul of her eyes. The softest strokes. Gentle hues hovering under arched brows. Lips, shape of a wide slanted heart. The tip of the brush gliding long, swerve, then curve. Inward. Outward. Hips, dip with the tip of her crevice. Swirl. Dab. Dip. Stroke. Feather. Flutter. Stroke the left breast. Sign . . . Trust. Frame. Knuckles to nails, I traced each finger of Honey's hand in my mind. I could describe every part of her body in detail.

I'd dozed off dreaming about Honey. Turbulence caused me to open my eyes. Glanced at my watch, then out the window. "Is this the right time?" I asked Jada, lifting my head from her shoulder.

"Yeah, our flight was delayed. We sat on the runway for a long time. Didn't want to wake you. You smiled a lot. You must've dreamt about Honey."

I nodded and smiled praying Honey was safe.

Jada sharing with me how much she'd loved Wellington gave me hope that Honey and I would soon experience that inseparable, immeasurable, unbreakable, never-ending love. I wondered if Jada regretted not having a child for her husband. I alternated resting her head on my shoulder. I wanted a platonic friend, a confidant.

"Jada?"

"Yes, Grant."

"What if?"

"If what?"

"What if everyone in the world had one solid relationship built on trust? A relationship that doubt could not stain, where lies would not exist, and infidelity would never penetrate. One perfect union amidst an endless sea of imperfections. One —"

"True love," she whispered. "Sweet as a songbird humming. A love so strong the eye, one eye, our third eye would weather every storm, together. One —"

"— Ness," I said. "A bond. Unbreakable. An eternal light of not forgiveness but understanding."

We both whispered, "What if?"

"Grant?"

"Yes," I said, afraid of where we'd gone. What she'd say next. As our plane landed on the runway, I didn't want to mislead Jada but the words we shared were melodic.

"You'll find Honey. I'll help you. And I should tell you you're a wonderful man."

"And I should tell you, you're beautiful."

I traced her cheek to her chin with the back of my pointing finger, then held her hand tighter. My thoughts shifted to the first day I'd met Honey. Honey was my age. Jada was twenty years our senior, old enough to be my mother. Jada's energy resonated with me, making me create a reason to prolong our time together. Perhaps because she reminded me in ways of my mother. Maybe because I feared the unknown. *Ding.* I unbuckled my seat belt, stood, stepped back, then waited for her to step out in front of me.

"Do you have anything in the overhead compartment?"

She smiled, pointed. "That's my laptop bag."

I retrieved the silver bag with the initial B inside the letter D. A diamond sparkled in the center. Brilliant marketing. I hung her bag on my shoulder, placed my hand above her hip, on her waist, waited for her to exit. My hand drifted from her waist to her hand during our journey to baggage claim. Our connection was natural and innocent, I thought.

"Let me know which suitcase is yours." Facing the carousel, I stood three feet behind her.

"If you're always this pleasant, I can see why a woman has captured your heart. I should be so lucky," she said, glancing over her shoulder, penetrating more than my eyes.

Down, boy, down. This was inappropriate for my dick to stand up. I was attracted to Jada's intellect, success, beauty, energy, and her magnetic appeal, not her vagina. Not many women possessed so much yet remained humble. But I was ready to find my Honey.

"You're phenomenal. I can see why Wellington cherishes you," I said.

"Correction," she said softly. "My husband is deceased."

I leaned toward her, hugged her from behind, then said, "Not in spirit. He's still protecting you."

Batting back tears, she said, "Oh . . . that bag is mine," pointing at her customized luggage with BD on the front as she backed into me.

I stepped around her, picked up her bag. "I need to make a few calls. It was wonderful meeting you. I'll give you a call later when Honey is safe."

"No bags for you?"

"I have a home here."

Her smile ignited mine. "Me too, but I always need something."

She'd opened a door that I had to close. Slowly, I smiled at her.

"Take your time, Grant. I'm in no hurry. I'll wait for you. Inside the bookstore, whenever you're ready."

I took a deep breath, exhaled. "Thanks. I won't keep you. I'll call you later."

Sitting on the edge of a bench outside the bookstore, I powered on my cell, dialed back the number Benito had called me from. The phone went straight to voice mail. I ended the call. Dialed again.

"Hey, bro. You late. You here?"

Grinding my teeth, I answered, "Yes, I'm here."

"Man, I'm dead broke. I mean dead like a copper Lincoln. Can you let me hold a few thousand? I'll pay you back. I need a place to stay."

There was no reason Benito should be

broke. He had multiple football champion-ship rings he could pawn. His last name should've been Simpson for more reasons than their being brute but not so bright star athletes. Benito blew his money trying to impress everybody except his son and his son's mother. Our parents kept his ass out of jail by paying his child support and he still had his empty hand out.

"Look, where are you?" I asked him, resenting bailing him out again.

"At this fleabag motel, bro, gettin' bit by bedbugs and stuff."

Grinding my teeth, I nearly fell off the bench. Sitting back, I asked, "Where is the motel?"

"Oh, I'm at . . . on Piedmont Ave. Not far from the botanical place."

"Stay there. I'll meet you. I'm going to set you up in one of my one-bedroom furnished condos for three months at Buckhead Pre-mier Palace. I suggest you get your act together by then or you'll be back at that fleabag motel."

"Thanks, bro, but can I get a two-bedroom? I'm with a male friend. We can't share one bed."

What the hell? I was so damn mad I stood up. "What the fuck you need two bedrooms for? Let him get his own place. Your trifling ass is never satisfied."

"My boy Valentino needs his own space. Seriously," he said. "But one is cool if that's all you got. We can share. He can sleep on my couch."

His couch? "Sure, no problem. I'll see you around seven."

I hadn't figured finding Valentino would be that easy. I'd postponed asking any questions about Honey until I was face to face with Benito and Valentino. I prayed I'd find Honey at the motel with them, rescue her, and take her home.

"Nah, man. We got to meet Sapphire and Red Velvet at Stilettos at eight. Can you come sooner? Oh, and I need to use one of your cars too. My prepaid phone is about to die. Can you get me a cell phone too, bro?"

I wanted to throw my cell phone into the store, knock the books down like dominos. I looked up and saw Jada smiling at me. Instantly I became calm. "I'll be there at six," I said, then ended the call before he asked for something else.

I realized I still had Jada's suitcase. Rolling her bag into the bookstore, I stood behind her at the counter.

"That'll be six dollars," the cashier said.

I placed my hand on top of Jada's. "I got

it," I said, handing the cashier a ten-dollar bill.

"For you." Jada handed me a cold bottle of water. "It's hot outside."

"Thanks. Look I have a lot on my mind —"

She interrupted. "But I'm not ready to leave you. Would you mind joining me for a quick bite? I can send a few text messages to my people. See if we can locate Honey."

There was that beautiful inside-out smile again, warming my heart. Jada's lips parted. I held my breath, hesitated then said, "Sure." I didn't want to rush to meet Benito. Plus I had to send a few e-mails to make arrangements for the two-bedroom condo, a car, and cell phone for him.

"We have to take a taxi, if that's all right with you," I said.

"My driver is outside. He can take us, if you don't mind," she said.

Damn, what else should I have expected from such a classy woman? I steadied her laptop atop her luggage, then followed her to the limo. The driver held open the door. I put my hand on Jada's waist, waited until she was inside, then I walked around to the opposite side.

When the driver closed my door, Jada moved closer to me. She placed her head on my shoulder and once more, I left it there. Tapping the e-mail icon on my iPhone, I e-mailed my management company and my personal assistant to meet me at the motel with keys to the condo, my Benz, and a new iPhone.

Continuing to respond to other e-mails, I recalled how Honey felt about emotional infidelity. I ignored Jada's head on my shoulder.

Chapter 14
Sapphire

Why did women in love play games, pretending they were not in love?

All men had symptoms of sexual ADHD. If her ass detoured, he'd disappear. Women had to learn, "Say what you mean and mean what you say." Women needed to save their tears for worthy causes. Men on earth did not have the patience of Job. Men initiated pursuit but they really wanted to be pursued, wanted women to pick up their slack on building a solid relationship while they scoured for new pussy. Women wanted men to pursue them. Women feared being judged as easy or sleazy so they'd hold out a second too long and let a good man get away. That would send him into the arms of someone else.

Was Santonio in the arms of someone else? When was he going to call me? I may have been a bit anxious but I wasn't in denial.

Honey wasn't fooling anyone except herself. She not only wanted Grant, she loved and needed him in her life. My job as her friend was to honor what she wanted and never tell her my truth. I'd fucked her man. She probably knew or had sensed the sexual tension, but I was over Grant. Every pussy battle wasn't worth the fight, especially if a woman won the war but lost her man.

Exiting the freeway, my ring tone played, "Can't be gettin' mad! What you mad? Can't handle that! . . ." A 212 area code appeared. I started to let the unrecognized number go to voice mail but then decided to answer. "Hello?"

"Hey, beautiful. How are you?" he said.

"You must have the wrong number," I said. Who'd call me beautiful?

"It's Santonio Ferrari. Maybe my greeting was too personal for my first time calling but you are beautiful."

I blushed. This man was off to a good start. "It's okay. Good hearing from you."

"I have a meeting in a few minutes so I can't talk for long. But are you available for dinner tomorrow night?"

I had so many questions for Santonio. "I'll make time," I said. Feeling like an infatuated teenager, I smiled.

"Great, I'll call you when I get to Atlanta. I can feel your smile. Bye, beautiful."

The detective in me wondered if he'd called me beautiful because he'd forgotten my name, didn't want to call me the wrong name, or if he referred to all women as beautiful. I added his 212 number in my phone to the 704 area code I'd programmed from his business card.

Parking in the lot, I entered the fast food restaurant looking for Honey. I was happy to find her but wasn't prepared to see the woman I'd given fifty million to looking nearly homeless. Honey was seated at a table in the back corner of the restaurant. Clothes dirty. Hair slightly tangled. I sat in the booth beside her, noticed a small cut under her chin.

"My God, what did they do to you?" I hugged her, held her.

She cried in my arms like a baby. Other than myself, Honey was the strongest woman I knew. I sympathized with her. This was the side of a strong woman that men seldom saw. We bled. We hurt. We cried. We broke down. We did things we weren't proud of but more importantly, we survived the best way we knew how. We picked ourselves up, brushed ourselves off, and kept going.

Unable to speak, Honey swallowed her words.

"Let's get you out of here, my friend." I let her lean on me until we got to the car.

I helped Honey into my SUV rental, then I got in, started the engine, and drove toward Interstate 75, merged north. "I'ma make a quick stop at my favorite restaurant off the Chattahoochee River and order us seafood to go. I'm starved." A drive-through would've been more convenient but whenever possible I ate the best of everything.

"I hate this shit!" Honey yelled, throwing something out the window.

"Honey," I softly said. "What was that?"

"My gun." She cried. "Some creep named Ken Draper," Honey said, wiping her nose with her palm. "I shot him. I hope that bastard dies. I mean . . ." Her words trailed off as she twirled the tip of her hair around her finger.

"Honey," I said, "did you kill him?"

She snapped. Her head whipped in my direction. "I just shot the motherfucker in his hands, I didn't kill him. God, I pray I didn't kill him."

"His hands?"

"Yes, his hands. They happened to be covering his dick," she said, staring out her window.

Okay, she was just getting started with her retaliation against men. I undetstood her so well because Honey was like me. Once I became angered and started knocking off pimps, I couldn't stop until I changed my environment. My current hit list was a dozen long. In order to stop killing, I needed to retire but I couldn't. I was addicted to my job. I had to help Honey calm down before she went insane.

I called my boss.

"Bleu, you in Atlanta yet?" he asked without saying hello.

"Boss, I need a condo in a gated community and a personal bodyguard in one hour. I have to place Honey Thomas in protective custody. And, yes. I'm here."

"You found her already, Bleu? How?"

"Yes, but until I arrest Valentino and Benito, I have to protect her. I'll give you details later. And see what you can find out about a shooting involving a Ken Draper."

"I'll call you back with the location within the hour. Ken Draper?" he repeated.

"Correct," I said, ending our call.

"I don't need no protective anything. Changed my mind. Take me home," Honey insisted. "I want to sleep in my bed."

"I know. With Grant. And you will, but right now my priority is to keep you safe," I told her, exiting the freeway.

"Grant won't want me after he finds out

138

who I really am and what I've done. I don't deserve him. Call my mother, my father, and Grant, and tell them all that I'm dead," Honey cried.

Yep, she was losing control. "You're making me nervous. You're not making any sense. Why do you want to lie about being dead?" I asked her, then said, "I have to keep you safe for a few days, so why don't I just tell Grant you're missing? We don't need to get your parents involved. After Valentino and Benito are incarcerated, and you're mentally ready, I can let everyone know you're safe. Actually that's a great idea. Everyone will be excited to see you. Is that okay?"

Honey yelled in my face, "Hell, no! You calling me crazy?"

"No, sweetheart. You are not crazy. You're stressed. You can do whatever you like. I'm recommending a safe place for you to stay for a few days. You decide."

"Fine," she agreed. "A few days, that's it."

Entering the parking lot of the restaurant, I self-parked facing the river, hoping the water would calm Honey. "Stay here. Do not get out of the car. I'm going to get us something to eat. What would you like?"

"Nothing," she said, folding her arms and

squinting. She stared at the water, squinted more.

I got out the car, locked the doors with the remote. I'd hear the alarm if she got out. "Can't be gettin' mad! What you mad? Can't handle that! . . ." I checked the ID, then answered, "Yes, boss."

"I've got your condo and Hunter is your personal bodyguard. You ready for the location?"

Damn, Hunter was already here? He was the one who'd be in protective custody from his bookies. Honey might be safer going home. I went to the bar, grabbed a napkin. "Ready," I said, writing the address and suite number for a condo at Buckhead Premier Palace. "Thanks, boss."

"Ken Draper was found in a cemetery an hour ago and rushed to Grady. He's in intensive care and being charged with first-degree murder. That's all I have for now. How are you involved in this, Bleu?"

"I'm not. Your ass is covered. Thanks, boss." I ended the call. By the time commuters drove over Honey's gun on the freeway, her .45 would be destroyed. One phone call and I'd make sure Honey was never associated with Ken. I was already preoccupied with finding Valentino and Benito. The police could handle Ken.

140

I ordered a broiled seafood platter, gumbo, clam chowder, a Caesar salad with chicken, and a Bloody Mary. I held the drink under my nose, inhaled. Santonio . . . what was he like? In bed? Out of bed? I took a sip. "Umph, umm." I bit the celery stick.

Fucked one now and then, but I'd avoided dating cops during my career. Figured we had too much in common. Would I be compatible with Santonio? What was I going to wear to dinner? My glass was half full when my order arrived. I paid the bill, left a generous tip, removed the lid from the clam chowder, crushed a sleeping pill, stirred it in, sealed the lid.

Carrying two bags out the door, I hurried to the car, pressed the button to silence the alarm. "Honey, what are you doing? I told you not to get out."

"Look," she said, pointing across the river. "Over there, between the trees. That looks like the car Valentino and Benito were in."

Oh, great. Now she was hallucinating. "Honey, get in the car. You're tired." I put our food in the backseat.

"Just look," she insisted.

I opened my glove compartment and got my binoculars, peered through them. "I'll be damned. There is an SUV over there."

"With the windshield blown out?"

"Yeah," I whispered in disbelief. It was eerie how things were happening.

"That's the car they used to kidnap me. I shot the windshield out before they drove off."

"Get in," I told Honey, then phoned the local police, reported the abandoned SUV. "Let's eat here. Wait until they arrive."

I gave Honey her chowder, ate my gumbo. We shared the seafood and salad. Honey told me about her day. I told her about mine, about Santonio. When the police arrived, we left. I'd call them later. Before I entered the freeway, I looked over at Honey. She was asleep — perfect. I prayed she'd stay asleep until I arrived at her condo. That way she'd have no idea she was less than six blocks from her house.

CHAPTER 15
RED VELVET

Should a woman stay in an abusive marriage for better or for worse? Was *or* the operative word? Had Onyx's husband been abusing her before she married him? There must have been warning signs. Isolation. Control. Did her husband tell her what to wear? Did he start off slapping her? My mama had told me slapping was not a sign that a man loved me. If a man slapped, he'd punch. If he punched, he'd stalk. If he stalked, he'd kill. Good thing Onyx left him or he may have killed her before she could've killed him. Spending each day in fear was no way for a woman to live.

Some men needed to present a note from their mother: "May cause nausea, diarrhea, vomiting, abdominal pain, migraines, weakness, heartburn, depression, low self-esteem, retardation, epilepsy, insanity, bleeding, muscle pain, thoughts of suicide, allergic reaction, bruising, rash, hives, hypertension, itching/swelling (especially of the face, tongue, and throat), dizziness, trouble breathing, heart attack, and mortality in women with high self-esteem. The risks of your marrying or dating my son are greater than the benefits. If you can survive his side effects, you are one helluva woman."

I had lots of questions but after almost suffering whiplash when she slammed on the brakes, I wasn't initiating a conversation with Onyx about anything. One day I'd like to marry a good man who'd love my son and me. Maybe I'd meet him in Hollywood and marry him before I achieved stardom. That way I'd know he wasn't marrying me for my money.

"Make yourself at home, Red Velvet," Onyx said, standing at the foot of the stairway in Honey's mansion. "Eat, sleep, chill until it's time to go to Stilettos. You've got one hour to relax. You can nap on Honey's chaise but do not get in her bed." Onyx trotted upstairs.

Goddamn! I tripped out big time. Touring Honey's first floor, I was amazed at her foyer, her kitchen, her office and hallway. I could not believe the countless number of C-notes lamenated beneath the clear marbled floors. If the hundred-dollar bills were real, we could rip out the floors to pay her ransom.

"Now this is a mansion worth featuring on a major cable show. I'd call it Divalicious Cribs, with your host Velvet Waters. Forget all those famous rappers and ballers, they need to highlight how female millionairesses do it up," I said, stretching across the white mink spread on Honey's bed.

I scrambled to the bottom of my purse, pulled out my cell phone. Nine missed calls. I left the ringer on mute, called my mother back first, to check on her and my son.

My mom answered. "Velvet Waters, child, where are you? Your agent has called here three times saying you're not answering your phone. Ronnie is worried sick. And you know I'm worried too. It doesn't take that long to celebrate with Honey. Lunchtime ended hours ago."

"Ma, Ma, please calm down. I'ma call my agent next. I'm fine. Honey is missing. We're trying to find her," I explained, hoping my mother would understand.

"Missing. As in lost?" Mama asked. "She's a grown woman. Grown women don't just come up missing."

"No, Ma. As in kidnapped. Valentino is holding her for his fifty-million dollars. He wants his money back."

"Lord, Jesus. Yes, indeed. Protect my baby

and Honey. Velvet, you're not making sense. None. Honey is too smart to be missing. Do not get involved in her games. You have a lifetime opportunity in front of you with this movie. Don't blow it. Ronnie deserves this break. Me too. Get yourself home right this minute."

My mother had started researching private schools for Ronnie, a nice home for us to buy, good stock investments, and a retirement plan for me. I was only twenty-six. I did not need a 401(k) plan. We lived in a good neighborhood a few blocks from the Twelve Hotel where I used to work. Ronnie was in a decent public school. Having money, millions of dollars, would afford us a better lifestyle, but Mama said it was up to us to live a better life.

"Sorry, Mama."

My mother scolded, "Sorry my behind. You don't owe Honey anything."

Was my mom serious? "Mama, you didn't feel that way when you asked Honey to find Alphonso, make him pay child support so I'd quit stripping for extra money. She found him. She got me seventy-two thousand from him and she didn't charge us one cent. I can't come home, Ma. Not until I know Honey is safe. I love you. Kiss my baby and tell him I love him. I'll be home soon. I promise. Bye, Ma."

"Vel—"

I hated hanging up on my mother but there was no sense in arguing with her. I wondered where Honey was, whether or not Valentino had hurt her. "This mink is nice," I said, rubbing it. I couldn't sleep. It was almost time to leave for Stilettos and I hadn't heard from Sapphire or Grant. Mama called back. I let her call go to voice mail. She wasn't changing my mind.

I called my agent. Got his voice mail and left a message. "Hi, this is Velvet Waters. I apologize for the delay in returning your calls. I had a family emergency. I'm still on schedule and will be in LA in a few days. Call me back." Felt like I was rambling so I ended the call. Better go upstairs and see if Onyx would let me wear some of her clothes. Honey's bed felt so good, I couldn't move. I lay my head on her white mink pillow, then closed my eyes.

Tap. Tap.

I rolled over, then called out, "Come in."

Onyx opened Honey's bedroom door. "What the hell! Are you deaf! I told you not to get in Honey's bed," Onyx yelled.

I had to straight stare at her for five minutes before responding. If I kept being passive, Onyx would think she could talk to me any way she wanted. If I replied to her in the same way she approached me, either she'd hear how crazy she sounded and stop it or I'd have to fight my way out of this situation and take my ass home.

"Onyx, what is your fucking problem? I have a child. I am not yours. You said, 'do not get in.' I'm *on* the bed, not *in* the bed. *In* means under the covers, not on top of the covers." I got up off the bed. Stood by the edge in case I had to hit her ass with Honey's gold lamp.

"Don't make me beat your ass," Onyx said, staring at me.

Moving closer to the lamp, I said, "And you know me well enough to understand I ain't going out without a fight. I'll stomp your ass if I have to." Bitch done lost her mind.

Onyx's lips tightened. Casually she said, "I apologize. It's just that I'm so stressed. Come with me. Let's get you dressed."

Cautiously following Onyx into her room, I asked, "You hear from Sapphire or Grant yet?"

"Grant called. Said he'd meet us at Stilettos. He might be a few minutes late. He had to take care of a few things first."

Why hadn't Grant called me? "What could be more important than finding

Honey?"

"Exactly," Onyx said, walking to her bedroom closet. She opened the door to a mini boutique, said, "Find something sexy to wear," then quietly sat in her rocking chair by the window.

I stood in the closet's doorway. There were dozens of dresses with tags on them. Onyx had dresses from simply sexy to formal, casual, and high fashion. Above her dresses were stacks of Michael Kors, Jimmy Choo, and Marc Jacobs shoes.

"I was thinking about asking Trevor if I could strip tonight. Lure Valentino in with a lap dance, then Sapphire can do her thing," I said.

"Not tonight." Onyx kept staring out the window. "Velvet, I keep telling you this is not a game. We're —"

I interrupted her. "Why you keep talking to me like I don't understand?"

"Because you don't. You have no idea what's really going on. We're dealing with a pimp and murderer who seems nice and charming but he won't think twice about killing us for his money. Valentino will charm your pussy off you, then cut your throat. My life depends on what you do and you're not stripping tonight. Shaking your ass on stage will make you an easy target for anyone in the club to take you out." Onyx walked to her nightstand, opened the drawer. "Put on something sexy, and keep this with you," she said, handing me a .9 and a holster. "Strap the holster high upon your thigh."

Staring at the gun in my hand, I thought, *I am no murderer.* I'd never pulled the trigger on a gun, not even at a shooting range. I wanted my mommy. "I'm going home."

Onyx handed me a short black dress, then said, "Like I told you, you can go home *after* we find Honey. If Valentino doesn't bring her with him tonight, I'll have to put you and the other girls on a stroll or two."

"I ain't no prostitute," I told her. "I'm not strolling anywhere."

"I won't keep you out there long. You'll only have to solicit information."

"Don't get me confused. I used to be a stripper, not a ho," I told her.

"Bitch, don't make me go there," Onyx said with a stern face. "Shut up and get your ass dressed . . . now! Sapphire is on her way."

Good. I was tired of trying to reason with Onyx. Maybe I could talk sensibly with Sapphire.

CHAPTER 16
VALENTINO

A toilet. A motherfuckin' porcelain pot with a plastic seat. Whosoever created this bitch was sho' nuff my nigga. Sitting down, the tip of my nuts marinated in the bowl and I didn't give a fuck. For a nigga who was used to dumping his insides three times a day, pissing around with Lace's ass this morning, then dealing with Benito, I was backed up. Lifting my balls, I tightened my abs, took a deep breath, then let it all out.

I'd locked myself in the bathroom to keep Benito from walking in on me. That nigga didn't have manners. How the hell did Lace live with him for three years? Those two couldn't have been more wrong for one another. Nigga's dick must've been a magic stick.

"Oowee! Look at that pile of shit," I said, flushing my defecation, urination, and frustrations. "Who was the recipient of all the shit and bullshit in the world?" Maybe I could chop up Lace's body, then literally flush her ass.

I turned the shower handle to H, stepped in, put my head under the water, then closed my eyes. I was in a one-star motel. I'd give this cheap-ass place no stars, if that was a rating. This was the kind of joint johns rented by the hour to get their trophy waxed, bang a bitch's skull against the wall — cause the headboard was so damn cheap it would break — then go home to their wife and kids. One day soon, I'd build another mansion bigger and better than my spots Sapphire seized in north Las Vegas. I'd take my chances trying to overpower Lace but I wasn't fucking with Sapphire. I bet if I looked between her legs she'd have two giant intimidating jaw-breaking balls.

I admired my naked body. The push-ups I'd done in prison the short time I was in that hellhole cut a nigga in the right places. A clean ass, asshole, and a close shave had done wonders for my fucked-up attitude. Staring in the mirror, I told myself, "Tonight is gonna be smooth." I began blow drying my hair, then the boxers that I'd hand washed in the shower. I felt crisp, like new money.

Flapping my silk underwear, I held them in front my nose, sniffed the crotch, then put them on. I was happy, smelling good, revitalized. Damn. The only thing missing was some good tight pussy and a bottle of cognac. I'd never worked this hard to get shit.

Knock. Knock. Knock. "V, pack yo' shit, man," Benito said, grinning as I walked out of the bathroom slinging my hair.

I asked that nigga, "What are you talking about? I ain't got nothing to pack. You neither."

"My brother is on his way, man. To pick *us* up. Said we could stay in one of his condos in Buckhead rent free for three months — a two bedroom. And we can leave that stolen car across the street at the mall. Grant said we can use one of his cars."

Should I kick Benito's dumb ass or kiss him for telling Grant where we were? "How you know that nigga ain't settin' us up?"

Benito shook his head. "Our mama wouldn't like that."

"Your mama?" I swear I wanted to smack him upside his head. "You mean the white lady you despise? That mama?"

"She still loves me. My stepdad too. I'm irresistible, V."

"Check this shit here out, nigga. When your brother gets here, we don't know shit about Lace being kidnapped. He'll believe us because she's not with us. And even if she shows up here with him, act like you haven't seen that bitch in a long time. Kiss her."

Benito bobbed his head. "Oh, you want me to play dumb."

I shook my head. "Shut the fuck up and listen. Let me do the talking. Can you handle that?"

Benito scratched his ass, nodded.

Sniffing the air, I said, "Go wash your resistible ass, nigga, before he gets here."

Chapter 17
Grant

Choice. Free will. Every man had it. Few women exercised it.

It was a man's world. The disproportionate number of confident, competent, and caring women made it that way. I could date Jada, sex Jada and marry Honey, sex Honey and marry Jada, or date them at the same time, brainwashing them with empty promises of becoming Mrs. Grant Hill, but I wasn't a user.

No matter what men did, women heard what they wanted. A man could explain or apologize his way back into a woman's heart before her tears dried. Women could not take their expectations out of the equation long enough to tap the core of men. Women's expectations were rooted in learned behavior from their single mothers, widowed grandmothers, unmarried siblings, out-of-relationship girlfriends, and nosy ill-intent coworkers. Women were pre-programmed for relationship failure.

I wanted to marry the woman who was an extension of me. She'd complete my thoughts, my sentences, my goals . . . my life. Honey was that woman. But could Jada do the same?

No doubt, I'd fantasized about fucking Jada. Most men's dicks functioned on autopilot. I was no exception. Sex bonded women to men. Beauty bonded men to women. Having a wife that other men envied made a man stand tall, stick out his chest, hold her hand, beg her to stay after he'd messed up. If a man didn't fight to keep his woman, he didn't love her. For my Honey, I was ready to go ten rounds nonstop.

My concern was women incubated their issues for days, weeks, months, and years. Would Honey remind me that I'd fucked Red Velvet? Would I tell Honey I had sex with Sapphire before proposing to Honey? After? Was Honey dead? Alive? Would I drop the flawless five-carat diamond solitaire in Honey's champagne glass, toast, then propose to her? Home was where the heart was. My heart was with Honey. My hands were on my iPhone. Jada's hand was on my thigh.

Jada's driver parked in front of my favorite restaurant on the Chattahoochee River.

Tucked away on the water, I loved the serene ambiance of this place. It was my getaway to dine alone or with my clients. I considered Jada a potential client. I held the door for her, led the way to the bar, pulled out her stool, then made sure she was comfortable. Jada had an elegance about her that resonated, "I am a WOMAN." I was proud to be in her company.

"I think I heard the bartenders talking about a car being stolen," Jada said as she kissed my cheek, barely missing my lips.

I shook my head. "Here? Not here."

"I think so," she said.

Not my car. Not my problem. I was solely concerned about finding my woman. I had to wait an hour for my personal assistant to meet me at the motel, wasn't sitting in a bag of fleas with my brother that long. Eating made sense since I didn't know if I'd have that chance later. "What would you like?"

Jada's eyes softened along with her voice. "A stiff one. A stiff one would be really nice."

Hmm, innuendos. I was not following her lead. "A bottle of champagne, two salads, and an order of crab cakes," I told the bartender, then asked, "Was someone's car stolen from here?"

"We're on top of things. This has never happened before." He handed me a business card. "The license number, make, model, and color are on here. If you see the car, give us a call." They couldn't be too on top of things if he expected me to look for the car.

The pianist started playing. Jada smiled. "Um, I love Ricardo Scales."

Impressive — she knew the artist. Beautiful, smart, and she enjoyed smooth jazz. Nodding, I sang the jazz rendition of Roberta Flack's "The First Time Ever I Saw Your Face."

Jada gazed into my eyes. "I'll never forget the first time I saw your face. When you rushed onto the plane, I looked into your eyes, looked at you . . ." She paused, then said, "And I saw the most handsome man. But I also saw worry in your eyes and I prayed your seat was next to mine."

Was I blushing? Yes, I was. I placed my foot on the bar beneath her stool. "Why did you want me to sit next to you?" I sipped champagne while listening to her sultry voice.

She sang, "The first time ever I kissed your mouth." This time Jada kissed me on the cheek as I turned my lips away from hers. "Honestly, no man has captured my attention the way you did. I was instantly drawn to you. I tried making things work with Darius's dad after my Wellington passed away." She shook her head, exhaled, then continued, "What I realized was, I didn't want to be with Darryl. But I didn't want to be alone either. He helped me through the tough times, then I let him go. Wellington was my soul. . . ." Her words trailed off.

Honey was my soulmate. Quietly, I held Jada's hand. Gave her, gave us, a moment of silence to reflect on what was going through our minds. The first thing I'd do when I saw Honey was tell her how foolish I was and let her know how much I loved her.

Sipping champagne, Jada's smile returned. "I like you, Grant. Honestly, I want us to be more than friends. I hope you can make it to the game tomorrow night."

As in lovers? "I could use a platonic friend right now," I said. "But first I have to find my Honey. I love that woman so much. I don't want to mislead you or ruin your impression of me."

Glad the food was placed on mats in front of us, I began eating my salad.

Jada gently rubbed my thigh. "Not at all. I admire your determination to find Honey. I wish more men were so loyal. There'd be fewer heartbreaks. But if you don't mind me saying, I'm attracted to you. And I also want to know about your Honey. You see, once a woman gets an image of another woman in her mind, she can never erase it. If you tell me about Honey, I will never forget her. And I look forward to meeting her one day."

The pianist started playing "A Taste of Honey" by the same artist. Drifting into the melody, I devoured my crab cakes, tossed my napkin on the plate when I was done.

"You ready?" Jada tapped my hand. "Are you ready?"

"Oh, I apologize. I zoned out for a moment. What did you say?"

Jada clung her flute to mine, took one last sip. I had another fifteen minutes before I had to leave. I closed out the tab, then suggested, "Let's take a short walk along the river."

We walked outside, sat on a bench facing the river, and shared our philosophical opinions about love, our dreams, and aspirations while watching the sunset.

"You have any children, Grant?"

"No, but Honey and I plan on having two, maybe three," I said, thinking about how beautiful Honey would look pregnant with our children. Her golden belly would radiate like a ball of sunshine. I'd rub her stomach every day while talking to our child inside her womb. I was going to be the best dad, just like my father. "You want more kids?"

"No. It's a little late for me, agewise. But it would've been nice to have reared Darius in a home with his real father. Wellington was my second husband. My first was Lawrence, a great man who did all the right things for me. I ruined that marriage, ruined him. I simply wasn't ready for marriage but I was tired of raising Darius by myself."

I talked with Jada like I'd known her for years. After a while I noticed whenever I mentioned Honey, she'd rant about Wellington. I changed our focus. "What's it like being the mom of a professional basketball player?"

Jada laughed. "I encouraged Darius to be whatever he wanted. That way he'd have no regrets about what he should've done with his life. He's married and has the perfect wife for him. Fancy was the only woman who held Darius accountable for his promiscuous actions. Then I have a stepdaughter by my first husband. Her name is Ashlee." Jada fanned the air. "That's a long story. That poor girl has lost her mind behind

Darius. She's angry he didn't marry her after she had his baby —"

We'd taken a wrong turn in the conversation. Jada's life was too dramatic. My thoughts had drifted back to Honey. The sun faded, exchanging places with a rising moon. I could tell that the story was going to be long and convoluted, so I interrupted, "I need to get going. Have to put my brother up in one of my condos." I smiled, escorting Jada back to her limo. "I guess we both have interesting stories. I'll have to tell you about my brother, Benito, at a later time, over drinks, at happy hour."

We laughed together.

Settling in the backseat, again she lay her head on my shoulder. When we arrived at the motel, I wasn't ready for our time together to end but I had to deal with reality. Quickly, she kissed my lips.

"Bye, Grant. I'll check on you tomorrow and let you know if I find out anything on Honey."

"Thanks." The driver opened my door, and in front me Benito stood grinning.

CHAPTER 18
GRANT

Benito lowered his head. I closed the limo door.

"What's up, bro? Was that Honey? You could've let her speak to me," he said.

"None of your business who that was," I answered, scanning the motel lot for my car and my personal assistant. "Where's Valentino?" I asked Benito, dialing my assistant.

"You're there?" my assistant asked.

"You're not," I replied.

"Too many propositions going on over there, Mr. Hill. I'm down the street at the mall. Be there in a minute," he confirmed.

Couldn't blame him for not waiting here. Rusted trucks, dented cars, and broken down women in slanted heels consumed the pothole ridden parking lot. The _OOMS __ABLE __ABLE __UZZI__PA sign flickered, leaving one to fill in the blanks. A woman in a short tight pink dress with high white heels approached me. "I'll suck your dick

over there behind that car for ten bucks."
She smiled and removed her dentures.

"How much for me?" Benito asked.

Digging in my pocket, I handed her a
hundred, then said, "Take the day off."

"Thanks." She sucked in her teeth, then
went into the lobby.

Valentino trotted down the steps as my
assistant parked in the driveway. Another
car parked behind my assistant.

"Here's the keys to your car, your condo,
and here's your iPhone. I'll be in my car
waiting for you," my assistant said.

"You can leave. I'll get home," I said,
handing Benito the black box with his
phone inside and the keys to the condo.
"I'm leaving this car with you."

Benito started grinning. "Thanks, bro.
That red convertible we kinda borrowed
from that restaurant on the Chattahoochee
is across the street at the mall."

Amazing. Don't know why I was surprised
Valentino stole that car. I slid my hand
inside my pants' pocket. Made sure the card
the bartender had given me with the vehicle
information was still there. I'd report the
location of convertible to the police when I
got home. My brother wasn't that smart. I
knew he was along for the ride.

"Wait!" I ran to my assistant's car. "Meet

me at this address in thirty minutes."
Valentino and Benito were not dropping me
off at my house.

I walked back to Benito, noticed his face
was clean, clothes not really dirty, but dingy.
The knees of Valentino's pants were scuffed.
"Come here," I told Benito. I held his
hands. Flipped them over. No scratches. His
face — no marks. My Honey would've
definitely fought her kidnappers.

He pulled away. "Wha'cha doing, man?"
Benito asked, opening the box. "Yeah, just
what I wanted for my birthday. Yo, V. Look
what I got. This is my brother, Grant.
Grant, this here is Valentino."

"Sweet, nigga."

After the introductions, Benito sat in the
front seat of my Benz. Valentino followed
me to the driver's side.

A petite woman in boy-cut shorts, a tank
top, and high heels raced to my door. "How
much?" Her eye was swollen, jaw bruised.

I dug in my pocket. Valentino held up his
hand. I checked for scratches, cuts, signs
he'd been in a struggle. Nothing. "Don't
give her ass shit. Bitch, roll."

"Please," she begged. "You gave her a
hundred for doing nothing. I'll do it all."

Valentino shook his head. "Bitch, step.
Let's go, G. You're not used to all this," he

said, waiting for me to get in first.

"Here." I handed her a hundred, got in my car, headed north on Piedmont.

"You're too soft, G. That ho just gon' give that C-note to her pimp. Make that nigga think she's holding out on him. He's liable to beat her ass again."

Was he telling the truth?

"That's why I'm allergic to cheap bitches," Valentino said. "No telling what she's got. Thanks for picking us up, nigga. I owe you. And when Valentino owes a favor, a nigga has got your back. Never know who you gonna need in the fucked up world."

Me need him? Never. "I'm not your G or your nigga. My name is Grant."

That was my first time meeting Valentino. Minus the profanity, he didn't seem like the type who'd kidnap Honey or beat a woman. He was charming as hell. I understood how this man was a pimp with escorts versus prostitutes on the street. My Honey actually worked for him. I wondered if she'd ever fucked him? Hoped not. Didn't want the answer to that one.

"Straight. No problem . . . Grant."

"Bro, was that Honey in the limo you got out of?"

"Stop with all the *bro* stuff before I drop your ass off at the police station for kidnapping Honey. You tell me, where is Honey?"

Benito hunched his shoulders. "Why you so sensitive?"

Valentino said, "We haven't seen her."

"Then why are the two of you in Atlanta?" I asked them.

"Unfinished business. A nigga gotta get some ends," Valentino said then reiterated, "When you see her, let her know I got something for her. Ain't no telling where she's at. That's how we roll in this lifestyle. Here today. Gone to motherfucking morrow. I might be up outta the ATL by tomorrow myself. Seriously, Grant we haven't seen Honey."

I said, "Yeah, like you haven't seen that red convertible across the street in the mall's lot. When you leave, take Benito with you."

Valentino slapped the back of Benito's head.

Benito blurted, "Sorry, V. Bro, I was hoping you'd invite Honey to dinner so I could apologize for outing her in front of Mom and Dad. You talk to Mom today? I'ma call her on my new iPhone you just gave me," he said.

Yeah, right. He didn't have any numbers programmed in his phone.

Benito tapped the screen, paused for a

moment. "Hey, Mom. It's me, your next to favorite son."

"You are not talking to Mom," I told him. "Press the speaker button."

I heard, "Grant baby, you okay? Your father and I are worried you haven't returned our calls today."

"What about me, Mom? You worried about me too?"

"Grant sweetheart, where'd you find your brother?"

"I didn't, Ma. He found me. Love you. I'll call you later. Promise. Bye."

Benito yelled, "Bye, Ma. Grant and I are coming home. I'll see you soon."

"Don't think Mama can save you. Onyx said your friend Valentino back there demanded fifty million dollars for Honey. Said the two of you kidnapped Honey from her house this morning."

"That," Valentino paused, then continued, "Onyx is a pathological liar. Why would we be in your car if we had kidnapped your girl?"

Driving into my development, I parked in front of a rental condo in the middle of the complex. "That's what I want to know," I said. I handed my brother the keys to the condo and car.

"Your unit is upstairs. You've got ninety

168

days. That's it."

"Sweet," Valentino said. "If you ever need me G, let a nigga know."

"Thanks, bro."

I shook my head, got in my assistant's car. Honey was too smart to be kidnapped by Benito or Valentino. Until I found out the truth, I didn't know who was lying. Valentino? Benito? Onyx? Sapphire? Or Honey?

CHAPTER 19
SAPPHIRE

Was I jealous of Honey?

Tangled hair and tattered clothes didn't detract from Honey's beauty. She slept peacefully. I hated slipping that pill in her food, but had to do it to keep her calm. Keep her from freaking out again. Keep her location unknown to her until the mission was accomplished.

If I weren't her friend, I could take her man and her money the same way I'd taken Valentino's money.

What was wrong with me? "Let it go," I told myself. "Give Santonio a chance." My wicked thoughts weren't predicated on having Honey's money or Grant. It was the power. The excitement. My ability to control others. Valentino got what he deserved, had a lot more coming. My new challenge was to find Valentino and Benito. No one made a fool of me. When I put a criminal in lockup, they stayed there until I approved letting them out. Valentino outsmarted me but not for long. His ass was going back to Nevada's prison, hopefully tonight. Benito didn't pose a threat to anyone but himself. Multiple counts of stupidity would warrant a lesser sentence.

Honey hadn't asked for Valentino's money. I gave it to her. By doing so, I had endangered her life. I had the power to blackmail her for the hundred million, get all of her money, and put Valentino away for kidnapping her. That setup would squash the rumors that I had Valentino's money. I could marry Grant, an upstanding citizen never in trouble with the law. Have his babies. Live happily.

Regardless of how screwed up my thoughts were, I could never harm Honey. Honey was sweet. The few months I'd really known her, Honey never complained about her mother or childhood, her life as a prostitute or a madam. Twelve-plus years in the business, Honey had her own money — not as much as what I'd given her but she was a multimillionaire before we'd met. She'd fought her way out of every situation today. First Valentino, then Ken.

Approaching Buckhead Premier Palace, I glanced at Honey. Her head hung toward her lap, bounced as I rolled over the speed bump and entered the gate. I texted Hunter: We're here. Open the garage door.

I parked. He pressed a button, the garage door closed.

Damn! That chocolate, bald, sexy man stood in the doorway like a framed picture of seduction. Hunter made my pussy throb. Santonio, he was nice but no pussy throbs, pulsations, or palpitations for him. Hunter could pull my hair, push me against the wall, fuck me numb. I looked at Honey. Contemplated going inside, fucking Hunter right quick, then coming back to get her. Shit, my fantasizing about Hunter let me know I was overdue for a good fuck.

I got out the car. "Come get her," I said. "She's knocked out."

Hunter opened Honey's door, slid his arms behind her back and under her knees. Honey lifted her head, opened her eyes, looked around, stared at me, closed her eyes. Her head fell forward.

"Put her in the bed," I said, going to my trunk. I opened my suitcase, gathered a pair of sweats, a T-shirt, and socks, then went inside.

Starting in the living room, I surveyed the condo. Peanut butter leather sofa, matching reclining chair. Track lighting on the ceiling illuminated a combination of two large mirrors and two unframed oil paintings hung on one wall. Wall-to-wall snow white carpet brightened the room. Seeing Hunter brightened my spirit.

I made my way to the bathroom, which contained a Jacuzzi, separate shower; both could comfortably accommodate two. I smiled with thoughts of the things I'd do to Hunter in that bathroom.

In the bedroom was a king-sized bed with four high posts, almost a dozen black and white pillows. Honey was laid atop the black faux-fur comforter. A white sham draped to the floor. I returned to the living room to find Hunter reclining in the chair with his legs spread wide, hand on his dick.

"Get comfortable there," I told him. "This was supposed to be a two bedroom. I don't want you fucking her."

Hunter stood, his crotch centered in front of me. Baggy sweats flowed over the hump of his dick. Hands big, thick fingers that could firmly grip my ass like he'd done before. "No one tells Hunter *how* to do his job. If you don't think I'm the man for you, hire someone else."

Yeah, right. Obviously he didn't know I was aware of his gambling debt. I took a deep breath, positioned myself away from Hunter's dick, tossed the clothes in my hand on the sofa. Those would have to do for Honey until I made it to her house to get some of her clothes.

"Where in the hell am I?" Honey entered the living room stretching her arms above her head.

I should've put two sleeping pills in her food so she'd sleep into the night. Her waking up early dismissed all chances of my getting fucked by Hunter. "This is your new home," I told her.

Honey shook her head. "No, it's not. I'm going to the bathroom and when I come out, you are taking me to my house." She stared at Hunter. "Who the hell is that?"

Hunter grinned. "I'm your bodyguard."

"Damn. I might have to rethink leaving until the morning," Honey said. She went in the bathroom, closed, then locked the door.

I stared into Hunter's deep-set brown eyes, squinted, then looked away when Honey came out of the bathroom. "This arrangement is just until Valentino is under arrest," I reminded her. "How are you going to be missing if you go home?"

"Fuck that bitch Valentino," Honey said, pacing in front of the coffee table. "Punk ass sneaking up on me. Balls too small to confront me." She pulled out a .22, held it with one hand, pointed at me. "I don't know who the fuck to trust. But I will say this. Any motherfucker that crosses Honey is catching a bullet with my name on it." She sat the .22 on the table.

"Make that your last time pointing a gun in my face." Annoyed with Honey, I phoned my boss.

"Bleu, you there yet?" he asked. No hello.

"We're at the location. Thanks, this spot is really sweet. I'll call you later."

"Bleu, do your job and get outta there safe. And let Hunter do his job. You aren't his boss, I am. Bye," he said, ending our call.

The hell I wasn't. Boss was a man of few words and a huge heart for me and his other employees. I cared about him too. Almost wished he weren't happily married with kids. My reset biological clock was pushing toward my goal of having a child by the age of thirty-two. My original plan was thirty.

"Honey, this is Hunter. Hunter is here for whatever you need. Whatever you need," I repeated, then said, "except sex."

Soon as his assignment was over, Hunter was going to frisk me all over. "Pat her down," I told him. "Take any other weapons you find."

Hunter smiled. His hands roamed

Honey's body. I was jealous.

Honey stared at me. Her lips tightened, eyes narrowed.

When Hunter's hands stopped moving, they were empty.

"You missed a spot," Honey said, tapping her pussy.

"I know you're engaged and in love with Grant. Hunter knows that too. I put it in your profile," I lied. "I'm defining the rules up in here. This is strictly a business arrangement. Actually, it's more of a favor from me to you, Honey. You can have your gun back when all of this is resolved."

"Fuck a favor. I ain't no damn charity case. That toy gun is not mine. It's Valentino's. And stay out of my personal business. I can handle Grant."

"Obviously not." I looked at the gun. Valentino's? He really was doing bad.

Honey wished she was engaged to Grant. What was my problem? I came to Atlanta to rescue Honey. Now that I knew she was safe and felt she was trying to control the situation, I decided to play my own games.

Hunter sat in the recliner. "The rules are, you cannot open any doors or the alarm will sound. You cannot open the blinds or I will mouth off at you, and trust me, you don't want to hear me yell. You will not be alone for one second, even when you're in the bathroom. And these," Hunter said, holding up a set of hand and ankle cuffs, "are for when you sleep."

"Well, why don't you wipe my ass after I shit?" Honey asked sarcastically.

Nodding, Hunter replied, "No problem. I'd be delighted."

"I'd be delighted for you to test those handcuffs on me," I said, eyeing Hunter. "Make sure they're not defective."

This time Hunter shook his head. "That won't be necessary."

"Honey, you make the call," I said, reverting to my professional persona. "You still want to follow through with the plan of my telling everyone you're missing? Or do you want to go home?"

Was my personal reservation for Hunter being cancelled by him? Men had a way of letting women know when they were not interested. Then again, Hunter could've been oblivious to my advance. I had to make sure. Damn, wasn't I the one who said I wouldn't chase another man after Grant slapped me in the face with his love for Honey?

"I need this assignment," Hunter protested. "She's not going anywhere until the boss says so."

Honey was my age but looked younger. She was cute, with a golden complexion and long curly blond locks. She had a cupholder booty that jiggled when she wiggled, and her cheeks separated just enough to command every man's — straight or gay — attention. She was so gorgeous Grant knew but didn't care about her jaded past.

"Absolutely I'm missing. I want to find out if Grant is loyal to me and I don't want to risk being kidnapped by those fools again," Honey said, sitting on the sofa.

Telling Honey about the meeting at Stilettos tonight wasn't a smart idea. Checking the time on my phone, I realized I had to meet Onyx at Honey's house soon to go over our plan.

I looked at my caller ID, then said, "I need to take this call in private." I placed my clothes in Honey's lap, then went to the bedroom. I heard them close the bathroom door as I closed the bedroom door. "Hey."

"Any word on Honey yet?" Grant asked.

"Not yet. I'm wrapping up a call with my boss on the other line. Can we talk in say, thirty minutes?" I had to get out of that condo before I embarrassed myself with Hunter again.

"Wait," Grant said.

"Yes."

"What time should I meet you at Stilet-tos?"

"I don't want you to come. Honey is already endangered. I don't want anything to happen to you."

He asked again, "What time?"

"If you insist, eight o'clock. But I don't recommend you come. I'll call you in a few. Bye." I had to end the call. Didn't want Honey to walk in on me talking to Grant.

Valentino wasn't going down easily. What-ever the outcome, I hoped it didn't cost Honey her man. Grant could get shot, killed, scared, or disgusted. I tapped on the bathroom door.

Hunter peeped through the crack. I heard the shower in the background.

"Hunter, do your job right and you might get a bonus to help pay off your debt," I whispered, winking at him.

"No worries. Honey is making it easy for me to do my job. I might not ever let her out of my sight. That way I could get a fat bonus."

I glanced down. His dick was harder than the doorknob. I considered calling in his replacement immediately. If Honey gave Hunter a taste of her pussy, he'd be the one in protective custody. Bitch had all of us catering to her. Hunter need not confuse Honey with the one signing his damn check.

CHAPTER 20
SAPPHIRE

Don't take your money to your grave.

Honey's ass had it going on. Unlike me, she was not hoarding her money. I drove up her long driveway, parked the front of my rental facing the exit for a fast getaway if necessary. Her damn resort home blinged like a Vegas casino. A row of luxury cars, none under eighty grand, lined her driveway. Neither my house nor my car in Vegas measured up to any of this.

I got my suitcase, carried it a few steps. Onyx greeted me at the door before I touched the doorbell. I pressed the platinum cobra and heard the sound of chimes blowing in the wind. Stepping in the foyer, I asked, "How did Valentino and Benito get in?"

Onyx retorted, "Girl Six was the last one to leave and I need to know if she left the door opened. If she's involved. Now I can't find her. She's not answering her damn phone."

Was Girl Six involved in Honey's disappearance? She was the last escort to move in with Honey. The only one who'd stayed behind in Las Vegas. The only one that Honey had beaten. The last one to leave the house this morning. How much did any of that matter now that Honey was safe? I wasn't interested in arresting Girl Six. Had she refused me, knowing she'd made a deal with Valentino? How much did any of that matter now that Honey was safe?

"We're upstairs," Onyx said, leading the way.

I regretted how badly I'd treated Girl Six when she was a guest at my Las Vegas home. Girl Six and I had had sex, watched movies together. She was my company. She was the only one of Honey's girls who had come to me and confided in me how brutally Honey had beat, kicked, and stomped her. Told me Honey's beating had fractured a few of her ribs. Hearing that pissed me off. I had changed my mind about letting Honey keep the money and insisted Girl Six accept Honey's offer to live with the other girls in Atlanta. Revenge came in many forms. What if Girl Six had volunteered as Valentino's informant? I couldn't blame her. What if

182

she'd preplanned walking out of Honey's house for good this morning not knowing about the kidnapping?

Entering a conference room filled with Honey's girls, the same girls I'd seen in Vegas when I handed Honey the cashier's check for half of Valentino's money, I said, "Good evening, ladies."

The girls greeted me in unison. I nodded at Red Velvet. Good to see she was on board. But this was no time to be friendly. "Okay, listen up," I told all the girls. Slowly circling the sofas in the family room, I looked each of them in their eyes. "If any of you know anything about Honey's kidnapping, this is the time for you to speak up."

All the girls were quiet. Red Velvet raised her hand.

"Yes," I said, noticing her shapely legs. I guessed stripping did wonders for the body.

"I have to be in LA in a few days for my lead role in a movie. How long is this search for Honey going to take?" she asked.

Onyx answered, "As long as it takes."

"See, I'm not seeing eye-to-eye with her ass, that's why I asked you."

"She's right," I said, not wanting to agree with Onyx, but I couldn't support any of the girls disrespecting her.

"We'll see about that," Red Velvet commented.

No need to acknowledge her. Red Velvet was determined to have the last word over Onyx but she'd best not try it with me. "I'm taking half of you with me to Stilettos and the rest of you will stay here. Onyx," I said, curling my finger.

We stepped out of the room, and I closed the door. "How many of the girls have handguns?"

Onyx laughed. "Of course I have mine, and I gave one to Red Velvet, but all of the girls have forty-fives."

"Perfect. I need you to pick four girls plus Red Velvet. She's the only one who knows Trevor well and she's on our team. I like her." I opened the door.

"You, you, you, you, and" — Onyx pointed at Red Velvet — "you. Come with me. The rest of you are on standby. If we need you, I'll call you."

Standing in the foyer, I instructed, "When we get to the club, split up. I'll handle the arrest. Your job is to prevent Valentino from trying to escape. Trip him, push him down, shoot him if you must, but don't kill him. The same goes for Benito. Let's go."

We arrived at the club. The girls did as I'd told them. All except Red Velvet. She was having a reunion with the strippers, laughing and chatting with Trevor. Onyx's lips were tight.

"Let it go. You can't control her," I said, but knew the burning sensation disrespect created.

Eight o'clock. I walked outside, patrolled the parking lot. No Valentino. Went inside and sat by Onyx. "Anything?"

"No," she said. "I have another plan."

"I'm listening."

"If Valentino is broke, he'll revert to pimping. We can put the girls on a quick stroll by the hot spot near the theme park. See if we get any leads," Onyx suggested, then said, "I'm really disappointed in Grant. He gave his word that he'd be here. He lied."

I remained quiet, listening to the crowd chant, "We want Red Velvet!" The louder they'd chant, the more Red Velvet smiled but she was smart not to get on the stage.

I maintained focus on my surroundings. Nine. Ten. Eleven. Twelve. The hours passed slowly. No Valentino or Benito. "Gather up the girls. Put Plan B in motion. I'll have the hotel rooms waiting."

CHAPTER 21
HONEY

All my adult life I'd taken care of myself. I'd never been protected or in protective custody. I was a proud independent woman. The second I'd stop living my life my way, I'd die. I sat on the couch watching Hunter massage his big dick. It seemed automatic for him to touch himself frequently. He was engrossed in watching the morning news. I was turned on watching him. I'd seen, touched, smelt, fucked, and jacked-off so many dicks, Hunter's actions didn't offend me.

Most men couldn't relate to my wealth and I couldn't comprehend their ignorance. "I don't care how much money a woman makes, I'm still the man." I saw straight through that bullshit. Translation: "I wish I had your money but since I don't, I'm going to dick you down real good and convince you to give me access to all your shit so I can impress my boys and other chicks."

A dick and balls didn't make a man, but Hunter had me hot. Made me curious. I wanted to see his dick. See if it was big like my favorite porn star's, Lex.

The news had begun interfering with my sexual energy. Every other person was shot, killed, raped, homeless, unemployed, and so forth. I went into the bedroom, got a throw pillow, returned to the sofa, faced Hunter, and lay on my stomach. The T-shirt I wore, the one Sapphire had given me, barely covered my naked booty. Closing my eyes, I trampled through my mind creating my newsworthy highlights.

If a woman selling her body to keep a roof over her head was considered a prostitute, then what were the men called who solicited pussy in exchange for cash? Why were male prostitutes glorified as gigolos if they were heterosexual? Ostracized if they were homosexual? Yet if a woman, irrespective of her sexual orientation, was promiscuous, she was a ho, no explanation needed. Society had been bamboozled by a bunch of hypocrites.

I glanced at Hunter, exhaled. His hand roamed inside his sweats, stroking his dick. I squirmed, redirected my attention to the television.

"Breaking News" scrolled at the bottom

of the screen.

"Do we have to watch this?" I asked Hunter.

"The news may not be what we'd prefer to hear but it's real."

I countered, "It's propaganda."

A reporter standing near the flagpole where I'd shot Ken announced, "A man identified as Ken Draper has been charged with four counts of rape, and one count of first-degree murder. He's listed in stable condition after suffering a gunshot to his genitals. It's alleged that Ken's last victim shot him before fleeing the cemetery. An unknown person e-mailed this video clip of a woman wearing a red suit shooting Ken Draper. Anyone with information on the alleged victim is asked to call this number. . . ."

Hunter stared at me. "Guess I wouldn't like the news either if I was on it. That's the suit you had on. That's your hair. And your ass," he said, admiring my butt. "I'm all ears. What happened?"

Thank God my face was not in the video. Whoever taped me had done so from behind. Hunter was not getting that close to me. Relieved that Ken was alive, I ignored Hunter. Ken deserved to suffer, but I didn't want to have another man's blood on my hands, on my conscience.

I began fantasizing about what to do once I got out of this web Valentino had created. Maybe move to California, where same-sex marriages were once recognized by law, cannabis clubs were legally thriving for medicinal purposes and prostitution was on the brink of legalization. Instead of men traveling to Amsterdam and Brazil, I could bring the women to America, host conventions in San Francisco and invite swingers and swappers to join in the fun. The demand for sex wasn't going away and women should have the right to choose prostitution as a career so hopefully men like Ken would freely pay for pussy instead of raping women.

"Fine, don't answer," Hunter said, interrupting my thoughts. "But if you change your mind, seriously I want to hear from you what happened today."

"I hope Sapphire has Valentino in custody so I can go home to my man."

Hunter said, "Not me. I want to get to know you," resuming his massage.

Successful women were prey for fast-talking, good-looking, shiftless men in search of free rides and riders. Most men didn't know how to fuck or make love. The way Hunter's hand grooved up and down

189

his shaft, he had good rhythm. I'd been with enough johns to testify firsthand that too many men were horrible in bed. They didn't know the purpose of a woman's clit, where her G-spot or erogenous zones were. Men wanted to control women but didn't know how to control their dicks by prolonging their erection until their women were satisfied. Had Hunter learned to prolong his pleasure by constantly stimulating his dick? I wanted to see him masturbate.

Having to create my own happiness without my parents or a man, part of me felt miserably trapped in this condo with Hunter. The other part of me felt like a celebrity hiding from crazed fans. Was being married going to overwhelm me? Maybe I was better off being unconditionally single than being conditionally married. Would Grant help with the kids? Or would he be a part-time husband and dad expecting me to become a stay-at-home mother while he stayed away from home? How long should I pretend I was missing? If I called off the charade, I could leave now.

I continued lying on the sofa. I watched Hunter recline in the oversized leather chair, spread his legs wider. His pelvis sunk between the arms. His long legs stretched beyond the footrest, neck wrestled with the headrest in search of comfort. Remote control in one hand, dick in the other. Gun on the end table beside him, pointed away from me.

Hunter's lips were succulent, mustache neat. I imagined him kissing my pussy. I understood Sapphire hitting on him but her approach was self-destructive. Hunter was a man. Men were hunters. Hunters enjoyed the chase, take away the chase, take away his interest.

"Hunter."

"What would you like?" he asked, watching me and the news at the same time.

"I'm going crazy cooped up in here." I stood, stretched. "I need to get out. Breathe fresh air. Take me for a walk . . . outside."

He stared at the imprints of my nipples under the loose-fitting T-shirt, witnessing my excitement. The T-shirt Sapphire had given me was all I'd slept in and all I'd worn since showering this morning. Last time I'd asked, two hours ago, to stretch my legs, Hunter created an obstacle course in the living room, then selected yoga via on-demand.

"Make this temporary arrangement easy on us. Stop asking for what you can't have," he said, sounding annoyed.

"Okay, I'll stop asking if you tell me where I am."

"That would defeat the purpose of my being your bodyguard and violate my contract. You wouldn't want me to breach my contract, would you?"

Honoring his responsibilities was a good indication that Hunter could be loyal. "Fine, then talk to me. Tell me about yourself," I said, plopping on the couch, spreading my thighs. "I can't sit here on the sofa all day watching you entertain your dick and watch television." I was used to getting up, showering, getting dressed, and leaving my house every day, unless I was in bed with Grant.

Hunter smiled, glanced between my legs, then asked, "What would you like to know?"

Did he prefer bald or hairy pussies? Some of my johns hated hairless pussies. Said the smoothness reminded them of girls, not women. My Brazilian wax never stopped a man from fucking me.

"Back into it. Start from today, then tell me how you became a bodyguard, then tell me about your childhood, and conclude with telling me about your parents."

Hunter reclined, lowered his sweats under his balls, squeezed his dick, pumped three times, then stroked. "Not sure if we have enough time for the entire debriefing. I'll do my best." He turned off the television, pulled up his sweats, moved to the opposite end of the sofa facing me. No smile. His elbows leaned on his knees. He had this hypnotic stare. His eyes were set so far back they seemed to hide from his face.

He exhaled. "I seriously need to talk about my life."

Oh, God. I prayed he wasn't one of those men who badgered women with their depressing problems. I asked for it but I didn't have to take it. If Hunter was a chronic complainer, I was prepared to end our conversation.

He stared at the white carpet. "Every time I say, 'I'm getting out of this business,' someone makes me an offer I can't refuse. Boss told me this was easy money. I'm not going to lie. I do need the money. Boss said I wouldn't have to kill anyone unless your life was in jeopardy. My game high points scored when I played college basketball was seven."

He sucked at basketball? To laugh would've been rude so I laughed on the inside.

Hunter looked at me. "Protecting my clients, I've killed more than seven people. It's my job but I'm tired of playing God."

Seven wasn't a large number. Having killed one person, I couldn't imagine multiplying that by seven. Hunter's eyes penetrated my spirit. I understood his pain. Courage pulled the trigger when I shot Ken. I wanted to avenge the women Ken had murdered but vengeance was not mine.

Hunter moved to the middle of the sofa. Placed my feet in his lap. "I didn't expect you to be so beautiful," he said, massaging my foot. "After seeing you, I wouldn't hesitate to kill anyone who'd attempt to hurt you. Best you don't tell me what Ken Draper did to you."

He was not getting me to tell him about Ken. "I haven't killed seven people, only one. Would kill again if I had to, but I don't want to kill again," I said, lying flat on the sofa. Hunter's foot massage relaxed my body. "You had a good childhood?"

"No. I had a great childhood. I have two wonderful parents but they have no idea what I do to earn my keep. I split my time between sting operations and protecting people like you. My parents think I'm an exterminator." Rotating his thumbs on the ball of my foot, Hunter blinked repeatedly.

"Can't relate to the parent thing. I was never a child," I said. "You are an exterminator of sorts. But I get it. They think you kill bugs, I mean pests. You know what I mean. You've covered that one."

Hunter mumbled, "More like about to be exterminated." His hands moved up my leg, massaged my shin. "You're the first woman I've met that I like, who can relate to how I feel. And you're so beautiful." He strummed the back of my knee with his fingertips, making my pussy quiver.

I pulled away, tucked my heel under my ass. I'd be safer at home if the person protecting me needed protection too. "What did you mean by 'more like you're about to be exterminated'?"

"Part of the business. Eventually someone will come after me. Sorry I mentioned it. I'm curious," he said, scooting closer.

"About?"

"Can I do a taste test? See if you really taste like your name?"

I placed my feet flat on the sofa, parted my knees, closed my eyes. Hunter couldn't replace my love for Grant, but I wanted Hunter to take the edge off my sexual frustrations.

His moist lips kissed my shaft. His tongue spread my lips, then gently touched my pearl. "I don't know who's prettier," he said, kissing me again.

I moaned, "Suck her for me, Hunter. I'm

so fucking hot, I've got to cum or I'ma explode."

Hunter eased his finger inside my pussy, strummed my G-spot, sucked my clit.

"I'm cumming already," I moaned.

The door opened. We looked up at Sapphire. Damn! Bad timing. I sat up, clenched my pussy muscles, slid to the edge of the sofa, exhaled, and released the rest of my orgasm. Hunter picked up the remote, moved back to the recliner, turned on the television.

Sapphire sat on the sofa between us, closer to Hunter, turned to him, then lamented, "I told you to protect, not service her."

"Did you arrest Valentino?" I asked.

"Neither Valentino nor Benito showed up last night. I'll find them by tomorrow but I'm going to need the fifty mil to lure him. You'll get it back," she said, looking at me.

Tomorrow? I didn't believe her. "How do you know Valentino will give back my money?"

"Because he'll never get it," she said.

Hunter's eyes widened, mine closed.

I asked her, "Then why do you need it?" Opening my eyes, I searched hers for the answer.

Sapphire turned her back to Hunter, faced me. "Are you saying you don't trust me?"

I stared at the ceiling. I was not giving her my money. "I trust you —"

"But?"

"But we both know how shit can go wrong. What about Grant?"

Sapphire stared into my eyes. "He didn't show up at Stilettos either."

Tears burned my eyes. I scratched my brow, rubbed my neck, tugged my shirt. "I need a last will and testament."

"Honey, you're not dying. This arrangement is only for a few days. I —"

"I can take care of that for you if you'd like," Hunter said. "Whatever you want. That's why I'm here."

Ignoring Hunter, I asked Sapphire, "Did Grant call you?"

"No. Honey, all I can advise is to be very careful with Hunter, darling. Grant loves you." Sapphire stood, pointed at Hunter. "I know what you're up to," then told me, "You're grown. You decide what's best for you. I'll be back later. Next time I'll knock first." Sapphire slammed the door behind her.

Hunter sat at the computer for fifteen minutes, printed a few pages, sat beside me on the sofa, handed me a blank last will and testament document.

"Let's start with your beneficiaries," he said, holding a pen.

"Hunter, I don't have any. I gave each of my girls a million so they've got theirs. I hate my parents. I'm uncertain about Grant. I guess I could leave something to my sister's son and maybe Red Velvet. Or divide everything equally between my girls. This is sad that I have lots of money and no one I want to leave it to."

Hunter held my hand. "I prepared the will for my parents. It's simple, and what's great is you can always change it. I'll help you decide for now. Let me call your parents. Tell them you're dying and they have to come to Atlanta right away. When they arrive —"

I shook my head. "That won't work. They won't come."

"Trust me, they'll come."

"My money?"

Hunter smiled. "Yep. My suggestion is, when they arrive you let me interrogate the shit out of them. I'll tell them you need a kidney and one of them has to give it to you and neither of them is leaving until your surgery is a success. Then I'll ask who wants to volunteer. If they volunteer without reservation, you know they love you. I say give them a check on the spot and name them in your will. If neither one of them speak up, I say give them a check —"

I shook my head.

"Wait, hear me out. Take the check back, tear it up, and tell them you're not giving them a penny."

"That's not a bad idea but you don't know my parents. It won't work. Think of something else. I'm going to take a cold shower," I said, heading to the bathroom.

"Can I join you, Honey? I'd like to finish what I started."

I could remain faithful to Grant. Or have sex with Hunter. That little peck earlier wasn't cheating. I stood in front of him, then turned my back to him. Then slowly removed my shirt, dropped it to the floor. I needed the comfort of a man. But that man wasn't Hunter.

"I'll pass." I closed the bathroom door, stood in the shower and cried.

I wanted to see my parents at the same time. That was something that had happened once in my lifetime, at my sister's funeral. I had a right to know why they were such horrible parents. Seeing them could close the void in my heart. No matter how cruel and cold they were to me, they were still my parents. I didn't want to die regretting I'd never cursed them out. My parents would die before saving my life and I wanted to let them know, I'd do the same.

CHAPTER 22
GRANT

Surrounded by silence and memories of times shared with Honey, I cried.

I sat in darkness in my living room, placed my hands over my face, and shamelessly let my tears flow. I let out the loudest, "Oh, my God!" ever. "Please, keep my Honey safe."

Holding Honey's scarf in my hands, I buried my tears but could not escape the pain in my throat, my head, my heart. Placing the silk against my nose, I sniffed her scent, remembering the good times. The times when we lay in bed making love, sharing ice cream, laughing at Huey, Riley, and Grandad. I missed her so much that I couldn't watch the *Boondocks* anymore.

Little things reminded me of Honey. Wind and fire. Rain and sunshine. Thunderstorms and rainbows. I loved Honey. I'd always love Honey. Jada was a lovely woman but she couldn't replace Honey.

Sniffling, I turned on the light. Throughout my home the pictures of Honey — on my mantel above the fireplace, my dresser, my desk, my kitchen wall, and in my foyer, bathrooms, and guest bedrooms — gave me hope that I'd see her soon. I went to my master bath, turned on the shower, waited for the steam to rise off the water, then stepped in. Hot water from each jet pulsated against my head, neck, shoulders, back, ass, thighs, and legs. I washed my face over and over.

Ding, ding, ding, ding, dong.

I stepped out the shower, stuffed wet feet into dry slippers. Wrapped a black towel around my waist en route to the front door. I wasn't expecting anyone. Maybe Jada had come to visit. I hoped not. Jada showing up at my house unannounced was grounds for my termination of all contact with her. I opened my living room door, entered my enclosed sunporch area, unlocked my front door.

"Hey, Sapphire, come in." I hugged her, lifted her off her feet, and twirled her around. "Gimme the good news! Where's my baby?"

When Sapphire didn't answer, I put her down and said, "Have a seat."

Tucking my towel tighter, I walked outside. Looked inside her SUV. No Honey. I went to the kitchen, poured one goblet of orange juice and filled the other with cranberry juice, then joined Sapphire in the living room.

Sapphire was seated in my blue plush upholstered chair. I put the glasses on coasters atop the round table between us, sat in the black chair. "Which would you like?"

"Cranberry." She took a sip, then continued, "Grant, I don't know how long it's going to take to find Honey. Could be a few days, a week, a month, longer."

Adjusting my towel, I asked, "What's taking so long?"

"A better question is where were you last night?"

"I couldn't make it," I said swallowing hard.

Last night was rough. I struggled with going to Stilettos. The strip club was wild enough without adding in a public hostage exchange where everyone except me would've probably had a gun. I questioned if Honey would be there. Who'd really kidnapped her?

Sapphire's eyebrows raised as she asked, "Couldn't or wouldn't?"

"Look, obviously physically I could but what I couldn't handle was if Honey was already dead. Besides, you told me not to come. I want you to find her. Bring her home to me will you?"

"Are you serious? Is that why you didn't show after saying you would?" Sapphire asked as though calling me a punk.

"Uh-hmm." I cleared my throat, gulped my orange juice, swiped my brow. "An even better question is why didn't Valentino show up?"

"Who said he didn't?"

"If he had, you wouldn't be sitting here without Honey. Agree?"

Sapphire rubbed the arms of the chair. "Yes, I mean no, he didn't show. He called me. Said he has Honey. Won't tell me where they are until I get his money."

Liar. Quietly, I sat for a moment. I knew where Valentino was and suspected Sapphire knew exactly where Honey was. Valentino said he hadn't seen Honey. Someone was lying for real and I was more inclined to believe him. How far would Sapphire take this before she told me the truth? I asked, "How much?"

"Fifty million," Sapphire said.

"How soon?"

"The sooner the better. Why so many questions?" she asked, shifting her hips along the cushion before crossing her arms and legs.

"Because I know if you wanted to you could give Valentino your fifty million." On the edge of my seat, I yelled, "Don't! Play! Games! With me! Do you know where Honey is?"

"Do you?" she asked.

"No. If I did, you wouldn't be here. I'd be here making love to Honey."

Women were the biggest liars. Sapphire knew where Honey was. I saw the truth in her shifting eyes that searched for lies. "I'll give Valentino the fifty million. Call him right now and tell him," I demanded.

I picked up my cell phone, dialed my broker. "I need fifty million dollars. Take it from my construction development account. I'll call you back and tell you where to wire it." I ended the call.

Sapphire pressed a few buttons on her cell, then asked me, "Are you serious?"

"Oh, I'm dead serious. If this is what it takes to get Honey back, I'll have the money to Valentino first thing tomorrow."

How long was she willing to lie to my face? I knew where Valentino was and she didn't? Yeah, right.

"Valentino, I'll have your money tomorrow morning. All of it," she said.

Holding out my hand, I demanded, "Give me the phone. Let me talk to him."

Sapphire pulled away, ended the call. "I left him a message."

I stood. My towel fell to the floor. My heads hung. No big deal for her to see the dick she'd sucked and fucked.

Sapphire moved closer and hugged me. "You're a real man, Grant." She brushed against my limp dick. "I'll find her for you. I promise."

Peeling her clammy lustful arms away, I said, "I don't know how long I can manage without Honey." I went into my bedroom, returned naked holding my ring box. I opened it and handed Sapphire the loose five-carat solitaire. "I have to give this to Honey before it's too late. Don't walk away from me with Honey's diamond," I sternly said.

She admired the rock. Threw it at me.

"You're insane. Stop fucking playing games with me. I know where Valentino is. I know where Benito is. What I don't know is what the fuck you're up to. I'm asking you. Do you know where my Honey is?"

"You have no idea where Valentino is. If you did, you'd know where Honey is. Get the ransom money. Give it to me. I'll take care of the rest. I'll call you when I hear back from Valentino."

"I don't give a fuck about when Valentino

calls you back. If you don't have Honey, don't call me. I've got to get dressed," I said, escorting Sapphire to the sunporch. I waited until her car was out of my long driveway, then slammed my door.

That woman had always been jealous of Honey. She wanted everything that Honey had, including me. I was sincere about the money. I could put a moratorium on building my condominiums. I couldn't place my heart on hold. Getting dressed, I could not make sense of Honey's disappearance.

I left my house, drove to the arena to meet Jada for the game. Made my way to her suite. She had ten seats in her suite but we were the only two there.

"This is nice. Why don't you invite more people?" I asked her.

Pouring two flutes of champagne, Jada said, "When your girlfriend writes an unauthorized biography of your family's secrets, who can you trust? I've learned to appreciate my privacy. Fancy and my grandson might come up but she likes to sit behind the team for home games. You can invite guests whenever you'd like. Just let me know in advance."

"Thanks." I tipped my glass to hers. We sat in the middle seats.

I became quiet. The game started, the

national anthem played, the players were announced. I put my arm around Jada, then said, "I had to place my real estate development on hold today."

Jada redirected her attention from the game to me. Her pale yellow pants and cashmere sweater tapered her body well, not too loose or too tight. "Why?" she asked.

"Had to set aside fifty million dollars for the ransom money for Honey."

She sat on the edge of her seat, stared at me. "Speaking of Honey." Jada opened her purse, handed me two sheets of paper.

I scanned most of what I knew — Honey's real name, Honey's associaton with Immaculate Perception, her business Sweeter than Honey. What I wasn't aware of caused my jaw to drop as I read, "Honey Thomas, a married woman."

I interlocked my fingers, rested my elbows on my thighs, looked at but wasn't paying attention to the game. "I thought you were going to help me find Honey, not to go spy on her. I already know this," I said, crumbing the paper. "I told you my fiancée was being held hostage." I had no idea Honey was legally married.

"No, you said you didn't know where she was."

"Same thing."

"No, it's not. She's a married woman. What is she involved in that would make someone kidnap her? And why would you pay fifty million dollars for someone else's wife? That's ridiculous."

"That's none of your business," I said. Jada made me question if giving away that much money was worth it. Would Honey pay me back? Should she? Would I want her to? I decided all that was unimportant. "I love her enough to pay the money."

"You're right. It's not my business, but I'm entitled to my opinion and I think it's ridiculous. Grant, your involvement with Honey is relevant. You're placing my life, my son's life, and my family's life in danger."

Jada treated me like a convict. I'd never jeopardize her life or her family's. "Would you say the same about Wellington? Wouldn't he do the same thing for you that I'm doing for Honey?"

"Don't you dare bring my deceased husband into this machismo mayhem. I would never sleep with a married person," she said, twisting a verbal knife in my heart. "Get out. You're no better than the rest of the men out there. Just get the hell out of my face!"

"Mayhem? If I were doing this for you,

you'd love me. Since I'm doing this for Honey, you hate me. You probably hate her too and you don't even know her. Stand in front your mirror and take a long look inside yourself. You're no better than the rest either."

"You're insane. Leave, now!"

"Yeah, insane about saving the woman I love. Sounds to me like you're jealous." I placed my drink on the counter and walked out. Sapphire, now Jada . . . Every woman couldn't be jealous of Honey. How many times would I have to defend my love for Honey?

CHAPTER 23
RED VELVET

"Shoot me! I'm telling you, I'm not going back out there."

Onyx wasn't kidding. That bitch was certifiable. She was crazy for putting me on a stroll, putting my life in danger. I was crazier for going out there last night. Some things I didn't want to learn firsthand, and prostitution was one of them. I had a God-fearing mother, and yes, I have made some not-so-good decisions, but my mother taught me right from wrong.

Click. Click. Click. Last night my stilettos tapped the grimy concrete near the theme park. Horny men drove by, whistled, circled the block, came back to get me. Each driver lowered his window, asking "What's your specialty, baby? How much for head? We're in a recession, you offering any two-for-one discounts?"

Onyx told me Honey had paid her girls two grand a night. I barely broke two hundred last night taking those men into one of the six motel rooms Sapphire had reserved. In and out of the rooms for hours, I alternated with Honey's other girls, detaining and entertaining the men with lap dances until Sapphire came in to interrogate them. What bothered me the most about prostitution was knowing pimps beat young girls, girls that should've been in high school, some junior high. The pimps complained about the girls not making enough money. That was no way for anybody's daughter to live.

I sat at the dinner table, pushing green peas from one side of the plate to the other. "I'm exposing my precious body, for what? We still don't know where Honey is. This is not the way to find her. Sapphire, talk some sense into Onyx. You're the only person she'll listen to."

Sapphire remained quiet.

I wasn't ignorant. I realized teenage prostitution was an extension of some of the forty-five strip clubs in Georgia. My ex-boss Trevor was definitely an exploiter. But he paid me good money to seduce his high-profile clients and potential clients, like Grant. Trevor never put me on the street and he didn't employ strippers under twenty-one, although the legal age for strippers was eighteen.

Onyx spoke firm. "Red Velvet, you did good last night, sweetie. We're closer to finding Honey because of you. All of you. We are family. Family stick together no matter what our differences are. We are going out again tonight. Let's go."

I refused to move. "I'm not done with my peas." The other girls got up from the table, picked up their plates, and left me alone.

Where the hell was Onyx's husband? I wish I had her husband's number; I'd call him right now. The other girls left the mansion. Not me. I couldn't move. "Sapphire, please, I'm begging you. Talk some sense into Onyx. Tell her she's going about this wrong."

Sapphire held my hand. "Red Velvet, it's a matter of loyalty, sweetheart, and every woman has to pay her debt to Honey so Honey can come home, including you and me."

Sapphire didn't seem upset. She was too calm. "Sounds like you already know where she's at," I told her, then asked Onyx, "What happens if I go home instead?"

Sapphire answered, "You wouldn't want to find out."

"Excuse me in advance, but you bitches are crazy. Red Velvet is up outta this bitch.

See ya." I held my head high, marched out the door, and bypassed the four cars lined in the driveway filled with Honey's girls. I made my way to the gate, walked up Blackland to Roswell. Standing at the intersection, I waved farewell to Onyx and Sapphire. "Good luck!"

Onyx lowered her window. "Come here, Red Velvet."

I stopped three feet from the passenger door. That way I could back up if I had to. "What?" I leaned closer exhibiting confidence.

"Give me back my gun."

Small demand, worth honoring, as long as she didn't shoot me. People who carried guns all the time weren't living right. Gladly, I gave it to her, waited for her to drive off, then I looked in every direction before crossing the street to Piedmont Avenue and began walking toward Peachtree Street. Buckhead was a nice neighborhood. Better than that slum area the girls were headed back to by that theme park.

A four-door sedan luxury car slowed, drove beside me. I kept walking along the sidewalk, continued in front of an office advertising furnished apartments for lease. The passenger lowered his window and said, "Let us give you a ride."

"No, thanks. I'm fine." I strutted faster, bypassing the Manor apartments.

"Come on, girl," the driver said. "We're headed to the steak house up the way. Let us buy *you* some meat," he said in a charismatic way.

Yeah, there was Ruth's Chris and Morton's near Piedmont and Peachtree, across the street from Brides by Demetrios and not far from the Ritz. I smiled, hopped in the backseat, wishing I had that gun for backup. "I'm not hungry. I'll accept a ride to the restaurant, then I'll take MARTA," I said, fastening my seat belt.

"I'll get you wherever you want to go. We're from out of town. Where's a good spot to party?" the driver asked.

Based on their casual attire, I recommended, "You can go to Taboo 2. It's kinda middle of the road, never know who'll you see in there, but it's cool. Elevated dance floor next to the regular dance floor, four bars, twenty-dollar cover."

"So what's your name, sweetheart?" the driver asked.

"You can call me Red Velvet. And you are?"

"V, you called it man. You said she looked like one of Honey's girls."

"V? As in Valentino?" I asked, staring at

his ass in the rearview mirror.

"That's right, bitch, get comfortable," Valentino said, making a U-turn.

CHAPTER 24
HONEY

"Honey, come here, baby," Hunter called from the living room couch. "We need to talk."

Propelled by my endorphins, I kangaroo-hopped from the bedroom cheezing, titties and ponytail bouncing. A lot had transpired since our sexcapade this morning. I kissed Hunter on the lips. "What is it, you?" I plopped in his lap, gave him a hug.

Emotions were complicated. I loved Grant and I was falling for Hunter. Was proximity the reason coworkers had affairs? Working long hours side by side, sharing energy and stimulating intellect could ignite a sexual spark that ordinarily wouldn't exist. Even Valentino's sexual charm lured me to sex him once. Would I have fucked him again, had we continued working together?

I knew I'd only met Hunter a few days ago, but spending every second of every day with him made me appreciate him emotion-

217

ally, sexually, and intellectually. With the exception of Sapphire's random drop-ins, we had zero distractions.

Hunter had a huge heart, a fantastic sense of humor, and a nice size dick with thickness and a slight hook to it. He knew when to take me seriously, when to hold me, when to brutally tell me the truth, and when to kiss me in the right places. And he'd orchestrated a brilliant plan for my parents' arrival tomorrow.

I still couldn't believe I let him talk me into flying my parents to Atlanta, but I did. "Yes," I said, kissing him again. "You summoned?"

"Sit here," he said, patting the sofa.

Okay, here we go. I knew things were going too well. Was our time up? Had Sapphire replaced him? I moved from his lap, snuggled close to him, then flatly asked, "What's up?"

"Here, read this," he said, handing me an article with the headline, *GA. LAWMAKERS PROPOSE FEE FOR STRIP-CLUB PATRONS.*

Patrons, not strippers. I scanned the article once, and again, searching for my name, Red Velvet's or her ex-boss Trevor's name. I hunched, shook my head. "What's this all about?"

"Stop skimming and read the entire article."

"Fine." I read, " 'A bipartisan group of Georgia lawmakers wants to slap a new fee on strip-club patrons to help fund rehabilitation programs for child prostitutes and sex abuse victims. . . .'"

Many proposals had been introduced from cutting budgets to increasing the legal stripping age from eighteen to twenty-one to expanding the definition of child abuse to include any person who allowed a child to engage in prostitution. All great, if you asked me.

"It's about time the government held all adults who exploit children accountable. Long overdue. And I support the five-dollar increase over three dollars. The patrons are going to make it rain on somebody with more than a few dollars so why not save a child in the process?" I looked from the newspaper to Hunter.

He held my hand. "Honey, don't think I'm crazy but hear me out. You want to help women in a big way, right?"

"I am helping women. That's why I started Sweeter than Honey."

"Is your company a nonprofit?"

Okay. Hunter was methodical and full of bright ideas. I'd learned that much about him. But it was too early for Q and A. He needed the point. "No, it's not. Please, Hunter. What is it?" I was on the verge of going back to bed, going to take a shower, or walking out the front door.

"Baby, you want everything instant."

"If that were true, I'd be gone. I'm still here, aren't I?"

"Honey, stop being so defensive. Everything is not about you. You personalize things too much."

I stood. "How dare you treat me like I'm a child!"

Gently he held my arm. "Please sit down. Hear me out. I'm not you. Our uniqueness brings us together, baby. But if we want to clone one another, we might as well be by ourselves."

Hated to admit he was right, so I didn't. I sat waiting, willing to hear what he had to say. Patience was making me impatient.

"You know I like to take my time. You have to learn patience and I need you to trust me."

"Can you get to the point, please?"

"Honey, I want you to create a five-oh-one C three. I'll help you. My friend has a business that does all the legal paperwork for setting up nonprofits. Then I want you to take every penny Sapphire gave you of

Valentino's money —"

I threw up my hand. "No," I said, shaking my head. I wasn't giving back or giving away anything. "Are you in cahoots with someone?" I wasn't very trusting. Refused to let him complete my last will and testament. He might have forged my signature and made himself the beneficiary.

He shook his head. "Can you be quiet and listen, woman? You're carrying this guilt for having Valentino's money. It's bothering you."

"No, it's not." I was a sensible woman. Guilt was not the right word.

I was empowered knowing Valentino was stripped of what most men worshipped . . . money. Men spent their lives, chasing money and pussy, and when they got either or both they didn't know what to do with it.

Valentino had hid all of his cash in body bags in his basement. He seldom left home fearing someone would rob him. He was a prisoner to things he perceived elevated his self-worth. In less than one day, one woman took every dollar. Men who worshipped things and money over women were idiots.

"Here's what I suggest you do. Set up your nonprofit bank account. We'll set up an account in Valentino's name. Make a lump sum contribution to Valentino's account, then transfer the money from his account to your nonprofit in the name of Valentino James. Transfer all of his money you have in your account, including the interest."

"It's not his money. It's in my possession and it's my money."

"I'm trying to get you to establish a track record that proves to the IRS you're legit."

"I didn't steal it. Sapphire gave it to me." What was this all about? Hunter was pissing me off.

"You're in the best position. Sapphire may not survive this ordeal when our boss gets the details. My job is to protect you but I've also signed a confidentiality statement that prohibits me from disclosing to you everything I know," Hunter said, peering into my eyes. "Your green eyes are gorgeous."

Back to not trusting anyone, I played along with Hunter. "Make the contribution in his name?" I maintained eye contact.

"Yeah. Valentino won't attack a nonprofit, if he's smart. The money you gave your former escorts was generous. You gave them more than enough to make it on their own. Let them go. The ones who want to work for you will stay. The others will leave. What you don't want is for them to feel obligated.

Honey, you've got to let them go. They're not indebted to you."

"Next you're going to tell me to come out of hiding."

Hunter smiled, touched my ass. "And share this booty with Grant? No way."

Hunter was so intriguing, I'd almost forgotten about Grant. I'd heard enough. Softly I kissed Hunter's lips. "I want some more."

"Me, too," he said. "Honey?"

"Yes."

"Let me make love to you," Hunter said, kissing my neck. "Let me start with an all over massage."

"Hunter?"

"Yes."

"Don't ever stop caring for me. You make me happy." I had to keep him close until I learned his motive. Did he think I was going to listen to him? What if in the middle of transferring my money, it got sucked into a black hole with the name Hunter Broadway on it?

We heard a familiar rattle, looked toward the front door. Sapphire walked in.

"At it again, huh? I give up. I stopped by to give both of you an update," she said, sitting between us.

"You could call first," I told her, scooting

to the edge of the sofa.

"You're getting cuter by the day, Honey. Anyway, all the girls have been strolling the last two nights trying to track down Valentino. He's somewhere in Atlanta but Atlanta is huge. Red Velvet bailed on me last night. I'll handle her personally. And —"

I interrupted, stood in front of Sapphire. "Wait one damn minute! You put my girls on the street? My girls are not street girls. And you will not handle Red Velvet! She's not a prostitute. She has the lead in a big movie and she needs to get her ass in LA. Good she left. This is all a mess. Sapphire, why are you mishandling everything?"

Sapphire stood inches from me, breathing in my face. "Bitch, I'm busting my ass for your safety and this is my thanks!"

Slap! I had no problem hitting first. Any bitch bold enough to get in my face and call me a bitch had it coming.

Slap! I expected her to hit back. I grabbed her hair.

She snatched mine.

I'd developed a lot of tension being on lockdown. Sapphire had built up animosity toward me because of my relationship with Hunter. I could fatally beat her. She could shoot me. Hunter stood, grabbed Sapphire. I slapped her ass again. A slap between two killers was an insult.

"Honey, stop it!" Hunter held Sapphire behind him, making it clear his loyalty was to her. She smiled as if victory was hers.

Sapphire's cellular rang. She checked the ID, then announced, "Lucky for us it's my man, Santonio."

"You wish you had a man," I said.

Answering the phone, she said, "Hey, daddy. We still on for dinner tonight?"

As she walked out the door, I yelled, "You need some dick in your life! Fuck him tonight!"

CHAPTER 25
VALENTINO

Bitches did not stick together.

Put money, a dick, or a good man between females and there was a guaranteed ten-round catfight underway. But a mismatch wouldn't last long. One bitch had signed up for a fuckin' knockout but she wouldn't know it until it was too late. I'd always bet on Lace's lucky ass to win. What was so damn straight-up lethal about her? Her ability to make alliances with every fucking body? Lace should've taught Red Velvet that shutting the fuck up was sometimes best. Bitch's mouth was more polluted than a septic system.

Red Velvet, that stank bitch was from a mutt breed. A little bit of this and a little bit of that all fuckin' mixed up together between her yipping and yapping. I sat in a dining chair, faced her ass sitting in a dining chair, staring at me. Benito had pulled up his chair, sat staring at her, then at me.

Back and forth his head pivoted every few seconds.

"Nigga, cut that shit out," Red Velvet said.

"Bitch, don't talk like me," I told her.

"What the fuck your bitch ass gon' do? I'm not telling you where Honey is."

"You know I'ma let you go on with all that. But trust me, your mouth has a ass whuppin' on layaway."

Sarcastically, she repeated, "Your mouth has a ass whuppin' on layaway."

I swear I could beat her with no reservations or regrets. Red Velvet was not my type. Her ass was so humongous I could sit on it. Waist so small, I could hug her with one arm. Lips too big for my liking. Nose pointed like a white woman's. Brown eyes hiding behind hazel contacts. Red Velvet was fine according to a black man's standard. Mine too if I was going to put her ass on a stroll to make me some change but she could never be my main piece. Lace could but she wouldn't. The one woman sexier than Lace was Sunny Day. Sure wish Sunny hadn't committed suicide. Wished Red Velvet would kill herself.

Fuck! Reflecting about Sunny made me think about my wife, Summer. I hadn't called her since I'd left Las Vegas in her car with Benito. Oh, well. Too bad for her car.

She'd probably reported the car stolen and bought another one with the insurance money.

"Hey, nigga. Stop staring at that bitch and get me the cell phone," I said to Benito.

"Yeah, nigga, get the phone. I need to make a call too," she said, staring me down.

Red Velvet was a weak opponent but her ass could outsmart Benito in a hot second. I had to watch him, watch her. She wasn't protecting Lace. She was protecting her own ass. Bitch kicked me in my balls last night when I dragged her in the condo. I would've backhand slapped her if I didn't need her to tell me where the fuck Lace was.

This was some fucked up sideshow circus shit. Grant suspected us. That nigga wasn't slick, he was keeping a close watch. I suspected Sapphire. And Sapphire, who did that bitch suspect? If the answer was nobody, then her ass was using Lace as my bait. Sapphire was the only person Lace would go to for help.

"Here you go, V. Be careful, man. It'll slide right out your hand."

"Whatever, nigga. Keep your eyes on that slick bitch," I said, dialing Summer's cell phone.

"Hello, this is Summer speaking," she answered, sounding all happy and shit.

"Hey, baby. It's your man, what's up? How's my seeds?"

"Who's calling? To whom would you like to speak?"

All right, maybe a nigga deserved some friction but her ass had better be joking. "It's your husband, Anthony Valentino James. Don't play, gurl."

"You definitely have the wrong number." Flatly she said, "I don't have a husband."

Red Velvet watched me, smiling, even fucking chuckling.

"What the fuck you looking at? Don't make me beat that stupid grin off your ugly face," I told her.

She smiled wider. Laughed out loud.

"Are you done with me? With her?" Summer politely asked. "I have to go to the hospital for my checkup."

I knew Summer would warm up to me. On the under she was trying to tell me she had a doctor's appointment for our twins. What kind of father would I have been if I'd stayed with my wife instead of coming to Atlanta?

"Bye. I believe you said your name was Anthony," Summer said. "Wait, Anthony Junior, mommy is coming."

"Sum—" before I got her name out, that bitch hung up on me. All women were bitches. Summer had probably sold the house, moved, and filed for an annulment. Advertised that shit in the paper and divorced my ass without my knowing.

Red Velvet hunched her shoulders, smiled at me with a blank "what now, nigga?" kind of stare.

"Tie her ass up," I told Benito. "Tie her ankles to the chair, her waist to the back of the chair, and tie her wrists together tight as you can, nigga. And this time do not use no fuckin' Scotch tape."

I stared down on Red Velvet. "I don't give a fuck if your ass never speaks another word. Get comfortable, bitch."

Red Velvet was smooth. No kicking, screaming, fighting; no reply.

"You don't seem so bad now. What happened to all that smart-ass talk you were spittin' before I got on the phone?" I asked her.

Red Velvet sat with her ankles bonded to the legs of the dining room chair, her wrists tied together, her hands in her lap. "Shut the fuck up. Your woman don't even want your sorry ass."

"V, I say we untie her. Let her entertain us, man. You know, booty clap for us," Benito suggested, nodding like a bobble head waving two dollars in the air.

230

Maybe if I was nice to the bitch. "Red Velvet, tell us where Honey is. We'll find her, then we'll let you go. You think Honey wouldn't give you up in exchange for her freedom? You crazy," I said.

Silence. Now the bitch was a mute mutt.

"Nigga, here. Take this scarf, wrap it around her mouth, and you shut the hell up."

Benito tied the scarf, I slapped a piece of tape over her mouth. "Let's go."

"Where?" Benito asked, his forehead wrinkled. "Shouldn't one of us stay with her?"

Smack! "Look at her. Does she look like she's going anywhere?"

An incoming call on the cell saved Benito from another smack upside his head. "I'ma take this outside, nigga. You stay here." I stood on the balcony.

"What's the deal now?" I asked. Sapphire was playing too many fucking games, procrastinating and shit.

"Grant has the money in an account but we have to deliver Honey to him first," she said.

"First, how the fuck we gon' do that when we don't know where she's at?"

"I might have a lead. But you have to split the fifty with me straight down the middle," she said.

"Your ass know where Lace is? Why you trying to fuck over everybody?"

"Not everybody, just you. Because I can. The money won't do you much good for long. You're still going to get your ass arrested. Where are you?"

Ain't that a bitch? A nigga had to consider making Benito custodial over my ends until I did my time? "Your psychic ass know so much, you tell me." I was so fucking heated I ended the call before I cursed that bitch out. That bitch wasn't fooling Valentino. Sapphire had no idea where Lace was. That bitch was just tryn'a get paid off my back, Grant's back, every damn body's back. I went inside.

"Where we going?" Benito asked.

That nigga was my fucking shadow. "Out to look for Lace, nigga. Let's go."

Benito pivoted Red Velvet's dining chair toward the television, turned up the volume. "That way if she tries to say something, no one will hear her."

On an occasion or two, that nigga made sense.

We headed out the door. "My brother owns a lot of real estate," Benito proudly said, stretching his arms.

232

"Yeah, nigga, keep it in perspective. Until I get my money back, I don't own shit."

CHAPTER 26
GRANT

Alone, I sat in my living room.

"What the fuck is your problem?" I asked myself, then answered, "You're too damn generous. That or you're fucking stupid!" I yelled, punching the air. I knew I wasn't stupid. I just felt that way. "You can't save Benito's trifling ass. You can't find Honey. And you're about to lose Jada's friendship."

I had to hear a voice of reason. I went into my study, where the mail was piled six inches high. The mail could wait. Talking with my mother couldn't. Pressing the speaker button, I dialed Mom's number.

"Hi, sweetheart," she answered. "Your father and I are worried about you. You took off out of the driveway like a madman. You hadn't answered or returned our calls. Benito had to —"

"I love you, Ma."

"Oh, baby, what's wrong? What's bothering you? I can hear it in your voice."

I forced back my tears, took a deep breath. My chest tightened. I took another deep breath, rubbed my aching shoulder. "I'm good. Just had to hear your voice."

"Don't you give me that, Grant Hill. You either tell me what's troubling you or . . . honey," she called out, "Come here, please."

"No, Ma, I don't want to talk to Dad. Maybe later. Right now I want to talk to you."

"You gon' talk to both of us," she insisted. "It's Grant, baby, go get the other phone."

The next voice I heard was my father's. "Son, where are you? What's got your mother all upset? I done told you don't stress your mother out. I can't do without her by my side."

My mother said, "We're listening, baby."

My lips tightened. I tugged at the left side of my chest. I was a grown-ass man. I . . . I . . . "Mama, it's Honey. She's been kidnapped."

Both of my parents replied at the same time, "Kidnapped!"

"And how do you fit into this equation?" my mother asked. "That girl has been trouble every since you met her."

"He doesn't," my father said, answering my mother's question.

I exhaled. "I love her so much I transferred

the money to pay her ransom."

"Put it back," Mom said.

"How much?" my dad asked.

"Fifty."

"Fifty dollars? Fifty thousand?" my mother asked.

I mumbled, "Million."

"Oh, hell, no," my mother, who never swears, said. "Lord, forgive me. Grant Hill the second, you come home right this minute."

My parents couldn't solve my problems. They reared me to make decisions and I had. "I'm not a child, Mama. I can handle this."

"You're my child until you die, if you don't kill me first," she retorted.

"Honey, calm down. Let me handle my son."

"Just hear me out, y'all. I can handle this."

I told my parents about putting Benito up in one of my condos. They knew I didn't like my brother and were pleased I cared enough to keep him off the streets. I told them about Valentino and how he'd allegedly kidnapped Honey but didn't say he was living with Benito. And I told them about Sapphire and how she was pretending Valentino had Honey in his custody. And finally, I told my parents about Jada. Of course they approved of her when my dad learned Jada was Darius's mom. I informed them Jada was just a friend.

"Get us some tickets to the game," Dad said as though he'd forgotten everything I mentioned prior.

"Transfer your money back to your business account and wash your spirit clean of that evil woman. She's been through too much for you to deal with her. She's not equally yoked, son," my mother said.

"You're simply not cut from the same cloth, son. Plus, your brother had her every way imaginable for three years. You don't want his leftovers. Let her go, son. Let that jezebel go," my dad said.

"Thanks, Ma. Thanks, Dad. I love you both. I'll be home soon. I promise."

"Bring Jada," my mother said. "We'd love to meet her."

"We love you too, son," my dad said. "Hang up and transfer your money back to your business account right now."

"Bye," I said, pressing the speaker button. I took a deep breath, trying to loosen up my chest. Then I opened my desk drawer, swallowed two aspirins, and decided to phone my broker.

Ding, ding, ding, ding, dong.

Hanging up the phone, I closed the door

to my study, headed to the living room. Sapphire stood outside my door. This time I'd invited her. Opening the door, I said, "Come in. Have a seat."

She sat in the same blue chair facing me. I sat in the black seat across from her, praying our conversation would not be a repeat. Honey had two strikes against her, my mom and my dad. I did not want to be the third but I'd grown weary of the search. I'd give Sapphire the opportunity to prove my parents wrong.

I told Sapphire, "I'll listen. You talk."

"Nothing has changed except that Red Velvet has abandoned the mission. She's missing and I'm not sure what to do with her when I find her. Everyone is expected to stay committed until we find Honey," she said.

Now Red Velvet was missing. I guess Sapphire would eventually call me and declare herself missing. What a damn joke. I placed my receipt on the table for the fifty million dollars I'd transferred.

"Either you arrange for me to get Honey today and deliver this money to Valentino today, or I'm abandoning this mission. I love Honey but you are playing games with her life and mine. I don't give a fuck about Valentino, Red, green, blue, or purple

Velvet. The only person I care about in this equation is Honey."

Sapphire snapped, "If you're so concerned about your precious Honey, why don't you find her on your own?" She picked up the receipt. "I apologize. This ordeal is stressing me out. I'll find her for you, Grant."

I was convinced my parents were right but I wasn't ready to give up on Honey.

"You know how much I love Honey and you mean to tell me you don't have any more information today than what you came here with yesterday? I don't fucking believe you. What I do believe is misery loves company. You were raped as a child. Honey was molested by her stepfather and raped by her ex-husbands. You became a cop so you could legally annihilate pimps. Honey became a prostitute, then a madam. You decided to quit your job and enjoy the money you stole from Valentino. Honey decided to get out of the business, use the money you gave her to help other women, and she gave each of those women who worked for her a million dollars each. Your fucking problem is if there isn't something in the deal for Sapphire Bleu, there is no deal. You've never helped anyone but yourself. So why don't you tell me what it is you really want, huh? What the fuck do you want!"

Sapphire eyes swept from one corner to the other. "Fuck you, Grant Hill. You don't know me. Mama's fucking boy. You're not even a man. You never had to fight for anything in your life. Probably never had a fistfight. Mommy and Daddy took care of their precious baby boy. You think you can buy your way out of everything," she said, ripping the receipt. Throwing the pieces of paper in my face, she continued, "Keep your money. I'll see what you're truly made of when I'm done with you," she said, flinging open my front door.

"Don't do me any favors," I said to her back as she left. That was stupid. I prayed her threat wasn't serious. I shouldn't have talk to her that way. "Shit." Sapphire could ruin my life in a second if she wanted but my frustration wasn't about Sapphire, it was directed toward my not knowing where Honey was. If Sapphire made good on her threat, life without Honey was happening.

The woman with so much fire, enthusiasm, drive, determination, brains, beauty, sex appeal, bedroom skills, a bodacious booty, her own business, and lots of money could give it all to some other man. My parents were right. I was beginning to wonder if Honey Thomas was the woman for me. I shouldn't marry into her insane lifestyle.

I walked around my house removing Honey's pictures from every room. I went into my garage, removed the lid, then trashed them. Picked up a small can, opened it, poured the red paint on top of the photos. I wasn't foolish enough to throw away the diamond I'd bought with Honey in mind, but I was certain my efforts would not go to waste.

My phone rang just as I was about to get into the shower.

"Hey, what's up?" I answered.

"Grant, I apologize for acting —"

"Childish. I was the one. Forgive me?" I asked Jada.

"Can we get —"

"Together later?"

"I'd like —"

"Me too. I'll see you in an —"

"Hour," she said.

"Can't wait." Instantly, the tension in my chest, arm, shoulder, and heart subsided.

I felt Jada's smile through the phone and couldn't erase my smile. Strange how a woman could make a man angry, cry, smile, and laugh all in the course of twenty-four hours. "Bye, Jada," I said, then ended the

call thinking Jada might just be sweeter than
Honey.

CHAPTER 27
HONEY

Inside dying to look out, I sat alone in the living room. Sun rays beamed between the slits of the closed blinds. Voluntarily incarcerated, I longed to trade places with the sunshine. What was it like always being exposed?

I reclined in Hunter's favorite seat, powered on the flat screen. The president was apologizing for the resignations of the health secretary and the chief performance officer. *Let he who is without sin cast the first stone.* Talking to the television, I said, "I wonder if God grants amnesty. If not, we are all going straight to hell."

Hell. Sin. Fornication. What if I was falling for Hunter and he was a broke bodyguard? What if all this nonprofit stuff was created to steal my money? I wanted to believe Hunter, trust him the way he appeared to trust me. We barely knew one another. My heart swayed toward reuniting with Grant. I picked up the cordless. Dialed nine digits, then pressed the end button. I had to see Grant's face.

Parting the blinds with my thumb and finger, I peeped out. "Aw, damn." I'd recognize that driveway anywhere. Buckhead Premier Palace. *What the hell?* All this time I'd been less than a half mile from my house. I could've been home in less than ten minutes.

I tiptoed to the bedroom and stood in the doorway. Hunter was asleep, lightly snoring.

I crept to the dresser, slowly opened the drawer, and gathered my sweatpants, a T-shirt, and my tennis shoes, no socks. Making my way into the living room, I quietly put on my clothes, shoes. I released the latch, turned the knob, opened the door.

"Where are you going?" Hunter asked.

"Insane." I ran out the door. Halfway down the stairs, Hunter grabbed me by the waist, picked me up with one arm. I kicked as he hauled me back inside. "Wait! Wait!" I screamed, pointing. "I see Valentino and Benito."

"Yeah, right. And I'm Lil Wayne. You are not going to ruin this contract for me. I thought I could trust you," he said, locking the door. "If you want out, you leave the right way. Don't make me look incompetent."

Dragging me into the bedroom, Hunter handcuffed my right wrist to the bedpost.

I sat on the edge of the bed, studying the handcuff, trying to figure out how to unlock it. "Seriously, I saw them entering the driveway. That was them in that Benz."

"I don't believe you."

"Fine." I placed my legs on the bed and started kicking the black and white pillows to the floor. "You shouldn't be so attached to money."

"Easy to say with all your millions." Hunter crawled onto the bed, sat in the center. "Baby, you need to calm down."

Beating his chest with one hand, I cried, "I'm going crazy in here. I can't handle this any more. Call Sapphire and tell her I want out of this arrangement."

His deep-set eyes scrolled with hatred. "I have obligations. I need this money. You've got yours. I'm making mine. You will not fuck this up for me."

Was this the same man I'd let lick my pussy?

"Your parents are coming today," Hunter reminded me, moving closer. "I'm going to get you back to normalcy. I promise, baby," he said, holding my chin. His lips moved toward mine.

I turned my cheek. I didn't want his kiss, I wanted Grant. Everything about Hunter was starting to irritate me. Hunter's touch was creepy, felt like when Ken pricked my chin and the blood trickled down my neck.

I cried aloud, "Just kill me. Please, kill me. All my life I've struggled. Why? What's it all about? If I lay down and never wake up, I'll be better off. Eventually I have to die. I'm tired, Hunter. I'm tired," I cried.

Hunter unlocked the cuff. "Baby," he said, holding me in his arms. "We all get tired sometimes. But if you hang in there another minute, another hour, another day, I promise I'll do everything in my power to make you happy." Hunter kissed my lips. "You take care of me and Hunter will take care of his baby."

This time it didn't feel so creepy. I kissed him back.

"I want you to know I'm vested in this assignment. I'm protecting my investment. Honey, I'm falling in love with you. I don't want to fall alone. Say you'll fall with me."

"I really did see Valentino and Benito entering this complex. You've got to trust me," I said, laying my head on his chest.

Hunter replied, "I know you did."

Was he intentionally fucking with me? I

closed my eyes and prayed. Brain? Courage? Heart?

CHAPTER 28
SAPPHIRE

Sexy mamacita!

Preoccupied with Honey, I'd neglected myself, forgotten the joys of being the vivacious bisexual woman that I was. I didn't have a preference of male over female or vice versa. Chemistry, physical appeal, impeccable hygiene, and sexual energy were how I selected my partners.

I had to rekindle my flame. Tonight, Santonio's eyes were going to pop out of his head when he saw me strut into the restaurant. Even if I didn't like him, I'd thank him. Our dinner date made me focus on my appearance, take time for me, and oh, my, he was going to get the best blow job if we hit it off.

A woman could dwell on what she didn't have to the point that she'd forget all the remarkable things the Creator had given her. Hands that could heal with a loving touch. Eyes that would soothe with a caring look. Lips that could command attention with a simply seductive curve. Hips that swayed to a rhythm that made a man want to know her first name, and change her last name to his.

Slap! I tapped my own ass. "Bitch, you are bad."

Dancing nude in my full-length mirror, I pinned up my soft curls, let a few dangle on each side of my face. I eased a sky blue thong against my clit, then between my butt cheeks. The matching lace-trimmed bra complimented my breasts.

I exhaled, admired myself as I slipped into my electric blue dress, which tapered to my shapely body. Not too short, not too long, the hemline hovered a few inches above my knees. Blue was the only color that complimented every complexion. The key was to select the perfect shade. When I strapped on the wide black belt, my breasts went from "look-at-me" to "all-eyes-on-these." I tugged my bra slightly, exposing the edges on the neckline of the dress. My plump juicy breasts were enmeshed close together. The twins, more like kissing cousins, convinced me I could have any man and his woman tonight.

Dialing the driver, I asked, "Have you picked up Mr. and Ms. St. Thomas yet?"

"We're on our way to the condo. We'll arrive on time," he said.

"Good. When you arrive, call me. Keep them in the car until I come and get them," I said, ending the call.

Why in the world was I playing along with Honey's ridiculous idea to confront her parents? They didn't love or even like Honey. Honey's decision not to leave them shit was unequivocally the right decision. Hunter. He'd gotten in her head and convinced her to do this dumb shit. I had to tell Honey the truth about Hunter tonight.

This was the last day I was dealing with Honey, Valentino, and Grant's bullshit. I stepped into my black pumps, strutted out the door, started my engine. I drove out of the garage of my town house, which was in a development near the Lenox Mall and Phipps Plaza.

En route to Honey's location, I called Santonio.

"Hey, beautiful lady," he answered.

Did he know my name? "Hey, Santonio. I have to make a business stop. Shouldn't take long. I'll see you shortly. Bye." I ended the call.

I wasn't good at small talk or dating. I usually invited a man or woman over, had a few drinks, sex, then never saw them again.

Grant was the exception. Girl Six, still hadn't seen her since the last time I'd fucked her with my double-headed dildo.

Buckhead Premier Plaza was quiet as I eased my car over a speed bump. I parked in the driveway, sat in my car contemplating how to culminate my stay in Atlanta. Hunter's hit had been arranged by his bookies. I tried but couldn't convince them not to include Hunter's wife and kids. They insisted, kids first, then his wife, and Hunter would be saved for last. Drying my tears, I had to dismiss Honey before Hunter's assassination. Grant, he had it coming. He didn't have to like me but he should've been smart enough to respect me or at least phone and apologize. Too late. Valentino, I'd leave him alone for now. Tonight I'd enjoy my date with Santonio. Maybe I'd let him do most of the talking. Try my best not to control our conversation. Why did I have the need to control everybody's life?

I could simply fly home to Las Vegas and never look back. I'd prefer to return to LA, spend a few months with my mother, but LA held bad memories of Alphonso and my burning desire to kill him. Was my control a side effect of having been raped and molested? Why did I latch on to Honey? Couldn't let go of my job? Clung to any-

251

thing except myself? I'd never latched on to Sapphire Bleu's blues. Never had a true sense of who I was. Never sat alone and mourned my pain and suffering. The time had come for me to trash other people's garbage. But how could I?

Pressing the garage door opener, I got out of my car and went inside. The condo was quiet. I searched the living room, bathroom, and finally opened the bedroom door to find Honey and Hunter naked, fast asleep in one another's arms.

I guess wherever this bitch lays her head is her home. Grant would be better off without her but I was not going to deliver the news to him about his Honey.

Honey's titties were golden, plump. Her caramel areolas surrounded gumdrop nipples. Her pussy was bald, stomach flat. Her ass beneath her gave a curvaceous hump side view. I wanted to spread her legs, taste her sweet pussy. I knew it was sweet based on how men responded to her. I imagined my tongue gently exploring her shaft, her vagina, then her clit. I wanted to strap on and fuck her while Hunter watched, holding his dick in his hand, rotating his palm up and down his shaft with envy. Knowing Hunter had fucked Honey, I was the envious one. But I was also the smart one not to fuck with her voodoo pussy.

"Wake up. This is not a honeymoon." I doubted Hunter had told Honey about his estranged wife and two kids. Bet that would make her see him differently.

Honey frowned at Hunter. They stared at me as though they'd seen me for the first time.

Now that I had their attention, I said, "Grant knows where Valentino and Benito are, but he won't say and I'm done searching. So the three of us have to come up with a different plan. Wash your asses, brush your teeth, and put on some clean clothes, 'cause I don't want to smell the remnants of your sexcapades. I'll be in the living room when you're ready. We have to devise a new strategy today. This is obviously not working."

"Damn, Sapphire. Is that you? You look good, baby," Hunter said, sitting up.

"Baby," Honey said, staring at me, not Hunter, "you look hot."

I squinted at Hunter before leaving the bedroom. I strolled to the living room, sat on the sofa, turned on the basketball game. The driver called, had arrived with Honey's parents. "Wait for me to call you back," I told him, watching the game. When Honey and Hunter finally entered the living room, I pressed the mute button.

"Honey, your parents are outside in the limo. I think what you're doing is senseless and childish. You don't like them. They don't like you. But since Hunter convinced you to do this, I'll go and get them. Tell them whatever you'd like. When you're done talking with them, I'm done with you. I'm bringing this assignment to closure."

Honey sat beside me as though we hadn't fought. "You look so beautiful, Sapphire. But what's wrong? Why do you seem so disgusted with me?"

I wasn't disgusted with her, nor was I stupid. That slick bitch was repositioning herself to resume control of the situation, get me to hang in until she was ready to quit.

"Because she needs a dick in her life," Hunter blurted, sitting on the arm of the sofa next to me.

"Too late for you to fuck me again," I said. "I have a date tonight. It's time I have some mind-blowing sex and happiness too instead of walking in on the two of you fucking like rabbits all day long."

"You two are fuck buddies?" Honey asked.

Hunter stared at me, shook his head. "Wouldn't call it that."

I felt amazing. Neither of them took their eyes off me. "Maybe you should ask Hunter's wife."

Hunter grunted, "You're crazy! You demented conniving . . ."

"What? Say it. I dare you."

"What's your problem, Sapphire? I haven't been with my estranged wife in three years. You know that."

"What about your kids? Haven't been with them in three years either?"

Shaking his head, harder this time, Hunter clenched his teeth, moved away from me, and sat on the edge of the recliner. "And you know I send a thousand dollars a week every week to their mother. I take care of mine. You also know my wife left me because she doesn't approve of my occupation of choice. Anything else you want to disclose on my behalf? Thanks for reminding me why I have to get out of this business. Too many damn background backstabbing checks. And I'm sure you know exactly where Valentino is at."

He couldn't squash my game. If I knew where Valentino was, I wouldn't have been sitting on my ass. "Occupation of choice or gambling addiction? You'd better pay your debt today. Your time is running out. And you're late on your child support payments."

Honey stormed into the bedroom. Hunter followed her. I walked to the window, motioned to the driver to send in Mr. and Mrs. St. Thomas. Opening the front door, I saw two of the most conservatively dressed folks I'd ever seen standing before me.

She wore a long-sleeve floral print collarless dress that damn near choked her. He had on a brown throwback silk suit that looked like he'd bought it in the sixties, and his fedora with a red and green feather was a mismatch. Despite his attire, the old man was handsome, but the woman's shifty eyes made her appear guilty until proven innocent.

"I'm Officer Sapphire Bleu. Please have a seat on the sofa."

"Pleased to meet you, Officer Bleu." She spoke in a country proper tone. "I'm Rita St. Thomas, Lace's mother, and this here is her father, Jean St. Thomas," the woman said, avoiding eye contact with my breasts. She sat two inches away from the man, who caressed my breasts with his eyes.

"Nice," he said, "to meet you."

"Stay focused." She jabbed him in his side with her elbow, then continued, "We miss our baby girl. Our firstborn died of a rare bone marrow disease. Now Lace is missing and some man named Hunter told us she might be dead." Her mother boohooed but not a single tear escaped her eyes. "We're her *only* surviving relatives. We loved our daughter so much." Rita wept on Jean's shoulder. "We should inherit all that money she has."

Jean said, "It'll help me take care of my only grandson. We're from a small town in Arizona."

"Flagstaff," Rita said, then asked, "Ever been there? Probably not. That's where we raised Lace before she ran away from home. I'm not surprised she's dead. That girl was horrible from day one. But we always loved her."

"Oh," Jean chimed in, "and if either of her two ex-husbands contacts you trying to claim our inheritance, let me handle them."

Yes, indeed. I was speechless, thinking I wanted to kick their lying asses back to Route 66. No one ever planned on dying but death was inevitable. Would Alphonso try to collect my money if he thought I was dead? Yes, the lowdown dirty bastard would. I had to put all my assets in my mother's name quick.

Honey and Hunter entered the room laughing like high school kids headed to

Disneyland for grad night. Rita's face tightened. Jean stood.

"Is this one of them 'you've been punk'd' pranks?" Jean asked.

"No, Daddy," Honey said. "Mama kicked me out and you slammed the door in my face when I came to you as a grown woman with my heart and arms wide open. You have just now proved my point. You're exactly like all the other leeches out there. You don't give a damn about family until you think they're dead and left you something. You have the nerve to feel entitled to my money? You don't deserve shit from me. I'd leave my millions to charity before I'd give the two of you one cent to split. Know this: if I die before you, you're not getting anything. You can leave now. Both of you are making me sick."

"Nice almost meeting you both," Hunter said, following Honey into the bedroom.

"Lace! Lace! You get your ass out here right now," Rita yelled. "I am your mother and you will not speak to me in such a way. I need your help. My husband Don is sick and I just got laid off from my job."

Rita stood, faced the bedroom, took a few steps in that direction.

"I wouldn't do that if I were you," I told her.

258

Rita faced me. "You had us come here for nothing?"

"It's never too late to learn to love your child. But you can't put a price on Honey's love," I said. "And if you feel you came here for nothing, if you're disappointed she's alive, then you don't deserve anything from her, ever. Personally, if you were my mother, I wouldn't have wasted my time."

"Her name is not Honey. Her name is Lace. I'll go to the police and report her. Have her arrested for —"

Jean interrupted, "Let it go, Rita. You were a horrible mother."

"And what the hell were you? Huh? Left me with your kids while you went off to enjoy the single life with those loose women. Huh? No conditions on you. You didn't wipe her ass, I did. Now you wanna man up? Tell Rita what to do? Huh?"

"You put her out, I didn't," he said.

"Can't put out what you never took in," Rita answered, "you sorry-ass good for nothing trifling piece of shit."

Damn. "We're going to have to bring this session to a close," I said. "The driver will take you to your hotel. Honey has prepaid for your room. Your flight departs in the morning."

"Did you say 'room'? As in singular?" Jean asked.

"Please don't make any more babies," I said, ushering them out the door.

Rita shouted, "Her name ain't Honey."

Both of them were pathetic. They argued to the limo, banged the doors shut. I hope Honey and Hunter were satisfied. "Y'all can come out now," I said.

Hunter grabbed the remote, turned up the volume on the TV, then leaned back in the recliner. I sat on the sofa next to Honey, held her hand. "You have my sympathy. Girl, your parents are insane."

Hunter grunted. "Y'all made me miss the first half of the game with that madness. Unbelievable. Can't trust anyone these days."

Honey and I stared at the television. The picture on the flat screen was what was unbelievable.

The commentator said, ". . . There's Jada Diamond Tanner looking like a jewel."

Another commentator said, "Yeah, since Darius's mother has been sharing her suite with her new gem, she seems happier."

"Oh. My. God. That dog!" Honey yelled. Grabbing the remote from Hunter, she hurled it at the screen. "He's not looking for me. He's moved on with some prim and proper stuck up looking bitch."

"It's not what you think," I told her. "Grant truly loves you."

Honey snapped. "Don't tell me what the fuck you think. Tell me what the fuck you know about Grant, Hunter, Valentino, that bitch he's at the game with . . . tell me every fucking thing or I swear I'ma kick your ass so bad your mother won't recognize you."

I exhaled, stood, then answered, "Oh, you mean the same way your mother recognized you?" I reached into my purse, ripped the corner off an envelope, jotted an address, handed it to Honey.

Honey's misery was not going to accompany me, not tonight. "I have a dinner date at the Ritz and I'm not about to let you fuck that up too. If you want your man," I said, pointing to the piece of paper, "I suggest you go and get him."

CHAPTER 29
VALENTINO

Babysitting a grown-ass woman during the game was not halftime entertainment. Benito moved Red Velvet's chair into the living room in front of the black leather sofa, removed the tape and scarf from her mouth, then fed her a bite of our pepperoni pizza with extra cheese.

"Oh, damn. Darius scored again! Nigga, you are missing the game of the mother-fuckin' season over there trippin'."

"She's gotta eat too, V," Benito said, twirling a strand of cheese onto his finger. "Open wide."

Red Velvet's eyes narrowed. "I don't know where your finger has been. You could've pissed, shook your dick, then left the bathroom without washing your filthy hands. You eat it. Give me another bite of the part you haven't touched."

"Nigga, I say let her ass starve. Oh, damn. Darius has scored again. This game is beyond spectacular."

Why hadn't I heard from Sapphire? Had she collected the money from Grant? Cut me out altogether? She could be back in Las Vegas. I wasn't going to California, Arizona, Utah, Oregon, Idaho, or any contiguous state that tipped that bitch-ass state of Nevada, ever again in my life. Summer would have to pack up our shit and move to Atlanta after she had the twins or she'd have to raise them by herself in Nevada. Where was that crazy-ass wife of mine and what was she up to? All I knew was Summer had better not have another man up in my house, sleeping in my bed, telling my son what the fuck to do. Women were more trouble than they were worth. If it weren't for pussy, titties, ass, getting head, and birthing babies, women were not necessary. Men could enjoy sports 24–7 without interruptions.

"Untie me," Red Velvet complained. "I've gotta pee."

That was exactly the distractive shit I was thinking about.

Benito put the pizza on the cardboard box, wiped his hands on a napkin. "Okay."

"No, nigga, no. What the fuck are you doing? Do not untie her ass until I say so."

"He'll change his mind in a minute. It's

got to be his idea not yours," Benito said, feeding her another bite.

Was that nigga a double agent? Benito's loyalty was solid as quicksand. But that nigga Darius Jones was faster than a cheetah. Darius was my new nigga. I had to see his ass shut down that damn arena in person. Halftime highlights — that nigga had a triple-double — points, rebounds, assists. The cameraman zoomed in on an exotic international-looking bitch and a black goddess.

My anaconda slithered down my leg. Midthigh, I grabbed the head, squeezed my dick tight. "Slow down, nigga." I'd like to fuck both of them at the same time too. "Look at these bitches here, nigga," I said to Benito. "Damn, they are straight solid. I'd do them both." I stood. Red Velvet stared at my dick. "You know you want some of this."

"I'll pass on that there shit, nigga. Don't look like you've had your rabies shots yet," she said.

The commentator said some shit about, "That's Darius Jones's mother, Jada Diamond Tanner, looking like a jewel, and his wife, Fancy Taylor, a flawless diamond, and that's his son."

The second commentator dipped in, "But

that's not her son. Sure takes a woman to raise another woman's child. The biological mother, Ashlee Anderson, is reportedly not doing so well."

I walked over to that trick Red Velvet, raised my hand to smack her in her big mouth, as the first commentator said, "Yeah, since Darius's mother has been sharing her suite with her new gem, she seems happier."

"V, stop. Look at the television man." Benito stared at the screen. "My bro! Got himself another rich woman. I think she was the one in the limo that day. That's how we do it. You think Lace knows?"

The second commentator asked, "Wasn't Ashlee Darius's stepsister?"

"I believe so. Back to the real highlights here," the first commentator said.

Grant had impeccable taste. He'd better not introduce me to Jada or Fancy. I'd fuck them so good they'd be callin' my name in their sleep. "Nigga, I don't care if Lace's ass knows or not. I'm glad your brother is smarter than I thought. Lace is bad news. Definitely not his type." She was more like mine.

Red Velvet kept her eyes focused on the television. There was something in her eyes — lust.

I told her, "What? You think you can score with Darius? A man that successful would never let a trick like you suck his dick. You're not good enough."

"Don't say that, V. She's not so bad. I kinda like her. If I don't get back with Lace maybe Red Velvet and I can hook up." Benito resumed feeding her pizza. "Can I untie her now? She's wiggling in her seat."

"No, nigga, no. Let her ass burst. She's got to release information at some point. I'm tired of playing her game," I said, then yelled at her, "I'm Anthony Valentino James, bitch. I don't have to beg for nothing. You don't have to talk to me. I just decided. It's time for your trouble-making ass to going home." I dialed 411.

"What city and state, please?" the automated system asked. Red Velvet's ass gave me a newfound appreciation for a preprogrammed bitch.

"Atlanta, Georgia."

"Business or residence?"

"Business," I said.

"What listing please?"

"SPCA."

"Would you like me to automatically connect your call?"

"Yes."

A few seconds later I heard, "SPCA."

"Yeah, is this the dog pound where you guys hired that inexperienced motherfucker to run things?" How the fuck did an animal shelter hire a nigga with no animal rescue skills?

"Sir, I have no idea what you're talking about. How may I help you?"

That bitch knew exactly what I was talking about — the shit was all over the news. "I've got a female bitch over here who's got me heated. Best y'all put her to sleep before I do."

"Is she an endangerment or terminally ill?" the woman asked.

"Damn straight, the bitch is foaming at the mouth. She can't stop barking and she doesn't obey commands."

"Have you tried obedience school?"

"Bitch, have you? Just send the fucking dogcatcher to fetch her ass before I put her to sleep my damn self," I said, ending the call. This was not bitches of the world unite day.

Laughing, Benito rolled on the floor, scooted under Red Velvet's chair. His head was aligned with her ass.

"What's so funny, nigga?"

"You, V. But I have to see if Red Velvet pussy smells like the cake before the dogcatcher comes to get her." Benito rubbed

267

Red Velvet's ass.

"Nigga, you at the wrong end."

"Her ass so big it's kind of hard to get the right angle unless I tip her over," Benito said, grinning.

"I'll tip the bitch for you." I pushed the chair on its two front legs. Benito repositioned himself to the front end and smiled.

Water flowed over the edge of the chair into Benito's mouth.

I laughed so hard my stomach hurt. I damn near dropped the chair on him. "That's what you get, nigga."

Benito slid from underneath the chair. "That wasn't nice. I should beat you senseless for that," he lamented at Red Velvet. "I'm the one who fed you and that's the thanks I get?"

That nigga may never learn. You can't treat a bitch like a lady. I shook my head. *Smack!* I slapped that nigga upside his empty head, grabbed the scarf and tape. Gagged that bitch, slapped a wide strip of tape over her mouth. "Go wash your pissy-ass face, then come help me put this nasty bitch on the balcony to dry out. And you are going to clean up her piss."

That bitch ruined my appetite. I tossed the pizza in the trash, watched the game. "That nigga DJ keep this shit up he gon' fuck around and get the league's MVP. Most valuable pussy." Somehow, I was getting in that suite with Grant and Jada on the regular. Had to change my strategy.

An hour later, the game ended. Darius had half the team points. I had to find a way to make Grant respect me. Maybe I could take my money when I got it and partner with him on a few real estate deals. Do some legitimate business and shit.

Benito came back smelling fresh. That nigga had dressed up, black slacks, black button up shirt, and rubber gloves. Couldn't blame him for doing it up. Nigga had to get his ego intact after having a bitch give him a golden shower.

"Help me carry her ass, chair and all, out on the balcony," I said, holding my side of the chair with a bath towel.

Benito grabbed his end. Red Velvet bucked like a horse. Made us lose our balance, slip and fall into her piss.

"Bitch, I will pick your ass up, chair and all, and throw you over the balcony. Do it again."

"Untie her. Let me handle her, V."

"Nigga, you're the reason both of us have to take a damn shower. Now! Buck again, bitch. I dare you," I said as we picked her and the chair up again.

We straddled her chair across the threshold. I shoved the sliding door firm against the side of her chair so tight she couldn't move a fraction of an inch. "Go shower again, nigga," I told Benito. "I'ma go take one too. Hopefully by the time we get dressed that damn dogcatcher will be here. If not, we're dropping her ass off at the pound. She's useless."

CHAPTER 30
RED VELVET

Valentino was insane. Benito was obnoxious. Grant was wonderful. Seeing Grant on television rekindled fond memories of our sexual adventure. I prayed Honey was safe and she'd reunite with Grant before that Jada woman stole his heart. He did seem happy with Jada though.

I heard the showers running in both bathrooms. This was my time to escape these fools. I bucked but the chair hadn't budged. Bucked harder. Harder. The chair hadn't moved with me. I scanned my surroundings. The knives were six feet away on the counter. I twisted my hands in opposite directions. "Ow." That wasn't a good idea. Tears burned my eyes. A burst of air hit my face. A breeze emerged, chilling my wet ass.

Footsteps drew closer. Valentino was in his bedroom, Benito in his. Who was in the condo? I kept quiet. What if Valentino really had called the pound? What if it was a robber? Or Valentino's wife? Or one of his enemies? He had to have many, my being only his most recent. My heart thumped. I quieted my breathing. What if it was Sapphire?

The pointed tip of a canary yellow shoe appeared. Then I saw the squared toe of a black leather shoe stop beside the yellow one. Then a pair of red pants flared against a pair of black slacks. Next I heard the front door close.

The draft abruptly stopped. No longer funneling my body, the breeze brushed my back one last time. The woman and man stood side by side in the dining room. He was my onetime lover. She was the older woman from the suite at the game.

"What the hell is going on here?" Grant asked.

Frantically shaking my head, I cried, "Please untie me. Hurry."

"Oh, my gosh, this poor child. I thought you said your brother lives here," Jada said, peeling the tape from my mouth. She untied the scarf, went to the living room, took a few deep breaths, then said to Grant, "You can explain this later."

Turning his head sideways, Grant inhaled, untied my stinky ankles, then exhaled as he stood. "Where are they?" he asked.

"In their bathrooms. I had to pee. They wouldn't untie me so I pissed on them."

Grant shook his head, then laughed. "Those two deserve to be pissed on."

"They tried to force me to tell them, but I swear I don't know where Honey is."

Jada untied my wrists. Grant untied my waist.

"It's okay. You're safe now. I believe you. I don't know where Honey is either." Grant hugged my upper body, avoiding below the waist contact.

"Baby?" Grant said.

Jada and I both answered, "Yes."

Grant smiled. He kissed Jada, looked into her eyes, then said, "Baby, I need you to take Red Velvet home, then come back and pick me up."

Jada kissed Grant. "My car? You want me to take her home in *my* car?"

"Please," he said.

"If I didn't care for you —"

He answered, "But you do. And I care for you too. You have to —"

"I do trust you," she said to him, then asked, "Sweetheart, is there a towel or something she can sit on?"

Grant went into Benito's bedroom and returned with a cashmere camel-colored blanket. Jada grabbed the blanket, then said,

"Let's go."

Grant held my face in his hands, focused on me as though we were the only two in the room. "Velvet Waters, you have a wonderful mother, beautiful son, and promising future in acting. I can't let you leave without asking."

My eyes widen, heart palpitated.

"Did my brother or Valentino sexually assault you?"

What the hell? I wanted to lie, wanted Grant to beat their asses, but I couldn't lie to Grant. "No, they were annoying but they didn't hit or rape me or anything like that," I said, hoping Grant would hug me again. He didn't.

"Go home, get yourself together, and get your family to Los Angeles so you can start filming, because Hollywood does not wait to make an unknown actor a star. Trust me, if you don't show up when you're supposed to, they have a replacement ready to take your part."

I smiled. He remembered I was leaving. Then I frowned. Was he trying to get rid of me?

"But Sapphire and Onyx said they'd find me because I've abandoned their mission to find Honey. Sapphire and Onyx had me and they might still have the other girls prostitut-

274

ing by the theme park every night. They're trying to find information that'll lead them to Honey and Valentino but Valentino is right here with you. Why haven't you called the police? Don't you still love Honey?" I asked, searching Grant's eyes to see if he cared more for Honey than he cared about Jada.

Grant stared through me. "If you need anything . . . money, travel arrangements, help finding housing —"

"I'll help her with all of that," Jada said, grabbing my arm. "I can see how much you're concerned about her well-being, sweetheart, so I'll take over from here." Jada's fingers tightened around my bicep. Firmly, she said, "Velvet, let's go."

"Bitch, let me go," I told her, snatching my arm, hoping she'd say, "Grant, you take her home."

Grant turned his back to me, sat on the sofa, and faced the flat screen as Jada escorted me out the door to an ivory-on-ivory gorgeous Bentley. She spread the blanket over the seat and floor. "Get in and try not to touch anything. I'll close the door."

Fine. I sat in the seat, wrapped my arms, torso, legs, feet, ass in the blanket, and waited for her to get in.

The animal rescue van parked in her space.

"Where am I taking you?" Jada asked, lowering all four windows. Frowning, she mouthed, "SPCA. Where are they going?"

I laughed to myself, gave her my address near Atlantic Station.

"So how did you get involved in this situation?" she asked, driving toward BPP's exit.

Glancing out my window to avoid looking at Jada's boogie behind, I saw a car backing out of a driveway. When the car faced us, I looked in the doorway of the condo and saw a lady that kind of looked like Honey. I stared in disbelief.

"Stop the car," I said, pointing. "I've got to get out."

The woman slammed the door. Jada kept driving.

I was so delirious I didn't know what to think or whom I saw.

"I'm taking you home. Once you get home, do whatever you like," Jada said.

"But I think I saw Honey."

"I know all about Honey, honey. Tell me about you."

My eyes opened and shut. My head leaned toward the window. My body ached from sitting in that chair overnight. I was exhausted but managed to say, "I have a six-year-old son. Ronnie is the love of my life. I conceived him because an older man raped me."

"Oh, you poor thing. That's horrible. But I meant tell me about you and Grant," Jada said.

I ignored her inquiry regarding Grant; I was not getting kicked out of her car before I got home. "Don't pity me. I'm fine. My son is wonderful. If you're jealous of Honey, you shouldn't be. What you should know is, Honey is wonderful. Either Grant wants Honey or he doesn't, but you could learn a lot from Honey. And the only thing you really want to know about Grant and me is did we fuck. Ask him. I'm young, attractive, and I'm about to make millions as an actress. Your feeling sorry for me probably makes you feel better about yourself. Thanks for the ride," I said as she parked in front of my place. When she kissed Grant, she'd be kissing Honey, Sapphire, me, and every other woman Grant had locked lips with.

Jada placed her hand on mine.

Sternly I looked at her. "Don't touch me."

"I apologize. You're right. A friend of Grant's is a friend of mine. Here's my card. If you need anything, let me know."

I opened my door. None of this madness was her fault. She was nice and I was being rude because Grant was with her. My mom would say, "Don't burn your bridges," so I said, "Would you like to meet my mom and my son?"

"I'd love to," Jada said, "but I can't stay long. I have to get back to Grant."

Jada followed me to my front door.

"Hey, Red. Where you been? Your mother is worried sick about you. I was too. What you all wrapped up in that blanket for? You're not hiding your stomach, are you? Red, you pregnant again?"

"No, Mrs. Taylor, I'm not pregnant. I'll be right out." I was going to miss her so much.

"Your mother and Ronnie should be back in a minute. They went to the store."

"Thanks," I said, unlocking my door, then told Jada, "Have a seat. I have to shower. Don't want my mother or my son to see me like this."

"I understand," Jada said, taking her cell phone out of her purse.

I was so happy to be in my house, I screamed. I scrubbed every nook and crevice of my ears, fingers, toes, thighs, arms, hair, and pussy three times over. I dried off, then towel-dried my hair. I covered my body with cocoa butter, put on a pair of sweats, a T-shirt, my tennis shoes, and dabbed on my favorite perfume.

"I'm ready," I said, joyfully bouncing into my living room.

Jada was gone. I walked outside. Her car was gone too.

"Red, no sooner than you closed your door, that woman left. She drove off like her life depended on it. Left tire marks in your driveway," Mrs. Taylor said, pointing as my mother and Ronnie drove up.

"Mommy! Mommy! Mommy!" was all my baby shouted.

I lifted him in my arms, gave my mother a big hug. We went inside my mother's house. I closed the door behind us, behind me, to all that was happening outside. I prayed Grant, Honey, and Jada were well, but I'd never neglect my mom and son again.

CHAPTER 31
HONEY

What was next?

Slam! I closed the front door. "Did I just see Red Velvet in a fucking Bentley with that bitch I saw at halftime scoring with my man?"

Hunter kissed me. "Baby, I thought I was your man."

Was that some sort of proposal for a relationship? Where had that conversation taken place other than in his head? I went into the bedroom, changed into my sweats, tennis shoes, and T-shirt. "I'm out."

Hunter blocked the doorway. "You know I have a gambling debt and you're seriously going to walk out on me? Not until my contract is complete."

"In case you weren't listening, it is done. Sapphire just told you so."

"She didn't hire me. She's not cutting my pay. Our boss hired me. So you're not going anywhere until I say so." Hunter picked me up, tossed me across his shoulder, carried me into the bedroom, then threw me on the bed. Turing on the DVD player, he said, "Let's watch this Lex video again."

Why? So you can fantasize that your dick is bigger than his? Hunter was well endowed but no match for Lex or me. I had tucked the piece of paper Sapphire gave me in my bra. "I've got to go handle this. I'll come back when I'm done. Promise."

Hunter threw the remote across the room. "Am I not man enough for you? What do I have to do to prove myself? If you don't come back, and you find me dead, it's all your fault."

Why was it when a man fucked up his life, it was a woman's fault? "This isn't about you! I had a life before I met you."

He followed me to the living room. "A fucked-up life. Your parents don't give a damn about you. Sapphire is using you. I'm the one trying to help you. My making love to you isn't enough? You want him. Fuck it! Go be with that nigga."

Hunter didn't scare me and that reverse psychology bullshit was not going to work. If he put his hands on me, I'd kill him. "Who the hell you calling a nigga? You don't know Grant."

"Apparently you don't either. He's got

another woman, a classy woman, not a whore. A woman who looks better than you. You can't compete with her. You should be happy that I want you."

I swear it doesn't matter how much money a woman had, there was always a man who'd try to put her down. I took off my shoe, hurled it at his head. Hunter caught my shoe, grabbed me, and threw me on the sofa.

"Get off me." I struggled to move him. I couldn't. Hunter left me no choice. I was so angry I spat in his face. "What is it? What do you want from me? I'm not your woman. You already have a wife, or have you forgotten about her? What else haven't you told me?"

Hunter became quiet. He stood. Wiped his eyes. Gestured with open hands toward the door.

I put on my shoe. Kept my eyes on him as I walked out. He trailed me to the front door.

"Do what you have to. I won't be back," I said, trotting down the stairs.

Slam! The door vibrated. I looked back. The glass shattered. I kept going. Whatever suppressed anger Hunter had flared in the wrong direction. Why was he striving to be my savior, my financial advisor, my companion, when he should've been a hero to his kids?

CHAPTER 32
HONEY

Digging in my bra, I removed the torn paper, read the address, strolled the complex in search of unit number 204. The condo development was magnificent, landscaping immaculate. I roamed each section, scanning the street names. The array of assorted flowers brought unexpected peace within me until I saw an SPCA van. "Aw, shit. There's a stray dog that might be on the prowl." I wasn't prepared to combat a four-legged animal.

Two men dressed in all white exited a condo. "We apologize for the confusion."

Relieved that whatever was going on had been resolved, I continued walking until I heard, "No problem. Sorry for the confusion." I stopped. The front door closed. Almost certain that was Grant's voice, I walked up the front steps, knocked on the door with 204 in gold numbers, stepped back, and waited.

The door opened. There he stood. That was my man. He was dressed well. I was casual. I couldn't move. I was happy, angry, excited, all at the same time. If I were so close, why didn't he find me?

"Honey?" Grant said, seeming more confused than excited to see me.

I wanted to hug him. Kiss him. But his reaction made me standoffish.

"May I come in?" I asked. Not waiting for his response, I crossed the threshold.

"Yeah. Yeah." Grant opened the door wider. "Of course. Sorry, it's just that I don't know how you found me when everyone else was searching for you."

"I didn't. Sapphire gave me this address," I said, stepping into the living room, not prepared to see Valentino and Benito. Casually making my way to Benito, I stood by him. *Whack! Whack! Wham!* Alternating hands, I slapped Benito upside his head.

Covering his head, Benito said, "Cut it out, Lace. It wasn't my fault. Valentino told me to kidnap you."

I picked up the closest object, a crystal elephant, and hurled it at Valentino's head. He moved in the right direction, and the elephant crashed on the carpet, broke in half.

"Damn! Bitch!" Valentino stood, looked at

Grant, then said to Benito, "Nigga, don't hold me accountable for your actions. You put the bag over her head. And, bitch, don't confuse me with Benito. Throw something else at me."

"Everybody shut up. Honey, sit down. And stop breaking up my stuff! We're going to work this out here and now," Grant yelled, standing over us. "Valentino, you go first. What does Honey owe you? And why?"

I protested, "I don't owe him shit."

Grant held up his hand. "You'll get your chance to speak."

"You ain't Judge Mathis, nigga," Valentino said. "If you were, I'd have my money from that bitch."

"And you don't pay rent here. Get out of my house," Grant said.

Valentino nodded. "Like I was getting ready to say before I was rudely interrupted, Lace worked for me as my madam. Both of you should be singing my name. I got the bitch off her back —"

"Who you calling a bitch?" I said, picking up a crystal paperweight.

Grant grabbed my hand, removed the crystal weight.

"That's what happens when you deal with brainless bitches. Bet Jada wouldn't do that," Valentino commented, rubbing his chin.

"Leave Jada out of this," Grant said. "And leave *bitch, nigga, bitches, niggas, mother-fucker, motherfuckers,* and all those words out of your mouth while talking to me. Or get out of my house."

Valentino was speechless for several minutes. "That . . . her . . . man, how am I supposed to tell you what happened?"

Grant said, "Maybe my brother Benito can explain for you."

"That . . . damn! Look, the short of it is, Sapphire and Lace set me up. They stole one hundred million dollars from me. And they were trying to set you up too. All I want is what's rightfully mine. I want my money back. All of it."

"Benito, what's your story?" Grant asked.

"I'm your bro. I don't need no story. You sexed Honey. I sexed Lace. You love Honey. I love Lace. You got a new woman — you might as well let me have her," Benito said. "End of my story."

I wanted to snatch that paperweight from Grant's hand and hit Benito upside his head. Grant's phone chimed to the tune of "The First Time Ever I Saw Your Face."

"Hey, baby," he answered.

I jumped up, snatched his phone. "Bitch,

this is Honey. He's busy," I said, then handed him back the phone.

"Hello. Hello." Grant stared at me. "You have no right doing that."

"How is it that I'm missing, and when you should be out looking for me, you're not only on national television with another woman, you're calling another woman 'baby'? You must've known her before you met me."

Valentino said, "Oh, this is about to be some real nigga shit up in here."

Grant flashed him a look.

"What? I can't say *shit* either?"

"I don't know who to believe. All of you are scammers," Grant said, digging into his pocket. "Valentino, you want money you don't deserve. Honey, you want to keep money you didn't earn. And, Benito, as long as you have a place to lay your head and wash your ass you're happy."

Grant opened his wallet, handed me a piece of paper. "I was actually going to give Sapphire fifty million dollars, to give him," he said, pointing at Valentino, "to rescue you when you weren't even missing."

My heart stood still. Grant loved me that much? "You did this for me?"

"Yes, I did. Fool me once, shame on you. Fool me twice, stupid me," he said, placing the paperweight on the coffee table. Grant eased the piece of paper from my fingers. "I actually transferred fifty million dollars from my account to give to him in exchange for you when you were never being held captive. I'd bet that Sapphire wasn't going to give Valentino a dime. She was going to double her money and leave you two to kill one another, then she'd claim your money. If she gave you my address, why didn't Sapphire show up here? Huh? I suggest the two of you split whatever money Honey has and call a truce."

I could give Valentino half, marry Grant, and come out ahead. "I'll do it, if we stay together."

"That's not what's going to happen," Jada said, entering the room.

Who let that bitch in? I looked up at Benito, then told Jada, "Bitch, get your own man."

"I am her man," Grant said. "I hope you keep your word to Valentino." He stared at me. "I tried loving you. You have no idea how much I've gone through over you." A tear fell from his left eye as he pointed back and forth between Valentino and me, then added, "That's your man right there. You two deserve one another."

No fucking way. Watching Jada stand next to my man, I wanted to hit that bitch in the head with that damn paperweight. Instead, I picked up the weight and hurled it at Grant. "I hate you!"

Valentino caught the weight inches from Grant's face. "Damn!" he yelled dropping it to the floor. "A nigga don't deserve that shit."

Grant said, "I could never hate you, Honey," then followed Jada out the front door.

I yelled at Valentino. "This is all your damn fault!"

I felt like a fool. I went to the doorway. Wanted to follow them down the stairs. Curse Grant out. Apologize for breaking his heart then curse him out again for finding someone else. Tears poured.

Valentino closed the door, then embraced me.

Shoving him away I punched him in his chest several times.

Valentino didn't try to stop me. "I deserve that. But as much as I've fucked up your life, you've fucked a nigga's life up too. Lace, I apologize for kidnapping you. But a nigga can't sit back like a bitch and let you pimp me out my money. Give me half and I'm straight."

CHAPTER 33
GRANT

A man knew when a woman was worth the wait.

Jada responded to Honey in a way that made me proud. She could've cursed Honey, attacked her reputation, or given me an ultimatum in front of her. Neither would've impressed me more than how she exhibited dignity, poise, and grace.

Touching Jada's hip, I opened my hand. "Give me your keys."

"How much more of this do we have to deal with?" she asked.

I opened the passenger door. "Get in." I closed her door, drove toward the exit of BPP. There was a contractor replacing a door with a shattered pane. "What is this about? Give me a minute."

I parked in the driveway, walked up to the door. "Hi, I'm a homeowner in this development. What's going on here?" I asked handing him my business card.

"Women, man. They're crazy," he said stretching his neck staring at the Bentley.

Glancing at my card, he nodded then said, "Developer, huh? Maybe we can partner on some things."

"You mind telling me what happened?" I asked.

"My girl wanted out. She wrecked the place, then left. I have no idea where she is but she will pay for this shit. Come in man. See for yourself."

Curious, I entered the unit. Surveying the living room, my eyes widened. The flat screen was broken in half. The leather sofa and recliner were slashed and the inside of the cushions protruded out. Mirrors were shattered.

"And you are?" I asked noticing bruises on his hands.

"Hunter," he said, adding bass to his voice.

"Damn, Hunter this is crazy. Domestic situation?" I asked, picking up the remote placing it in on the slanted TV stand. I walked to the bedroom entrance, peeped inside. Didn't want to ask if he'd call the police, I said, "Hang in there man." I walked out, got back in the car with Jada, and called the police, while driving off.

A woman could push a man to the edge,

make him do the unimaginable. Why would his girl Honey trash that place? Was it his place? Hers? The owner was irrelevant. That was why men were reluctant to let women into their space, their heart. Women were reckless.

In the beginning of my relationship with Honey, my love for her was strong. I defended her in the presence of my parents. Transferred money to save our love. For what? The second I didn't do what she wanted . . . Did I deserve this bullshit? The crazy part was I still loved her. But loving Honey was scary.

"Everything okay, baby?" Jada asked.

"No! It's not! She lied to me! Made a spectacle of me!"

"Grant, you had me looking for Honey when you knew where she was at?"

Merging onto the freeway, I sighed heavily. "No. I didn't."

"Well, if she knew where your place was, Grant, be honest. You had to know."

This was the first time Jada and I didn't complete one another. "I said I didn't know."

"Grant, I'll ask you one more —"

"Who do you think you're talking down to? Believe whatever the hell you want. Don't ask me another question."

The remainder of the ride to my home was quiet, awkward. The strangling tension made words travel from my mind, then lodge in my throat. We finally arrived at my front door.

"Grant, I apologize. You're right. Guess I'm so used to handling business I've forgotten how to be submissive."

"Nah, I don't want you to be submissive. But I do need for you to believe me and believe in me. I'm the one who owes you an apology. Please —"

"Forgive me," Jada said.

"Can I hold you tonight? I don't want to sleep —"

"Alone. Me either."

I escorted Jada to my bedroom, told her everything she needed was in the bathroom. Jada went inside the bathroom, closed the door. I heard the heavy flow of water into the Jacuzzi.

I sat on the edge of my king-sized bed. I ground my teeth when I heard *varoom.* I pulled my cell from the hip holder and saw who was calling. *I can't believe this shit.* I turned off my phone. There was nothing Honey had to say that I wanted to hear. Not right now.

"Grant," Jada called.

"Yes, you need something?"

"I need you," Jada said, with a sweet melody.

I entered the bathroom, froze. Jada was nude. Never had I seen a body so beautiful. Perky breasts. Her areolas were slightly darker than her breasts. Nipples hard like chocolate chips. Chocolate pussy lips with a hint of strawberry peeping between her thighs. Jada undressed me. She stepped into the tub. I followed her.

"Relax," she said, sponging my neck, my shoulders.

Jada's hands caressed my chest, my abs. She washed my thighs, my legs, my hair.

"Relax. Lean back. Give me your foot."

Her fingers started at the heel of my foot, eased into the arch. She pressed points that made me relax. Her thumbs rotated on the ball of my foot, in between my toes. Special attention was given to each toe, especially the big one as she eased it to her mouth.

"Do you mind if I gently cleanse your genitals?" she asked, massaging my other foot.

I smiled. My body floated. Jada was exactly what I needed at the time.

The sponge swiped between my butt, circled my hole, then floated and drifted. I closed my eyes as Jada rubbed my balls with her hands. Her hands fluttered up and down my shaft. Teased my head. Slid down my shaft, back up. Slid down. Circled the head. Her rhythm alternated up and down my shaft pressing against my underside vein. From the base to under my head, over and back. Over and back.

She applied pressure to my perineum and I released my sperm into the warm water and my heart into her hands. Was I with Jada because I wanted to be with her or because I couldn't be with Honey?

Chapter 34
Honey

Funny how you could fuck someone and at the same time fuck yourself.

Have you loved so hard you thought your heart would break?

Have you ever wished your foolish pride hadn't fooled you?

Have you mourned a lost love so deeply you thought you'd grieve to death?

Have you cried until you had no tears left?

Have you boxed with your mistakes to take the pain away?

Have you played games and had someone check you for your mate?

I was not letting Grant go. Jada may have won tonight but Grant was my man. Seeing him walk out the door with his hand on her waist irritated me. Benito sat across from me, nodding. I was too disgusted to pick up that paperweight. Wanted to give Valentino and Benito more than a piece of my mind. One paperweight, two targets. My losing

Grant was all their fault.

"Lace, you don't love me anymore?" Benito asked.

Valentino shook his head in disgust.

Untying and retying my shoelaces, I stood, removed the brown band from my ponytail. "Valentino, I will split what I have left of your money with you under one condition."

"How you gon' put restrictions on a nigga?" he asked. "That's my money."

I waited for the word *bitch* or *trick* to follow. When it didn't, I told him, "I could keep all of your money. And if you step foot on my property again without my permission, I'll shoot to kill."

"You should shoot yourself. All those years on your back and you've failed at keeping your man," he said.

A woman had to give up, in order to fail. I hadn't failed, had no intentions of failing. "That may be your truth, but the fact is I'm not broke. I can buy a man with your money." I gathered my hair into a fresh ponytail, stood in the doorway. "Think about it. Let me know by tomorrow, midnight, or forget about it."

Benito blurted, "What about me? Grant might kick us out because of you. Can I come live with you again?"

And do what? I'd already prayed that

Benito was not my destiny. In case God hadn't heard me the first time, I prayed again.

Valentino said, "You don't need her. I've got you covered."

"But I'm in love with Lace not you," Benito replied with droopy eyes.

Benito would never be my man again. Not seriously. But if I didn't get back with Grant, and if I lead Benito to believe we were dating, every holiday I could become a permanent thorn in Grant and Jada's life. I headed out the door, jogged back toward the condo, saw three police cars surrounding the unit. Hunter pointed at me. Pretending not to see him, I maintained my stride.

I turned right, jogged to Peachtree. Turned left, made my way to a restaurant, and went inside.

Observing my attire, the hostess frowned. "Excuse me, miss. May I help you?"

"Nope, I'm fine," I lied. I bypassed the entrance, scanned each section until I saw Sapphire seated with a handsome Italian man.

Sapphire noticed me right away as I approached her table.

Slap! My hand landed across her face, left a red imprint of my fingers.

Her date grabbed me and forced my

hands behind my back. The hostess came running to the table. Sapphire stood and emptied her Bloody Mary on my head. Ice cubes lodged in my ponytail.

"You jealous bitch! How dare you not tell me that Grant withdrew fifty million dollars from his account to pay my ransom? Let me go!" I yelled, struggling with the man behind me, hoping he'd leave Sapphire at the restaurant.

"It's called karma," Sapphire said.

Who the fuck was she to tell me about karma? Like her ass lived in a glass house. "You wanted Grant for yourself. That's why you lied. This is not over," I yelled, still struggling to get free.

"Yes it is, Honey. Let it go. Accept that Grant has another woman. That's not my fault. Move on with your life. I'm moving on with mine. At some point we have to let go of our past. I admit I made some bad decisions. So have you. I apologize. But you'll get through this. So will I. Take care of yourself, Honey."

"I hate you!" I shrugged my shoulders, jerked my arms. Tried to get closer to her so I could punch her this time. It was her fault.

"In case you've forgotten, you are the one who decided to declare yourself missing. I guess you really are. You don't hate me. You hate yourself. And you hate the fact that things didn't turn out the way you wanted. It's called life."

The hostess said, "Please take her out of here before I call the police."

The Italian man said, "I'm a police chief, I'll handle her."

"I'm going to report you," I yelled at Sapphire as the Italian man escorted me to the front door. The second he released me I ran away.

I ran fast. I ran long. And I ran hard. Tears poured down my cheeks. I didn't care. I was mad. At every one. Why me? Grant didn't know the meaning of abuse. The awful ways that abuse had fucked me up for life. Sure, he could recite the dictionary's definition. But what did he understand? And what had he survived?

I could've returned to the condo and let Hunter comfort me but he had anger management issues. I'd been abused enough to know the warning signs: His telling me how to invest my money, trying to make me stay until he released me, throwing me on the bed, telling me I was less than Jada, throwing the remote, slamming the door so hard the glass shattered. Going back to Hunter would be my volunteering for a volatile ass whipping.

Hunter's job may have made him angry. He was also mad at his parents, his estranged wife, not having enough money after paying child support or to pay his gambling debt. Perhaps he was born that way, grew up that way. Happy on the outside, angry on the inside. That was how most abusers were in public. I'd bet that his wife was doing well without him. Had another man raising his kids. She'd probably moved on with her life but he couldn't move on with his. Had to find himself a better woman than he'd left to prove to his ex he didn't need her when he was probably the one who'd messed up. Regardless, his problems were not mine.

I ran to my mansion. *Bam! Bam! Bam!* Relentless, I kept knocking.

Onyx opened the door. "Honey! My God! You're home!" She hugged me tight.

I hugged her lightly. "I've got somewhere to be," I said, letting her go.

"You just got here. I'm so happy you're safe." Onyx hugged me again, then yelled upstairs, "Honey's home! I'll go with you. I'm not letting you out of my sight."

That sounded so good. But I had to keep moving solo. I had one more stop.

My girls came stampeding down the stairs, smothered me with a group hug. I smiled, laughed. "Honey's home, girls, and I'm fine." A few minutes was all I spared before saying, "I've to go handle some business. Onyx, get me your cell phone."

I went into my room, locked the door, showered, washed and blow-dried my hair. I put on my red baby doll dress, red heels with the silver spikes. I curled my hair. Long golden spirals bounced freely. Layered earth-toned shadows on my eyelids. Brushed on red gloss.

I checked the purse that was left behind the day I was kidnapped, for my driver's license and credit cards. I picked up the keys for my white-on-white Jag. Went to my office, opened my desk drawer, removed my .45. Checked the rounds. Thirteen bullets in the clip, one in the chamber. I placed the gun in my purse.

Standing at the foot of my stairs, I called out, "Onyx, where's your phone?"

Onyx trotted downstairs, handed me her phone. "You look beautiful. You have a date with Grant?"

"Yeah, something like that," I said, then left.

CHAPTER 35
HONEY

Twenty minutes later, I was parked in Grant's driveway next to that bitch's Bentley. I got out and banged on his door with my gun. *I wish she would come answer my man's door,* I thought.

Grant cracked the door. "Honey? What are you doing here?"

"Open the door," I demanded.

"Nah, I can't do that. You should've called first."

Was he serious? I knew Grant hadn't gotten over me that fast. He'd have to prove it. I wasn't going anywhere.

My voice trembled as I held my gun beside my hip. "Grant, I need to talk with you now and I'm not leaving, so you might as well open the door."

He opened the door another inch. "You look nice. Look, call me tomorrow. We can talk then. Now is just not good for me, Honey."

Well, now was perfect for me and once I was inside, I'd change his mind. "For you? Or for that bitch up in there with you? I'm not leaving. Open the fucking door!"

"Fine." Grant opened the door, turned his back, walked into his living room. He tightened the black oversized towel about his waist.

I slipped my gun in my purse, closed the door, followed him, eyes glued to his ass.

He turned up the lights. I squinted, wanting to dim the lights back, set the mood for loving him.

"Baby, is everything okay?" Jada asked, entering the living room. "Not her again. Why is she here?"

" 'Her again'? 'She'? Bitch, you'd better recognize me," I said, clutching my purse to my side. "You think you gon' ease your way up in my man's house. Not without a fight."

"Ahh, not this again. Grant, where'd you find her? She's so ghetto," Jada said.

I stared at Jada. Opened my purse. Put my hand on my piece.

"Am I supposed to be scared? What are you going to do, shoot me?" she said, laughing.

"Baby, go back in the bedroom," Grant told her. "I'll be there shortly."

"Don't keep me waiting too long," she

305

said, leaving.

I sat on his plush gold cushioned sofa. "We need to talk."

Grant stood. "You talk. I'm listening."

"I need you to sit next to me," I said, placing my purse on the end table.

"I don't want to sit next to you," Grant said, leaving space between us to accommodate another person. "I'm listening."

"Baby, I'm sorry. You've got to believe me. I never meant for any of this to happen. We are so good for one another," I said, sniffling.

"Are you serious?" Grant asked.

I moved closer to him. "I want things between us to go back to the way they were before the kidnapping."

"We weren't speaking before the *alleged* kidnapping. Remember? I can go back to that. Are we done?"

No, we were not done. Grant was right but he knew what I meant. We'd left the hotel in Las Vegas, stood on the same elevator and hadn't spoken a word. How could that be, when the night before we'd made hot passionate love? I knew Grant was stubborn. So was I, but I had to take him back to that night. Back to our making love. Help him remember his true Honey.

I said, "True. But you came here to

Atlanta to rescue me. You did that because you love me."

"Correction. *Loved* you. That's what I thought. But the real reason I came was it was meant for me to meet Jada."

If Grant didn't love me, he wouldn't have let me in. "You barely know her!"

"That's more than I can say about you," Grant said, then asked, "Is there anything else?"

Jada entered the living room. "I'm going home." Grant stood. Jada held up her palm. "Don't, Grant. I'm leaving. Don't sweat the small stuff," she said, walking out the front door.

What the hell did that mean? I didn't care. I was glad her ass had left.

Grant looked at me. "Honey, what do want from me? Blood?"

I shook my head. "You. I want you back," I told him.

"I don't know how many different ways to say we are not compatible." Grant's eyes caressed my legs, my breasts.

We weren't compatible. We had different backgrounds, upbringings, lifestyles, but I loved Grant. Didn't love count? Couldn't my love for him, his love for me, sustain our relationship?

"I love you, Grant Hill."

"No you don't," he said. "What do those words mean to you?"

I had to think for a moment, then answered, "Being with you makes me happy."

"You, happy? What about me? Do you care if I'm happy? I'm looking over my shoulder every day worrying if someone that you've stolen money from is going to shoot me. Honey, be truthful. Can you honestly tell me that you love me unconditionally?"

Unconditionally? Silence lingered between us.

"You can't because you don't," he continued. "You want to be loved. You think I'm that man. I don't know if it's because of my looks, the great sex we shared, or my success. I'm not the man for you. You're gorgeous. Any man would be lucky to have you."

No, he wasn't trying to pacify me. I knew what I wanted and I wanted Grant. But he was right. I didn't love him unconditionally. I didn't love anyone unconditionally.

"Any man except you would be lucky to have me, that's what you mean?" I said. "Don't treat me this . . ." I couldn't hold back the tears.

"Honey, please. Don't cry." Grant sat next to me, held me in his arms. "I do love you. But remember that night in Vegas, you were the one who told me, 'sometimes love isn't enough.' "

I pressed my lips to his neck, my breasts to his chest, then whispered, "Make love to me one last time."

CHAPTER 36
GRANT

Fuck Honey — fuck up with Jada.

The chances of Jada finding out were slim, if Honey could separate sex and love, move on with her life, and let me be. Jada and I had already agreed not to sweat the small stuff. Fucking Honey, for me, would classify as small stuff. I wanted to fuck Honey. Her hot juicy lips were on my neck. Her nipples poked through her dress, pressed against my chest. I remembered how hot and wet she'd get for me. My dick hardened.

I cupped her breasts, pressed them together, bit her nipple through her dress. Red was definitely Honey's color.

"Umm, yeah," she moaned, then grabbed the back of my head with both hands. Pulled my mouth closer.

Lowering her shoulder straps, exposing the tips of her golden nipples, I continued sucking. My dick throbbed, lifting the towel. I should jack off, release myself on her titties, then ask Honey to leave. "This is our last time doing this." I couldn't say making love because I was going to take my emotions out of the equation and fuck the shit out of Honey. "Promise me you won't make me regret this night."

Her lips pressed against my ear, then I felt the tip of her tongue penetrate my ear hole. Precum oozed from my dick head. I eased my hand under her dress, prepared to push her thong aside, and felt it. The hot, juicy pussy I remembered was on my fingertips.

"Damn, no drawers? For me?" I asked.

"Yes," she moaned, gently pinching my nipples.

I stood and slowly unwrapped my towel to show her what she'd done to me. Hoping she was prepared for what I was getting ready to do to her, I laid my towel on the sofa, spread Honey's thighs, got down on my knees, then flickered the tip of my tongue on her clit. Holding her beautiful booty, the nicest ass I'd ever held, in my hands like it was half a juicy watermelon, I'd buried my entire face in her pussy.

"Damn, I miss my sweet pussy," I said, licking from her asshole to her clit.

There was something about a woman who made a man feel her pussy belonged to him and he could hit it anytime he wanted.

Maybe it was the fact that women allowed their exes an all-access pussy pass, or men were too egotistical to believe their exes didn't want the dick anymore. I was glad Honey initiated our last dance.

Her pussy lips ground against my tongue. Her back arched. "Don't leave me, baby," she cried. "I need you."

In the heat of our moment, I replied, "I need you too," softly suctioning her clit. I eased my middle finger insider her pussy, strummed her G-spot. "Damn, you're really getting wet."

"For you," she said. "Let me taste you. I want to feel your strong hard dick in my mouth. I want you to fuck in my mouth. Grant?"

"Yes, Honey."

"You can cum wherever you like," she said, and I almost did.

Honey knew exactly how to turn me on. I tugged my shrinking nuts away from my dick to release the tension. I wasn't ready to cum.

Trading places, I lay on the towel. I watched Honey play with her breasts, squeeze her nipples. She rubbed her titties on my dick, then sucked my head. "Don't move," she said, heading toward my kitchen.

She returned with an open champagne

bottle in one hand, a champagne glass filled with honey in her other hand. Unsure of what was next, I moved to the floor. Spread the towel underneath me.

Honey poured champagne in her mouth, sat the bottle and glass beside us, then slid her mouth over my head. Slowly she released the champagne. Bubbles flowed down my shaft, around my balls, between the crack of my ass.

She picked up the champagne glass and said, "A toast, to us." She tipped the flute to my head, tilted the glass, then drizzled honey over my dick, down my shaft, and onto my balls. Working her way from the bottom up, she teabagged my nuts, sucking off the honey.

Her tongue trailed up my shaft, then she rotated my head in her mouth. She gulped the champagne, then poured some over my dick. She tilted my ass up, proceeded to French kiss my asshole, then my money bag. Her tongue pressed hard against the dimple between my asshole and my nuts.

Just when Honey was about to break the bank, I said, "Aw, damn, baby, you gon' make me cum." I took several deep breaths to prolong my ejaculation. I wasn't ready to cum.

Honey straddled me and slowly lowered

her hot pussy from the head of my dick to my balls. Her ass rotated. Grinding her glorious booty against my pelvis, she sandwiched my nuts. Her pussy throbbed against my shaft. I lost it. I couldn't hold back.

I held her ass; she rolled her hips. I rolled her onto my dick, thrusting deeper inside her. She opened and closed her legs like a butterfly until . . . until . . . "Ahhhh. Ahhhh. Ahhhh. Cum with me, Honey," I moaned.

The moment we came, I was glad Jada was gone and Honey was where she belonged. Home with me.

CHAPTER 37
SAPPHIRE

The mission to arrest Valentino had gone awry but my date with Santonio Ferrari the night before was amazing. He reminded me how some cops lived on the edge, defying death. Death to a cop was a possibility each day he or she suited up and reported for duty. Maybe that was why I craved control.

Minus our minor interruption by Honey, we'd laughed, found we had a lot to talk about. I fed him crab cake. He spoon-fed me chocolate mousse. After the short drive to my house, I invited him in for another cocktail. He lit my fire and the fireplace in my bedroom. We cuddled under the sheets, fell asleep twisted like a pretzel.

"Morning," I said, prying my leg from between his thighs. "Gotta shower, then pack. Time for me to head to the City of Angels or Sin City." Had no idea where I wanted to go next but I appreciated being on my schedule, not anyone else's.

Santonio propped a pillow behind his back, leaned against the headboard. "Top of the morning to you, beautiful. You were energetic last night. Can we have one more hip-locking orgasm before you fly off into the sky?"

Typical. Men had sex on the brain all the time. Santonio was forty-five — fifteen years my senior — so energetic was relative. Riding him, I'd done most of the work, he'd done most of the talking. Not a bad combination, him keeping me motivated to buck through five orgasms. I rode him like I was a jockey but when it came time to get off his horse, I couldn't unbend my knees. I'd fallen off sideways. Inch by inch I'd straightened my legs. Next time I'd take a few Excedrins in advance.

Santonio told me he was previously married. Also that his wife had passed away a year ago and he hated being alone. He didn't like casual sex but casual sex was better than none, and sex with me was great. I'd agreed he was also a fantastic lover.

I was sure I liked Santonio. I wasn't sure I wanted to invest my future with an older man with two adolescent kids. A fifteen-year spread wasn't bad at my age but what about when I hit forty, fifty, then sixty and he's fifty-five, sixty-five and seventy-five?

My realization was that, I wasn't the motherly or marrying kind anyway so our age difference didn't matter.

"I guess that means no," he said, getting out of bed.

"Rain check?"

Santonio picked up my blue dress, sniffed it. "Can I keep it for a souvenir?"

Hell no. He knew better than to ask that of a cop. I had no idea what he'd do with my DNA. "How about I keep it for you?" I said, tossing the dress into my suitcase. "You can shower in the guest bedroom." I went into the master bath, took a fifteen-minute hot steamy shower.

He was already dressed, sitting on the edge of a stripped bed. "Hope you don't mind. I tossed the sheets in the laundry room hamper. Habit, you know. You decided where you're headed?"

"To check on the condo."

"No, I mean when you leave here."

Okay, hopefully Santonio wasn't one of those older men that suffered from CRS — can't remember shit. I just answered that. Probably some sort of cross-examination to see if I'd say the same thing twice. "Not sure. Vegas, maybe LA." I packed my clothes, zipped my suitcase, thinking, *New relationships are nice.*

"How about Charlotte?" he asked. "Come meet my kids. Be our guest for a week or so. You'll love my boys."

My loving them was not the problem. Would they like me? "Maybe another time."

"Come here. Sit next to me."

I made my way to the edge of the bed, heard, "Can't be gettin' mad! What you mad? Can't handle that! . . ." I glanced at my cell ID. Hunter could wait.

"Why are you so afraid to let me love you?" he asked, holding my hand.

Before I answered, Hunter called again.

"You'd better take that," Santonio said. "Might be important."

Trying to live in the moment, I said, "Not more important than you." I paused, then said, "What if I told you I was going to LA to kill my stepfather? Would you still want me to visit you? Meet your boys?"

Santonio didn't hesitate when he said, "Only if I could talk you out of it. Having a license to kill doesn't give us the right to a man's life. Killing is inhumane."

"So is molestation and rape. The Bible says an eye for an eye. What if he's out there raping another woman?"

He hunched his shoulders. "You decide," Santonio said, standing. "You have my number. If you kill him, don't call me."

Was this a conspiracy? I didn't need his help, his sympathy, his approval, his advice, his nothing. Santonio had no idea what Alphonso had put me through. I didn't owe Santonio or anybody else an explanation. What was worse was he didn't ask for one. "Then I guess we should say our good-byes now."

We hugged. He left.

I inspected the town house, made sure I wasn't forgetting anything, then tossed my suitcase in the trunk. On my way to the condo I called my boss.

"Bleu, what the hell is happening over there? You're not taking my calls."

My sexual high had diminished. "I'm on my way over there now."

"Judging by the pictures the police e-mailed, the damage is estimated at twenty-five thousand dollars. Where's Hunter? I'm not filing an insurance claim. I'm taking every cent out of his pay, Bleu. You hear me?"

"I don't care. It's not my money."

Hunter needed a wake-up call. Who better to give it to him than our boss? Being attached to money more than his family is what got him kicked out. Spending his money on cars, a big house, expensive clothes to impress others, he'd forgotten he

319

had a wife and kids. His fault.

"Boss, I just got here," I said. "The windows are boarded up. I'm removing the tape in front of the garage and going in."

"Where were you? You didn't answer your phone all night."

Turning on the light, I said, "Busy. Working my ass off." That was the truth. "Hunter really trashed this place." One peep inside the bedroom, and I bolted out of the condo.

Pacing outside, I said, "You won't believe what has happened."

CHAPTER 38
RED VELVET

"Quiet on the set!"

Those four words resounded in my mind . . . surreal. I'd dreamt since I was my son's age of being on television. Raven-Symoné, her role in *The Cosby Show* and her growth spurt to *That's So Raven,* inspired me to not so much be like her, but to do my best.

"Breakfast is ready," Mama shouted from the kitchen.

We were in temporary housing in Inglewood. A comfortable two-bedroom my agent leased for his clients. Pictures from *Chinatown, Glory, Diary of a Mad Black Woman, Titanic, Doubt, Slumdog Millionaire,* and more movies decorated the walls in each room.

Ronnie sat at the table. "Mommy, I want to be an actor when I grow up."

"Baby, you can be whatever you want, including the president of the United States of America," I told him. This was a proud time in our lives. Enthusiasm for our new president soared in the film industry. "Mama, have a seat. Let me serve you."

"Baby, you're the one who has to work. This is my job," Mama said, putting the platters of pancakes, eggs, and bacon on the table.

Mama sat at the table, said grace. "Dear Lord, thank You for blessing us abundantly. Let this food nourish our bodies so that we may better serve You. In Jesus' name, amen."

"Amen!" Ronnie said, reaching for the syrup.

"Have you gained enough weight for your role?" Mama asked.

Her question took me back to how I tried to eat half of Benito's pizza. "I haven't lost any, so that's good. We'll see. I still have two weeks before they start filming my part." My concern was how I was going to go from a DD to DDD cup size in two weeks.

I stuffed two helpings of everything down my throat, kissed Ronnie and my mom. "I've got to go. I'll see you later. Memorize your lines, sweetie," I told my son. Even if Ronnie didn't become an actor, memorizing lines from his books would help with his studies.

"I will, Mommy. Am I going to see my

daddy again?"

I stopped, looked at my baby. "Do you want to see him again?"

"No, Mommy. I don't want to ever see him again because he made you cry."

Batting back my tears, I kissed my son. "Then you don't have to. Nobody's going to make you," I said, then kissed my mom. If I ever had to cry on the spot for a movie scene, all I had to do was recall this moment.

"I love you Mommy. Bye."

There was no replacement for genuine love. I smiled, realizing how fortunate I was. Outside our door was a limo driver waiting for me . . . for me! I smiled again, got in the back, then stared out the window at luxury cars, limos, black Town Cars with tinted windows driving by and alongside us.

An hour later we arrived at my agent's office. I stepped out the limo, took a snapshot of my surroundings, then hurried inside the building.

The receptionist greeted me. "Hi, Ms. Waters. Here's your revised script and your check." The receptionist resumed working.

Taking my package, I said, "Thanks," then waited.

"Is there something else?" she asked.

"Yes. I have a meeting."

"Oh, your agent is in an important meeting right now. He'll get in touch with you later. If you have any questions about the revisions, give me a call."

She spoke casually, as if my meeting with my agent wasn't important. "Thanks," I whispered.

"You're free to go now," she said.

"Of course." I stepped backward without turning around. "Oh, I'm sorry." I'd stepped on someone's foot.

"Unless you have eyes in the back of your head, you've got to stay on your toes around here," he said.

I returned his friendly smile. "Thanks. I'll remember that."

"I'm Brennen," he said.

Before today, I'd known Brennen by name only. I closed, then opened my eyes. "Hi, I'm Velvet."

Brennen Mosely was the executive producer for *Something on the Side.* His filmography was extensive. The demand for him in Hollywood was high. This was his first time producing an "all black cast" film. I kept my hands at my sides.

"Relax, Velvet. I've heard great things about you. Are you busy?"

Wanting to be appreciative of my opportunity, I said, "Have to study my lines."

"You can study them over lunch with me," he said.

We arrived at a tall building in the limo, and Brennen dismissed the driver. In the elevator on the way to the penthouse, I became nervous, not knowing what to expect. Was Brennen expecting special favors for my role? We sat at a table for two by a window overlooking the city.

"Tell me your goals," he said.

His personal servers came and went at his command. Proving I was committed to gaining weight, I ate everything on my plates. We laughed. I shared my goals. Brennen shared useful information on how to stay in good favor with important people in Hollywood by saying, "Always say thank you, follow up with a handwritten thank you note, or send a tasteful token of appreciation, but never do either of these simultaneously."

I gobbled up this helpful advice along with dessert.

"Velvet, I'd like for you to be my guest at the private screening."

I bounced in my seat. Settled myself, then said, "I'm so excited and can't thank you enough."

"That's what I love about you, Velvet. You're stunning and sincere. Those are the two qualities I admire most in a lady."

A lady? That was a first, but hopefully only the beginning of many positive reinforcements.

Chapter 39
Valentino

Shit was stale up in this bitch-ass condo.

Benito was sulking over a bitch who didn't want his ass. I was legally married to a bitch that disowned me. Grant had me pretending I was a punk-ass nigga trying to speak like his proper ass. That lame shit was for softees, not me.

Slapping Benito's feet off the sofa, I said, "Let's roll, nigga," turning off the television.

"I don't feel like going anywhere. If you see Lace, tell her I love her."

"Get your . . . forget it. Stay here." I picked up the keys and cellular, put the remote on his chest, and left his ass on the couch.

Now that the chase for Lace was over, I had no idea where I was headed. The phone rang. Not this bitch. What the fuck did Sapphire want? I answered, "What's up now?"

"Got a proposition for you," she said.

Did I have *proposition me* airbrushed across my ass? "I'm straight. I don't want shit from you."

"Don't be so sure of that," Sapphire said.

"What? What?" I was so frustrated I'd repeated myself.

"I have an emergency. I've gotta get to the airport. Come over to the condo where Honey was."

"I don't know where you were hiding that bitch." Sapphire thought I was what, a fool? Thought Valentino James was her fucking gopher? "Come over there and . . . ?"

"And I'll tell you when you get here," she said. Sapphire gave me the address, unit number, then ended the call.

A nigga wasn't rolling over there on foot patrol. I drove Grant's Benz in case I had to get away with a fuckin' quickness. I was no fucking freeloader. Time had come for me to get my own spot, my own rims, my own hos. I parked parallel in front of a fucked-up bandaged condo that looked like a tornado touched down on that bitch and that bitch only. *What the hell happened here?*

Sapphire waved at me. "Come this way. Follow me."

My eyes narrowed, scanned left and right. I asked, "Who fucked up this spot?" Following her through the garage, into the bedroom, I said "Oh, hell, no! Damn! What the fuck?" A nigga's stomach rose up to his chest, then pressed down.

Sapphire said, "I want you to call the cops and paramedics, then stay here until they come."

"So I can get framed for this assassination massacre? Hell fuckin' no," I said. "I don't give a fuck what's in it for Valentino James. You can eat that shit."

In the bed were a man, a woman, and two kids. All on their stomachs. All with a bullet in the back of their head. That shit reminded me of that dude in California that took his whole family out after him and his wife lost their jobs. The recession was an opportunity for a nigga to regroup, then recuperate, not to fuckin' retire.

"I'll have all charges against you in Nevada dropped, expunge your record, and you'll be a free man. You can roam the world wherever you please. Even go home to your wife and kids."

That was a pretty package for a nigga to consider unwrapping, but in a few seconds? Not the wife and kids part — the part about being a free man. Either way my ass was fucked. I headed toward the door. "Let's step outside. Nigga can't inhale up in this bitch."

"What about the kidnapping charges?" I asked.

"Honey needed a sabbatical. You did her a favor. I'll do you a favor. I'll dismiss that too," Sapphire said. "I've got a flight to catch. Call nine-one-one from your phone," she insisted.

"This isn't my phone. It's Grant's."

"If I make the call, you're going straight to Nevada State."

Bitch had me by the fucking nuts. "How do I know you're not setting me up?"

"You don't," she said, dialing her phone as she said, "Nine."

"What the fuck am I supposed to say?"

"One," she said, pressing another button.

"Fuck it." I dialed 9-1-1.

Sapphire held up her pointing and middle fingers, kissed them, waved at me, got in her car, then drove on out.

Waiting for whoever the fuck was going to show up, I called Lace.

"Hello," that bitch sang like a canary.

"It's Valentino. I'm ready to hear your proposition." Might as well know all my options.

"Hey, Valentino. I'm glad you called. Are you home? Or I should say, Are you at my sweetheart's condo?"

I'm going to pray she hadn't fallen and

bumped her head on Grant's head because most dicks were diagnosed with amnesia. And when a chick got the raw end of a dick, a nearby nigga was the recipient of her backlash. I wasn't going to ask her shit about Grant. "Something like that."

"Good, I'll meet you there in a half hour. Bye."

"Wa — haaa."

Sirens blared in the background. A nigga had zero knowledge about what the fuck was going on with that dead family. What would happen if I left before the cops got there? Wasn't my fucking phone. Leaving was a chance a nigga was going to have to take.

CHAPTER 40
HONEY

Walking on sunshine.

Great sex with the man I loved made me feel I could walk on water. I opened my bedroom blinds, welcomed the sun rays, blue sky, white clouds. I slid back the patio door, invited in the crisp morning breeze. Grant was no longer torn between Jada and me. I put it on him so good he'd forgotten about her.

"Jada who? Jada what?" I said, then laughed. She could go find her own man to show off in her suite. I knew he'd call. I knew it! My lips spread wide with pride and joy. I waited, then answered on the third ring, "Hey, you," staring out my patio window.

"Honey, hey. It's Grant."

"I know. I'm glad you called. Baby, I apologize for all the confusion. I'm glad we're back together. Wanna come over tonight and explore my pleasure chest?" I said, opening the pleasure chest at the foot of my bed. I had to get some new sex toys. A triple bullet — two for me, one for Grant — would be nice.

"Nah, I gave that some thought and my coming over is not a good idea. Things between us can never be right." He chuckled. "Damn, you're the best. Obviously, I can't resist you. Look, I don't know the right way to say this but . . ." He paused.

Grant was not leading the conversation in a direction I wanted to follow. He sounded happy, like he was on his way someplace without me. But he also sounded like he'd made up his mind without my input, like he was pleased we were fuck buddies last night, but all good things must end. I prayed my instincts were wrong.

"But what?" I exhaled. My breath stopped at my throat. I wiped my tears. I was tired of putting my heart on a merry-go-round that abruptly stopped. I was tired of being the one getting flung off, waiting for him to make up his mind whether to let me ride again. I paced in front of my window.

"I've decided to ask Jada to marry me."

That was it! If there was ever a fucking straw, that was the one that broke my spirit. "What? You're not man enough to tell me to my face? You call me on the fucking phone to tell me this shit? You weren't calling that bitch's name last night when you came inside me. Why didn't you stop her from leaving your house last night if you want to marry her so bad?"

"Honey, listen. Truth is, outside of sex, you're no good for me."

"Fuck you and that black bitch!"

"I love you too," he said, then ended the call.

Brain? Courage? Heart?

I could go over there, burn his house down with him in it, then shoot his barbequed bones. I could confront him about why he'd fucked me last night, or confess my love one more time. I got in my car, went to my bank, requested a cashier's check for eighteen million dollars.

"Forget, Grant. I'm spent. She can have his ass."

"If you liked it then you should have put a ring on it," became my new ring tone. I took my finger off my ignition and answered, "Hello."

A soft voice said, "Madam?"

"Madam? Who is this?" I asked.

"It's me. Girl Six."

"Where are you?" I asked.

"I'm sorry. I didn't mean to leave the door open. I swear it was an accident. I thought you were leaving behind me. I —"

"Wait. Stop." I asked her again, "Where are you?"

"I'm good. At a homeless shelter," she said.

"I can't have any of my girls living in a shelter. Tell me where, I'll make arrangements to get you and bring you home."

"I'm scared. You're going to beat me again." Girl Six cried.

That part of my life, abusing, using women, was behind me. "I promise you that will not happen. Let me help you. I owe you that much." I wrote the address and number to the shelter, ended our call, and started my engine.

I drove along Piedmont, entered Buckhead Premier Palace. Eight police cars, two ambulances, and two coroner's vans surrounded the condo I'd stayed in with Hunter. "Every *man* for himself," I muttered as I bypassed the scene. I parked in front of Grant's condo, got out my car, and banged on his door.

Valentino answered. I asked him, "What's going on over there?"

"It's breaking news. Some nigga named Hunter, his kids, and his wife . . . shot in the back of their head."

Numbness consumed my body. That

335

could've been me. Kick it with the wrong man, marry him, have his babies, inherit his debt — credit cards, taxes, child support, gambling — all of that becomes yours. Becomes a monster you lose all control over.

Hunter was a good man who had made some bad decisions. And now he was gone. And so was my anger at him. The anger I had for Grant vanished too. I gave my heart a clean slate. Life was too precious. I wasn't calling him back.

I reached into my purse, pulled out an envelope, handed it to Valentino. "We have done some wild things together."

Valentino nodded. "Thanks. We sure have. That's why I always wanted you on my team. I apologize for kidnapping your ass. What do you say we start all over? Get us some new escorts."

"That's out." I shook my head. "Girl Six is in this shelter." I handed him the paper. "I want you to look after her. Go get her, set her up with a house, a car, and cash. Do something commendable for a woman for once in your life."

"I gave all them bitches equal opportunities to make good money."

"And indirectly you made them all millionaires. In your own way, you done good," I told him.

"Would've done better if you were my woman instead of my madam. Lace, don't take this the wrong way but . . . a nigga was feeling your ass."

The business we were in marinated in corruption. The kind of corruption that caused me to think I was better than Valentino, better than Sapphire, better than my escorts, better than my mother. Sometimes we all did what was best for us, forsaking all others. I could no longer judge Valentino without first looking in the mirror.

I kissed Valentino on the cheek. "You're okay in my book, Anthony Valentino James. I forgive you." I tapped the paper in his hand, got in my car, then left.

Good pussy could make the hardest nigga soft and the softest man hard.

Chapter 41
Grant

If I could kick myself in the ass for thinking with the wrong head, I would.

Honey knew what she was doing and she got exactly what she deserved. Good pussy was not the determining factor for my staying with her. Nor was her beauty, her body, or her booty. The drama she'd brought was lethal. Our relationship had ended before she showed up at my house unannounced last night.

I had no regrets for flying to Atlanta to find Honey. No regrets for almost paying her ransom. No regrets for falling in love with her. But I did regret fucking her last night. I was not proud of breaking Honey's heart by telling her about Jada. I was not proud of letting Jada walk out my door. I should've stopped her. I was not proud that my selfishness hurt two women that I cared for.

Despite my shortfalls, I was a good man

and deserved to marry a good woman.

Honey was the source of my frustrations, the reason my woman left my house. Did Honey think, "Jada's gone, I won Grant"? People won trophies, awards, medals, but not people. Follow my heart; be with Honey. Follow my head; fight for Jada. Men who married trophy wives masked their misery behind their egos. Eventually the mask had to come off. The only man I knew who'd never worn a mask was my dad. I had to call my old man for advice.

Mom answered, "Hey, sweetheart."

"Hey, Mom. Dad around?"

"Hold on . . . Grant! Get the phone . . . You okay?" she asked me.

"Yeah, Ma. I'm good. You?"

My dad said, "Hello."

"I'm good, baby. Come see us soon. We miss you," Ma said before hanging up.

"What's going on, son?"

I didn't censor what I had to say. "Man-to-man, Dad, I need your advice. Jada was here last night. Honey came by. Jada left. And Honey put it on me real good."

Remorse for my actions lingered. Honey deserved better. I should've been strong and resisted her. Too late.

"Son, you have got to take control of both situations."

"I know, but how? If I fucked Honey that easily, how do I know I won't give in to her the next time we're alone?"

Respect. If Honey disrespected herself, that did not give me permission to treat her the same way. I took advantage of her vulnerability. The pussy was great while my dick was hard. In retrospect, neither one of us benefited. Make-up sex is great. Break-up sex, all bad.

My dad said, "Next time she drops by — hopefully she won't — but if she does, don't let Honey in your house. If she's outside, you won't go outside. You're going to mess around and lose Jada before I make it to the game."

"Seriously, Dad. What should I do?"

Responsibility. I had to verbally acknowledge my obligations, exhibit control, and apologize to Jada and Honey. Why should I apologize to Honey?

"Son, if you care for Jada, do what I wanted to do with your mom but didn't."

"What's that?"

"If you believe Jada is the one, get her far away from Honey for as long as you can. Take Jada on a premarital honeymoon. Treat her like she's your wife before you marry her, then at the end of the premarital honeymoon, propose. Set a date, marry her, and take her on another honeymoon. Hey, thanks to this conversation, I'm going to take your mother on a second honeymoon and pretend it's our first. Thanks, son." Dad shouted, "Hey, honey, come here."

"Bye, Dad." I had to smile; their marriage was enviable.

I went to my office, called my travel agent, called my driver, packed two suitcases with casual wear, formal wear, swim trunks, sweats, and the diamond I'd bought for but never gave to Honey. I took a chance, had my driver take me to the florist, then to Jada's house. Sat in the car. Stared at my phone. Should I call? Should I knock on her door? How would I feel if she showed up at my house under similar circumstances?

"Haaa." I was here now. I rubbed my brows. Sat in the car.

After thirty minutes of contemplation, I picked up the flowers, got out the car. A doorman greeted me before I knocked.

"How may I assist you?" he asked.

"Is Jada here?"

"Is she expecting you . . . mister?"

"Grant. I hope so," I said, shifting the flowers to my opposite hand.

"Wait here." He closed the door. Moments later the door opened. "Ms. Jada

Diamond Tanner is unavailable for your presence."

I deserved but hadn't expected that. I handed him the flowers. "Give these to her for me."

"I'm sorry, Mr. Hill. Ms. Tanner does not accept unsolicited packages. Have a nice day."

Unsolicited? "Jada! Jada! Baby, please!"

The door opened wider. I smiled. "Baby, I'm —"

"Sorry-ass motherfucker, you'd better raise up off my mother's steps and make tracks outta here. You make my mother cry one more time, and I am going to beat your ass personally. Get the fuck off my mother's property and don't come back unless she invites you here," Darius said, then slammed the door.

That was cool. That was her way of punishing me for not stopping her when she left my house. I should've put Honey out. This was all Honey's fault. I hated her. She knew she was ruining my life — that's why she hadn't called.

"Take me back home," I told my driver. Getting in my limo, I called my travel agent. "Yeah, cancel my trips to the Grammys, the All-Star Game, and Fisher Island." I opened the ring box. One woman would love to have it; the other, I doubted she'd accept my proposal. I closed the box. Should I close this chapter in my life? Move on? Forget about Honey and Jada?

Approaching my house, I lowered the window. *What the hell?* Three police cars were in my driveway. "Stop here," I told my driver.

Two cops headed toward the limo. They placed their hands on their guns. What had Honey gotten me into now?

"Do you live here?" the taller officer asked me.

"What seems to be the problem, officer?"

"Is this your home? Are you Grant Hill?" he asked.

He wasn't friendly. I wasn't guilty of any criminal actions but I was extremely nervous. I answered, "Yes, but what's the problem?"

"Step out of the car," he said without answering my question.

I opened the door. Stood face to face with the officer. "What is the problem?"

"I have a warrant for your arrest. You have the right to remain silent. Anything you say can and will be used against you. . . ."

"Wait, there must be some mistake. I'm sure I can explain. What are the charges?" I'd paid all my parking tickets, moving violations. There was nothing I'd done or failed to do that would warrant my arrest.

"Four counts of murder. Turn around before I have to add resisting arrest."

This couldn't be happening to me. "I've never had a fight, officer, let alone killed anyone. This is all a mistake."

The handcuffs tightened around my wrists. He escorted me to his car, placed his hand on top of my head, then pressed down on my head, shoving me in the backseat. All I could think about was who to call first. Not my attorney. He'd delay the case to maximize his fees. Definitely not my parents — didn't want to upset my mother. Jada would either come to my rescue or terminate all contact with me. Benito would say all the wrong things. Valentino wasn't trustworthy. Honey. Honey would know how to get me out of this, and Jada would never have to know it happened.

CHAPTER 42
HONEY

Serenity. Me time. Home was sweet.

Beyond love, there was a place of clarity. If we searched, in the corner of the mind where one meditates, we found peace. To center all thoughts, erase them, sit in silence and wait, was powerful beyond love. In this precious moment where we learn to wait for truth, for hope, for faith, we come face to face with our Creator, where love begets love without judgment.

I lay in my bed gazing at the ceiling. Closed my eyes, discovered that when I was with me, inside of me, I was at peace. Truth was, there was no war inside of me, a place where fire and water coexisted. My recipe for truth, hope, and faith allowed me to love myself.

Exposing, sharing my ingredients for love, made me vulnerable, imbalanced, dependent upon others to deliver what I thought I needed from them. When I shared my truth, I trusted a man to do the same. Each time he'd lie to me, he'd strip away a layer of my peace, spoiling my recipe for love.

If I shared the hope that encompassed my dreams with a man who had no hope for himself, or a man whose only hope was for me to fail, another layer of my confidence was stripped away. Give my faith to a nonbeliever . . . perish.

Transcendent peace within my spirit, I sat alone in the corner of my mind, a tiny space whose sole purpose was to protect my heart. I pulled up a chair, visited with my spirit for a spell. I was at home with forgiveness.

I forgave Grant, I forgave Jada, I forgave my mother and my father, and I forgave myself. There was no room inside me, inside my home, inside my heart, for hate. Hate was far too great and could not survive without my explicit permission. I stood tall, picked up my sign marked RESERVED, placed it on my chair. I'd be back, but the time had come for me to move on, accepting that I could love Grant from a distance.

Tap. Tap.

I recognized the knock. "Come in, Onyx."

"You okay?" she asked, hugging me. "I can take care of Grant if you'd like."

I hugged her, smiled. "I've made peace with our past. I wish him well."

She shrugged. "If you love him, I like him. Dinner is almost ready. You joining us? Valentino is bringing Girl Six." Onyx cheered.

"I'll be there shortly. I want to make a call to a friend." Rolling onto my stomach, I dialed, pressed the speaker button, waited for an answer.

"Hey! Honey, how are you?"

I countered, "No, how are you?"

Her voice was crisp. Excitement streamed into my ear. "I'm doing so well. My agent says he's getting calls for me to read more scripts and I'm not done with this film yet. Oh, please tell me you and Grant are coming to the private screening."

"How's Ronnie?"

"He's so excited about his new school and he has an inseparable friend. My mom is good too. I pray for you all the time, Honey. I'm so happy you're safe. I haven't had the chance to thank you, so I'm saying thanks now for all you've done for me."

Tears formed in my heart, rolled down my face. I was at peace. "I'll be at your screening no matter what."

"And Grant?"

"You'll have to personally invite him."

"It's okay. There's good men out there. I'm dating my producer, Brennen."

My brows raised. "Brennen Mosely?"

Red Velvet chuckled. "Yeah. He's so nice to me, my son, and my mom. Well, I've got to get back on the set. I'll call you soon with the details for the screening. Take care of yourself, Honey. I love you."

"Sure thing. Bye."

I love you. Red Velvet had no idea how much her words meant. Wiping away my tears, I went to the dining room and joined my girls.

Onyx hugged me once again. "You okay?"

I nodded, refusing to complain about her constant hugs. Onyx expressed her love physically, Red Velvet verbally. I sat at the head of the table. Onyx blessed the food. I motioned for Girl Six to sit next to me. "You look good. You're family. My home is your home."

She smiled. "Valentino told me I could pick out my own house and he'd pay for it."

Onyx said, "Girl, take the cash and come stay with us."

"I'll think about that."

I interrupted. "I have something to say. I want y'all to know, each of you are free to leave here whenever you want. If you want to go back home to your families, go. You have my blessings. You're also welcome to stay and work at Sweeter than Honey, start

348

your own business, or work for someone else. It's up to you. Show of hands, who wants to move out?"

Onyx raised her hand and spoke first. "I'm never going back to my husband. I'm staying here with you and I'm going to file for a divorce."

Fifty-fifty. Half the girls wanted to go home but were scared to leave. I had no idea they were afraid of leaving me. The other half liked Atlanta, liked not living or being alone, and wanted to continue running the agency. Girl Six was undecided.

"We'll have a new beginnings celebration. Onyx can arrange the big bash here at the mansion, invite our clients, and all the who's who in the ATL," I said.

"I'm on it," Onyx said, smiling. "Including Lil Wayne?"

"Absolutely. Put him at the top of my list. One last thing. You are your sisters' keepers. Always take care of one another."

I heard, "If you liked it then you should have put a ring on it . . ." I raced to my bedroom and saw it was a blocked number. Reluctantly I answered, "Hello?"

"Honey, I'm glad you answered. It's Grant. I need you."

Grant's "I need you," seemed desperate. "I'm listening."

"I'm in jail and you have to get me out."

"What did you do? Get in a fight with Jada?"

"No. I'm in here because of you," he lamented.

"Me?"

"If Valentino wouldn't have used my cell to call nine-one-one to report the murders of Hunter Broadway, his wife, and two kids, who were all killed in the condo where Sapphire placed you under protective custody, I wouldn't be in jail. It's all your fault, so the least you can do is bail me out of this —"

I'd heard enough. Grant didn't need me. He needed an attorney. I ended the call, silenced my ringer, and returned to the dining room.

CHAPTER 43
VALENTINO

A nigga had a promise to keep.

Strange how one person's — out of the billions of people in the world — belief in me changed my heart. Keeping shit real, it was Lace's belief and the eighteen million she'd given me. Being broke, a nigga had a bad attitude. She hadn't given me the fifty million I wanted, but less than half was better than being homeless, and a nigga was appreciative.

This was my chance to impress Lace. I'd gone to her banker, got my ends straight, then drove straight to the address on the paper Lace gave me, picked up Girl Six, took her shopping at Phipps Plaza, got her the expensive shit I would've had her in if she was still working for me, brought her here to the condo, freshened her up, then dropped her off at Lace's place.

I wasn't invited to join them for dinner and sho' nuff wasn't inviting myself in. I headed back to the condo. When I opened the door, I found this nigga in the same spot I'd left him. *Smack!* I slapped his feet. "Nigga, get your ass up."

Benito sprung forward, sat up. "What, V? What time is it? I was having sex with Lace. You spoiled it. She was just getting ready to —"

I flashed a real Chicago roll of C-notes. "Let's go celebrate."

"Huh? We got enough money? Yeah, boyie," Benito said, dancing on the coffee table. "Hit me on the hip with a couple of those Benjamins, V."

"Nigga, get down," I told him. "Go get ready. I'll be right here."

I grabbed the remote, turned on the television, saw a picture of Grant, then heard, "Grant Hill, an Atlanta business owner, has been arrested. He's considered a suspect in the massacre of the Broadway family. Hunter Broadway, his wife, and their two children were found dead in a condo at Buckhead Premier Palace. Each family member suffered a single gunshot wound to the back of the head. The call made to nine-one-one was from a cell phone registered to Mr. Hill. Mr. Hill was not at the scene when police arrived. There are no other suspects in the murder at this time. Grant Hill is being held on a five-million-dollar bail."

"Nigga, get in here quick!" I yelled.

"What! What!" Benito yelled, running into the living room.

"Man, your brother is being charged with the murder of those people that were in the condo over there. How did that shit happen?" Damn, I'd used his phone. Made one brief call to Lace after calling 9-1-1. Hadn't used it since. *Fuck!* Just when a nigga get a clean slate, shit gets dirty.

"My brother? You sure?" Benito asked, staring at the television.

I switched channels. One thing for sure, Grant's story was breaking news on every station. The story was repeated almost verbatim on another channel with Grant's picture on-screen.

Benito opened the front door. "Let's go, V. We've got to get my bro out."

"Put your ass in a seat for a minute and chill. First off, our helping his ass could backfire. And it's midnight. We have to think this through before we make a —"

"Get me the cordless phone," Benito interrupted.

"You can use my cell. Nighttime minutes are free."

Tired of slapping his ass, I got the cordless phone my damn self. I considered going to Lace's house instead of calling her. That might backfire too. I dialed her number.

Good, she answered. "Hello?"

"Hey, Lace. Valentino."

"What number is this?"

"Condo. Landline. What's up with your boy?" I asked her, not mentioning his name. Never know when the corrupt-ass government is tapping ass or tapping lines.

"He's not my boy," she said, ending the call.

Damn. Cold-blooded. Mental note: once that bitch is on your side, keep her there. I made another call. It was only ten o'clock her time.

"Hello?" Sapphire answered.

"You hear about what happened to Grant? Were you setting me up for this shit?"

"You're a smart man. Wanna be his hero? Figure out a way to prove Hunter had a gambling debt that cost him more than he could afford. That's the truth."

"So how do I help Grant?"

Sapphire ended the call.

Damn, how was a nigga supposed to get involved without getting involved? I had to think fast.

"V, what they say, man?"

"Be quiet. Give a nigga a minute to think

this shit through."

With the ends Honey gave me, I could bail G out, but not if it meant trading places with that nigga.

Chapter 44
Sapphire

Valentino had the street sense to do the smart thing. He didn't have to take the fall, involve Honey, or mention me. The police arrested Grant because they found his business card at the scene. To find the murderers, the local government needed to roll over in their own beds. Hunter's family massacre was an inside job. Good luck to Valentino and Grant. Honey, like me, would outsmart the men.

It was time for closure to my situation with my stepfather. Permission from my mother wasn't warranted. Alphonso had raped my mother of me, me of my mom. He stripped us of years of mother-daughter hair days, shopping sprees, spa treatments, birthday parties, graduation, watching movies together, hugging, crying, feuding, and loving one another. Years impossible to recoup.

I sat in my hotel room on Century Boulevard, picked up the phone, dialed the transit office during the morning shift. "Yes, may I speak with Alphonso Allen?"

"Hold just a moment," a receptionist said.

Gun . . . silencer . . . extra clip — I tossed them into my sack.

I wondered what Santonio was doing. I was glad my mom was in her new home and that chapter of my life was closed. I'd never have to step foot in the hellhole she'd moved out of again.

"Hello. This is Big Al," he answered.

Disguising my voice, I said, "Hey, what route are you on today?"

"Who is this?" he asked.

"You don't remember meeting me? I'm the sexy young girl who rode your bus recently. You gave me this number."

"No, I don't give out my work number, baby. You must have me mixed up with another driver," he said.

"I wanna ride your bus today. What route are you on?"

Alphonso whispered, "If you do, I'm going to ride you." He told me his route and hung up.

A cold sweat accompanied my disgust. I ended the call, stood in the mirror naked, remembering his hands on my breasts, his body smothering mine. The pillow he used to silence my cries, smother my tears.

I whispered, "Showtime. Time to get dressed."

Opaque stockings, a flowered duster, comfortable white nursing shoes. A padded bra, salt and pepper wig, and black framed eyeglasses. I smeared on my red lipstick, slightly crooked, and slipped on my sweater.

"Can't be gettin' mad! What you mad? Can't handle that! . . ."

"Hi, Ma."

"Hey, baby. Where are you? You were gone when I woke up."

"I'll be back in a few hours."

"In time for lunch?" she asked.

"Yeah, Ma. I'll be back in time for lunch," I said, ending the call. Didn't want to delay my mission or change my mind.

"Can't be gettin' mad! What you mad? Can't handle that! . . ."

I was beginning to believe I was doing the wrong thing. "Valentino, what's up? I'm busy. Make it quick."

"Hunter's gambling debt was from a side bet in-house, Vegas, on a bowl game."

"Very good."

"Grant can get off if I —"

"Not if *you,* if *he* wasn't so damn onerous and condescending. Jail should humble him. I'll make sure he's released tomorrow morning. I sense you're changing for the better. The old Valentino was all about self-preservation."

"What about my charges?"

"I'll take care of that tomorrow too."

"You're changing too. Maybe we're getting old," he said.

"Speak for yourself. One more thing," I said.

"What's that?"

"If you love Honey, tell her." Valentino's chances were greater than mine. I wasn't interested in having a happily ever after relationship with a woman. My love for dick was too strong. But having a special female friend who understood me would've been nice.

"Thanks," Valentino said. "Wish me luck."

"Real men don't need luck." I ended our call, exhaled. My phone rang again. "Hey, I'm on my way to see a dog about not being a man," I told Santonio.

"I thought if it weren't too late, I could change your mind."

"You don't know me, have no idea what he's done to me."

"You're right. I heard you when we were in Atlanta but I wasn't listening. Where are you?"

Why did he care? Was this a power play to

break me down, gain control? Leave me hanging? Break my heart? I answered, "Los Angeles."

"I haven't been able to get you off my mind. I think about you day and night. Do me a favor, beautiful. Don't kill him. He's not worth it. I'm on my way to LA."

I tried blinking away the tears. I was a strong woman. Alphonso deserved to die. I was doing the world a favor. Or was I doing myself a favor? "We're so wrong for each other. Why do you care what I do?"

Santonio started singing, "If loving you is wrong, I don't want to be right."

I laughed out loud. "That was so corny. You cannot sing."

"Everyone can sing. And I made you laugh. Let me make you laugh every day. I'm on my way. I'll see you tonight. Bye, beautiful."

Removing the wig, I threw it in the trash. Did the same with all of my disguise clothing, showered, then called my mother and invited her to join me at the hotel for breakfast, a facial, and a massage. I was excited all over again. Felt like a woman again, knowing I'd see Santonio tonight. "Wow." The simple things that man did made me feel like a woman, and tonight I was going to make him my man.

CHAPTER 45
GRANT

Never question where your help comes from. That was my lesson. Jail was no place for me. I was never going back. Not to visit or stand trial for a crime I didn't commit. The cells were small, beds hard, toilets filthy. I'd slept standing, leaned with my back against the wall all night. The unwritten rule was nine out of ten black men would do time during their life.

I was determined to stay in the tenth percentile, be the one out of that ten that proudly said, "Man, I can't relate to prison, county, central." Crossed over before my thirty-first birthday but I was thankful they hadn't transferred me. One way in, no way out. I'd heard scary stories about inmates who ended up in GSP.

Before I needed Valentino and Benito, I didn't think much of them. My opinion was they were two freeloading grown-ass men who needed to get off their asses and get jobs. I worked for mine, they could work for theirs. They weren't handicapped, mentally challenged, or disabled. They were users. I also realized if I hadn't given them a place to stay, they may have ended up robbing me or someone like me. When I got processed out of jail and saw Valentino and my bro waiting for me, I hugged both of them.

"Not too tight, nigga," Valentino said, stepping back.

His olive-colored designer slacks, hand-stitched square-toe brand new shoes, buttoned down collared shirt — all appeared tailor made. Benito's mustard slacks and black shirt with mustard pinstripes were sharp. I'd expect Valentino, being a pimp or a former pimp, to have worn the bolder color.

I hated using the N word, but in a special way, they were my niggas. "Y'all niggas look good," I said.

Valentino shook his head. "Stay in your lane, nigga. You outta line. Shit don't even sound right coming outta your mouth."

He was right. I didn't feel right saying it, but had to say, "I owe you guys. Can you believe I called Honey and she refused to come get me?" I sat in the front seat of a new black luxury car. "Whose ride?"

"Who's driving, nigga?" Valentino said,

nodding. "And don't go hating on Lace. You burned your bridge with a ride-or-die bitch that would've had your back for life. See, that's the one thing y'all businessmen don't understand — hos are loyal. It's those pretty little rich daddy's girls and poor undereducated chicks with no street smarts that niggas gotta watch."

Yeah, guess he made a point, but I'd prefer that pretty little rich daddy's girl over a ho any day. Thinking of who really had my back, I said, "Benito, please tell me you did not tell Mom or Dad where I was."

"I heard what you'd done, bro, but I had no idea where you were. V said let's ride, and here am I."

"Get it straight. I didn't do anything," I told Benito.

Valentino was decent like that? Maybe I misjudged him.

"Clarify that shit for your brother, nigga," Valentino said, and I was glad he did because Benito hadn't answered my question. Benito should consider becoming a politician. He had all the qualifications. Every since we were kids, he could respond to a hundred questions without answering one.

Hanging on to my shoulder, my brother said, "I, Benito Bannister, did not tell Mom or Dad that their favorite son is a jailbird and their adopted son, whom they treat like a stepchild, has never been behind bars."

Interesting. So he could answer when he wanted.

"You got a point there, nigga," Valentino said.

Listening to Valentino and Benito, I was amused at their unique way of communicating. They were entertaining but I wanted to get home faster than Valentino was cruising along the streets, watching to see who was watching him.

"Bro, guess what?"

"Tell me," I said. We were ten minutes from my house and I was fifteen away from calling Jada. Listening to Benito helped occupy my mind, made me not think about Honey.

"I'm going to visit Tyra and my son tomorrow," Benito said with pride in his voice. "If our visit goes well, Tyra said I could start keeping him every other weekend."

I'd almost forgotten Benito had a son. He'd had a kid before me. He'd never been arrested. And if I got with Jada, I'd have to adopt. I was young, healthy, handsome, and I did not want to adopt kids. I wanted my own.

"That's commendable, brother. You think

you'll get back together with Tyra?"

"Since Lace won't have me back, maybe."

Damn, Benito had beaten me to a whole lot. He'd probably get married before me too. Long as he didn't marry Honey, I was cool. I'd almost forgotten my brother had dated Honey for three years. I cringed at hearing or thinking her name. As soon as Valentino stopped the car, I opened the door and said, "Thanks."

"We'll be out of your spot in a week," Valentino said. "I'll deliver your car and keys to you."

"No problem. Take your time." I was glad and sad they were moving on. With Valentino and Benito out of my life, that lessened my chances of seeing Honey. I went inside, closed my door. I'd shower in a few. Putting my phone on the charger, I waited for it to power on, then immediately called Honey.

"Hey, Grant," she answered, sounding exhausted.

"You are one selfish woman. Don't you ever call me, come near me, or speak to me again as long as you live. If you show up at my house again, I'm calling the police on you. I know you did this to me on purpose."

"Okay, Grant," Honey politely said. "I wish you the best," then ended the call.

What? No argument? Honey took the fuel

out of my anger. I listened to my voice mail messages.

"Hey, Grant. Jada. I'm trying not to sweat the small stuff. Truth is, I miss you. Call me."

That was what I wanted to hear. I called Jada right away.

"Hey, how are you? I —"

"Miss you too," I said. "Where are you?"

"Home."

"Pack your bags for two weeks. I'm on my way to get you."

There was still time to follow through with my initial plans. I showered, changed clothes, grabbed my suitcase, my diamond, and got in my car. En route to Jada's house, I called my travel agent. "Reinstate my travel plans for LA and Florida."

I ended the call, then called Honey.

"Grant, what is it now?" she asked.

"Nothing. Nothing," I said, ending the call before she did.

Chapter 46
Honey

The sunshine peeped in the morning, then faded, but not my spirit.

I arrived early at my office with Onyx. The other girls would be here soon. I turned on the lights and surveyed the office. Sweeter than Honey was immaculate, the way I insisted. A cluttered office was a sign of a dysfunctional operation. My personal life was in disarray, not my business.

Onyx brought me a cup of hot coffee with cream and hazelnut. "This is half. I have the other half," she said, handing me a stack of intake forms. "With so much going on, we haven't had time to contact any of these ladies."

The feeling of being at work, being in my office, brought me joy. "Thanks," I said, sipping my coffee. "Mmm, this is so good."

Onyx returned to her desk as I sat in my office prioritizing the forms. I began to sort my stack into three categories, then set them aside. "Onyx, come in here and bring your forms." I wanted to review all the forms, not half.

Moving to my small conference table for four, I held my coffee in one hand, forms in the other, gestured for Onyx to sit next to me. "Let's work on this together. I want a color code system. Blue for high priority. We'll stack those here. Red for medium. Those will go here. And white for low. Those we'll put here."

Onyx stared at me with a half smile.

"What is it?" I asked.

"Honey, you look so serene. It's good to have you back," she said, hugging me.

"It's good to be back. Now let's get to work before clients start walking through the door dividing our attention."

My policy was if the lights are on, we are open. Each case before us warranted immediate attention, but with one hundred new cases a day, we couldn't help them all at the same time.

I read, "Geraldine Spears. Twenty-six years old, rape victim, two months pregnant, needs abortion consultation."

"Blue," Onyx said. "We have to find out if she was raped while she was pregnant or if her pregnancy is the result of a rape. If it's recent, we need to find out if she has a rape kit on file, if there is a police report, if there's an active investigation in progress."

Impressed, I smiled, read the next one. "Tammy Nelson. Sixty years old, recently contracted AIDS."

"Red," Onyx said. "Unfortunate, but there's nothing we can do to change her status. We'll assist her with education on maintaining her health, medication, and make sure she's emotionally stable."

"Next is Cotton Candy. Sixteen-year-old stripper/prostitute."

"Red Velvet could help mentor some of these young girls," Onyx said. "White for Candy. She's probably a rebellious teen."

I thought about Sunny Day, then said, "Let's move Candy to blue. You're doing a great job. Keep sorting the forms, I'm going to call Geraldine Spears."

While Onyx continued working at the table, I sat at my desk and dialed Geraldine's number.

"Hello." The woman who answered sounded as though I'd awakened her.

"Hello. May I speak with Geraldine Spears, please?"

"This is Geraldine."

"I'm Honey Thomas. I'm calling from Sweeter than Honey. Are you available for a consultation today at noon?"

Geraldine perked up. "I'll be there. And thanks so much for calling me. See you at noon. Thanks," she said.

Scribbling notes on her form, I called Valentino to thank him for taking care of Girl Six.

He answered, "Hey, I was thinking about you."

A pregnant girl entered my office, stomach the size of a basketball. Too far along to be Geraldine. "How can I help you?" I asked.

She placed her hands on her stomach. "I want to give my baby up for adoption. Can you help me?" Her pink backpack hung on one shoulder.

"Valentino, let me call you back." I picked up a blank intake form and sat with the girl at my conference table. After taking her basic information, I said, "Tell me why you want to give up your baby, sweetheart."

She was fourteen. A pretty girl with short hair and bright eyes. Her hygiene was good, clothes clean.

"I heard you could help me. I'm scared. I don't know who the father is. My mother is always gone. She works two jobs, says she can't feed another mouth. Nobody will hire me. I don't have any money. I've never been to the doctor. And . . ." She started crying.

I hugged her. "It's okay, baby. Tell me."

"And I don't want my mother to sell my baby's virginity the way she sold mine." She wrung her hands. "I'm so scared. You've gotta help me. Please."

I got up, paced around the conference table, sat down. This was the kind of shit that made me want to kill a man. Who was this child's father? This mother-to-be was still a baby herself.

I looked toward the door. Onyx walked in with Valentino and Girl Six. This was going to be a very long day.

"Wait here, sweetheart." I stepped out of my office and closed the door. "Onyx, get her some tissue and a bottle of water."

Valentino handed me a bouquet of red and yellow roses. "For friendship and love in that order. Happy Just Because I Like You Day, Lace."

"Thanks." There was a card attached. I handed the flowers to Onyx as she passed by. "Put these in water for me, please."

"Bad timing?" Valentino asked.

"I have a crisis right now. Onyx, I need you to call Grant."

"Grant Hill?" she asked.

"Yes, Grant Hill, right now. I need to purchase two houses, six beds, six baths each, in Buckhead. I need the houses completely furnished. And ask two of the girls to move into one of the houses immediately."

"What's the rush?" Onyx asked.

"Do it now," I said. "We have to provide a safe environment for our pregnant fourteen-year-old client in there. She says her mother sold her virginity."

Valentino shook his head. "Shameful."

"She might be the first to come here but she's not alone. If we can house them together, they can emotionally support one another."

"Voice mail," Onyx said.

"Leave a message," I told her.

"Wait. Lace, let me find the properties for you," Valentino said.

"What?"

"I can and want to find those properties for you," he said.

"I'll help him," Girl Six added.

"Hey, Grant . . ."

"Onyx, hang up the phone. We've got our team."

CHAPTER 47
GRANT

Our flight landed in Los Angeles. The limo was waiting.

Giddy as a teenager, Jada asked me again, "Where are we going?"

"I keep telling you, you are not allowed to ask questions." The driver opened the champagne. I filled two flutes. "To us."

To us? Thoughts of Honey crossed my mind. I saw an incoming call from her office, didn't answer because I was with Jada. I knew Honey would call but there was nothing she could say to make me forgive her.

"Never sweat the small stuff," Jada said.

The driver parked on Rodeo Drive. I wasn't big on shopping, would rather have hired a personal shopper to assist Jada with her selections, but if I intended to be her husband, I'd have to get used to doing these types of things. I escorted Jada into one of the numerous designer stores on the strip where celebrities shopped.

"May I help you?" the host asked.

I initiated control before Jada spoke. "Yes, fit my lady with a gorgeous gown, shoes, a handbag, jewels, the works. Find her a fitted gown, mermaid style. And I need a stylish tuxedo and shoes."

I sat outside the fitting room as Jada modeled each dress. My choice was clear. She looked stunning in red. "Um, um, um. It's perfect," I said, staring at her ass.

Standing in the three-way mirror, Jada glanced over her shoulder. "You don't think the color is too bold? I'm more of a background type of woman. I'm accustomed to handling all the details and only stepping up when things don't go smoothly."

"We're stepping out, and if anyone has to step up, it's me."

She smiled, went into the fitting room, came out dressed in her aqua blue pants and long-sleeved blouse. I wondered what dress Honey would've selected to wear to the Grammys.

The host brought our bags and boxes to the limo. "To our hotel," I instructed the driver. I settled in with Jada, opened a fresh bottle of champagne. "A toast to your beauty."

I was certain that if Honey were in the

limo, I would've had my dick sucked, licked her pussy, or at least stuck my finger inside of her pussy for an appetizer. With Jada having so many clothes on, I didn't bother initiating anything sexual.

The limo arrived at our hotel. "Have our things sent up," I told the driver. "We're on a tight schedule."

We checked into the Wilshire, where I'd reserved a suite with a glass-enclosed master bathroom so I could watch Jada shower. She removed her clothes, and for the second time I saw the most amazing body, that of a woman my age, not her age. The bellman arrived.

Not wanting him to see my woman naked, I said, "Leave the rack." I rolled the cart in front of the sofa.

Jada stepped out of the shower and I stepped in. I wanted her to shower first in case she was one of those women that took forever to apply makeup, do her hair, and get dressed.

Surprised, by the time I finished showering, I noted the only thing Jada had to do was put on the red dress and silver stilettos. Once she did, she was absolutely ravishing.

"Shall we?" I said, extending my arm.

We made our way back to the limo, rode through heavy traffic. Jada finally figured out where we were going when we arrived at the security checkpoint.

"Ahhh! We're going to the Grammys."

"Roll down all your windows," the officer said to our driver. Several police officers looked inside. Our limo drove through two car detectors before arriving at the red carpet.

The red carpet entrance blazed with lights, cameras, and celebrities. Behind the roped area, *E!, Access, Extra,* and *Insider* interviewed a variety of stars. With so many interviews occurring simultaneously, it was amazing how the televised versions didn't have the background noise.

I escorted Jada to our floor seats. Next time, I told myself I'd get Level 1 or Suite tickets. It was fantastic to sit with so many celebrities on the floor level, but we were seated adjacent to the technicians' sound stage.

The show was spectacular. Jennifer, Lil Wayne, Alison, Jamie, and so many more artists performed with amazing passion. When the show was over we headed to an after party, where we were up close with more celebrities. I knew with Jada's contacts, she could've gotten us invites to the big-name parties, but she simply appreciated all I'd done to orchestrate the evening.

Jada looked amazing. Men couldn't take their eyes off her. I couldn't take my hands off her. The night was long. She was tired when we arrived back at our hotel and went straight to sleep. I lay awake, eyes open in the dark, staring toward the ceiling. I had to consummate our relationship before I proposed, had to know she was more than a pretty package.

I held my dick, stroked my shaft, and dozed off thinking about Honey.

CHAPTER 48
HONEY

Valentino was working his way into my heart, as my friend. I was tired of always being at odds with him. Didn't want to keep worrying about him coming after me. I kind of felt like we were two high school bullies who'd realized if we united we could build an empire. It was more uncommon for a woman not to have a best friend than it was for a man. Valentino made me realize I'd never had a best friend.

The more we talked I was amazed that his upbringing prior to pimping was similar to Grant's. Valentino had enjoyed the luxury of having two loving parents but lost them both in his senior year of high school. His way of making money had become his survival skills, first exploiting high school girls, then starting his business, Immaculate Perception. I felt my relationship with Valentino had grown from our being archrivals to buddies, like two kids who'd fought, then made up.

Onyx said, "Honey, delivery."

I looked up from the new pile of intake forms. Valentino handed me a bouquet of pink, yellow, and red roses. "For admiration, friendship, and love," he said, handing them to me. "Let a nigga take you out for lunch today."

I held the flowers, inhaled deeply. "These smell so good. Thanks." I stepped into the lobby, gave the flowers to Onyx, and returned. "I would love to but I can't," I said, pointing at the stack of papers.

With the rising real estate foreclosure rate, Valentino had easily located two properties within the same block, less than a mile away from my mansion. And he paid for one as a gift to me. Before closing on both houses, I made sure all twelve beds were obligated to homeless pregnant teenagers.

It took me a while to read the card he'd attached to the first bouquet of roses he'd given me. It read "I will always love you." I was shocked. Valentino confessed that he loved me. How long had he felt that way? I'd read the card attached to the bouquet he'd just handed me later.

"What you're doing is good, but it's no good if you don't take care of yourself," he said. "You've got to eat."

Appreciating his concern, I said, "Let me think about it. . . . Onyx, come here for a moment, please." Onyx stood in the doorway. "I need for you and Girl Six to go shop for furniture for the group houses. Bill it to my corporate account."

"You sure you'll be okay here by yourself?" Onyx asked.

"Don't you see a nigga standing here?" Valentino said, repositioning his chair so he sat behind my desk facing me. "I'll stay here with her."

I didn't need, nor did I want, any financial assistance from the city, county, or state governments to fund any of my projects. All the bureaucracy would delay my mission. But I was happy that Valentino volunteered to stay.

"I'll call and check on you while we're out," Onyx said, leaving with Girl Six.

I asked Valentino, "What do you feel are early warning signs of exploitation of young girls? There has to be some way we can reach them before they end up on my code blue list."

My mind drifted to Sapphire for a moment, wondering if she was happy.

"Let's switch seats," he said. Typing on my keyboard, he opened several Safari windows on my computer. "The Internet makes it fucking impossible to protect minors from sexual predators. We have to get major sponsors to place tons of banners that constantly remind females of the warning signs of exploitation."

I saw his wheels turning and matched his fervor. "Banners, pop-ups, quizzes, videos — okay, that would cover some territory. And we could push for 'Education on Exploitation' in elementary, middle, and high schools."

"And churches," Valentino said. "Let's not leave them out. Congregations are an intricate part of our communities."

My eyebrows raised. Was this the same man?

"Most exploiters, pedophiles, molesters, abusers, rapists, and pimps are professional charmers, and the majority of Americans are materialistic. Couple that with gullibility and any broke man can dangle a carrot in front of a woman and make it sparkle like a diamond. Why do you think it was easy for me to start pimping females when I was in high school? They offered to have sex with me because I was a straight-A student, looked good, dressed nice, and treated them well. But some women are so desperate, they beg to be with men who don't want them."

"Straight A?"

"Yeah. What — a nigga like me can't be intelligent? Hell, my nigga Lil Wayne was a straight-A student too. Americans judge too fucking quick. Those smart-ass niggas like Grant, who think they know everything, could learn a lot from a nigga like me. He was stupid. He let you get away. I'm not doing that."

Okay, I was not prepared to respond, so I didn't. I had work to do. I had to have a one-on-one with each girl, then facilitate group sessions. Passion propelled me to jump in, determination and conviction had to steady my course. Standing, I bent over to stretch my lower back and legs. The space in front of my eyes faded to black.

"Lace, Lace. Get up."

I heard Valentino's voice but I couldn't see him and I couldn't move.

CHAPTER 49
GRANT

Sunrise began a new day, new adventures. A week later Jada and I were in Phoenix watching one of the best basketball games I'd ever seen. I'd brought Jada but she had all the connections in her presidency position of the Basketball Moms Association. We were in the best suite with Fancy, her mother Caroline, Caroline's son, and Darius's son. Watching the toddlers play made me want my own son, or daughter, but preferably a boy.

Fancy was gorgeous; she wore her self-assurance in the erect stance of her average-height stature. The rock on her finger, in comparison to the loose diamond I was prepared to give Jada, was gigantic. Fancy's striking beauty and confidence reminded me of the late singer Aaliyah. Her mother, Caroline, was not equally attractive on the outside, but Caroline glowed from within.

Jada tapped my arm. "It's rude to stare."

"I wasn't staring, I was lost in thought. Baby, this is fantastic!" I said, kissing her cheek to avoid messing up her lipstick again.

Jada seemed unimpressed by it all, but her eyes sparkled when they rested upon her son or her grandson. I wanted to know that feeling.

"Wellington has a son too," she said. "Wellington the third. But his mother, Simone, refuses to let me see him."

I wasn't sure I'd heard her correctly. "Repeat that?"

She did and I began to believe all of our lives were complicated. The woman I had loved, Honey, was cloaked in layers of armor crowned with a tiara. I prayed Jada's past wasn't jaded like Honey's. If things didn't work out with Jada, I'd put my desire for marriage on hold.

Fancy held little Darius in her arms. "Look, baby. Daddy is MVP."

The little boy clapped as though he understood. "Daddy!"

Jada was so cool, like this was the norm. For her, I guess it was. For me, it was all new.

"Daddy! Daddy!" Darius's son shouted and kicked, reminding me of Ronnie. I prayed things were well with Red Velvet, that her acting career was going well. She deserved happiness. We all did.

"You ready?" I asked Jada, anxious to get to the airport for our trip to Fisher Island.

"In a minute. I have to hug and congratulate my son first. He'll be disappointed if I don't, and I never want to disappoint Darius."

"Of course."

Not having kids made me impervious to compassion for the little things that meant so much between mothers and sons. I reflected on my relationship with my mother. Would Jada always place her love for Darius ahead of her love for me? Would their relationship change ours? Would I be jealous of their bond? My first contact with Darius was disastrous. He made it clear that I was not to hurt his mother. What if his mother hurt me? I wasn't ready to spoil his excitement of being MVP by standing in front of him.

"Take your time. I'll meet you in the car."

En route to the car, I wondered what was bothering Jada. She had been excited at the Grammys but suddenly she seemed sad. Maybe memories of Wellington consumed her. A half hour later, Jada arrived at the limo and we headed to PHX.

CHAPTER 50
GRANT

Whisking Jada from Phoenix to Fisher Island, I was about to bust. Her dick massage was a good release but I hadn't had sex since I was with Honey. I wanted my dick in Jada's juicy blackberry on the beach tonight.

Sometimes a man wanted to be doggish with his woman. I wished I could throw Jada down on a blanket and fuck the shit out of her. Or drag her naked body into the ocean, put my dick inside her, and ride her hard. Jada seemed too reserved to fulfill my doggish side. I guess I could adjust but if I were with Honey, I could have it all. I hoped I didn't have to fall asleep another night jacking off my dick.

"You good?" I asked her.

"Yeah, why wouldn't I be?"

"You're just so quiet."

We arrived at Fisher Island Hotel and Resort. The driver removed our bags from the trunk. I tipped him. The valet placed our bags on a cart, then rolled the cart inside. I tipped him. Tipping the bellman, I said, "Baby, go get comfortable. I'll be up shortly," then handed Jada one of the room keys.

As soon as the elevator closed I went back to the check-in counter and asked, "Are my reservations and special accommodations in order?"

The hostess smiled. "Yes, Mr. Hill."

The moonlight, warm night, and ocean breeze were so inviting. But the flight and the time difference between Los Angeles and Miami snatched three hours of our time, making it impossible for us to sit on the beach and watch the sunset.

I hurried to the room, slid the key, opened the door. My smile vanished. Jada sat in the living room, seemingly deep in thought. Sitting on the sofa beside her, I asked, "Baby, what's wrong?" hoping her somber attitude wouldn't ruin my night, our night. Nothing was worse than my going out of my way to please an unappreciative woman. Made that mistake with Honey. I would not do the same with Jada.

Our room was quiet until she said, "I know we agreed not to sweat the small stuff."

"But . . . ?"

Gazing at a blank television screen, she continued, "But I can't erase that night you let me walk out your door with Honey sitting in your living room and you didn't say a word to me."

Here we go. Why couldn't Jada have brought this up before we left her house?

"I know, baby. She caught me off guard. I didn't know what to say." I refused to speak Honey's name, knowing that would make Jada feel worse.

Jada faced me, looked in my eyes. "Did you fuck her? Before you answer, let me say, I already know the answer."

Unless she was a fly on my living room wall, and she wasn't, Jada was not fooling me into believing she knew what happened that night. This was not the time for true confessions. I'd paid a violinist to play "The First Time Ever I Saw Your Face" during my proposal.

I took Jada's hand, led her to the balcony. I had to have fresh air. And time to deceive this human lie detector beside me.

"Jada, the moment I sat next to you, I knew you were a special lady. The more time I shared with you, the more time I wanted to spend with you. I never planned on loving you. So much transpired in my life before I'd met you. It's not always so simple to let go of a person you love. I don't love Honey anymore," I lied, then asked, "Haven't you ever backtracked?" hoping she'd reveal her demons first.

"This isn't about me," she said, eyes focused on the darkness blanketing the ocean.

"Are you unwilling to forgive me if I did?"

"Yes."

Is this a trick response? I kept quiet.

Jada said, "I will forgive you only if you were smart enough to use protection," she answered. "Because if you give me anything, you will regret it."

A part of me was already regretting that this conversation was taking place. A small lie was a small sacrifice for a huge future. "Yes, we used protection."

"Grant, I hope you're telling the truth. I've had my heart broken before," she said, a tear trickling down her face. "It's so unnecessary to lie and break a person's heart."

I kissed her tears away.

Jada cried more. "I let my guard down with Wellington, believing nothing and no one could come between us. Melanie Marie Thompson. She was beautiful, like Honey. Foolish me, I trusted Wellington. Melanie moved in, fucked Wellington, said she was pregnant with triplets, and he married her." Jada leaned against the patio window, slid down onto her knees, dropped her face in her hands and wept. "I don't know what I'd do if you did the same to me."

I motioned for the violinist. He stood in the sand below our balcony and started playing our song. I squatted in front of her. "Was the fact that Wellington did right by Melanie the reason why you let Wellington believe for twenty years that he was Darius's father when he wasn't?"

As delicately as I could, I had to let Jada know that she too had imperfections and was no saint. Her silence affirmed my implication.

I held both of her hands. "Jada Diamond Tanner, I, Grant Hill, promise to be your faithful husband. To forsake all others, to make love only to you, and to never have sex with another woman as long as we are one. I promise to never sweat the small stuff. I want to share my dreams, my goals, my life with you, never taking you for granted. And I promise you that divorce is not an option . . . if you, will you, Jada Diamond Tanner, marry me?"

Jada was quiet again. Patiently, impatiently, I waited for her answer. If she didn't answer soon, could I rescind my proposal?

She asked, "Are you okay with not having children? I know how important that is to you."

Honestly, no, I was not okay with not having children. I wanted to be a father and a husband. "Are you okay with adoption?"

"Yes, I am, and yes, Grant Hill, I will marry you."

I expected her response to lead us into a deeper conversation. I'd figure it out later. I removed the diamond from my pocket, placed it in her hand.

"I want you to choose your setting."

Jada smiled, hugged my neck.

I carried her into the bathroom, the Jacuzzi already filled with warm water, red and white rose petals. This time I washed her head to toe. I dried her off, carried her to the bed, kissed her feet. I kissed her ankles, her legs, rotated my tongue behind her knees. Sucked the inside of her thighs. Licked the crevices of her lips. Her chocolate delight detained me as I sucked her clit. I kissed her stomach, navel, breasts, nipples, underarms, collarbone, neck, ears, forehead, and nose.

While kissing Jada's lips, I thought, *Today is the last day I'll lie next to her stroking my own dick.* I slowly penetrated her.

Jada was dry as a box of shredded wheat.

CHAPTER 51
HONEY

Fatigued.

I'd learned Valentino was right. I wasn't superwoman. My body had to knock me out, slow me down, and make me take care of me first. I was thankful Valentino had stayed with me two days ago, when Onyx left to go furniture shopping. I could've been in my office alone, passed out, and been brain-dead before anyone found me. I had stayed in the hospital overnight but I refused to lie on my back any longer, having nurses constantly draw blood, run test after test with no conclusive results. As cute as they may have thought I was, I was not their guinea pig.

I'd never been hospitalized, hadn't been to a hospital since I'd last seen my sister alive. I had to get back to work and home, in that order. After I insisted I be released immediately, Valentino appeared, and it was only seven in the morning! He promised to take care of me and he did. Each time I pleaded to go to the office, he made me rest, saying, "After your follow-up appointment, if the doctor releases you to work, I'll take you to your office. Not before."

I was self-employed. The doctor couldn't tell me when to work. But I fought a battle that Valentino wasn't going to let me win.

My bedroom was my sanctuary. Quietly, I opened my patio door, went outside, sat on the deck. I'd almost forgotten about my Georgia peach trees. Red Velvet crossed my mind. I smiled. She had so much zest for life.

Zest. Other than Velvet, whom did I know who had zest? Not the women and girls I was helping. Not Valentino or Benito. Not Grant. Couldn't say definitively about Jada but I doubted it. Not my mother or my father. Not my girls. Not me. I guess one either had it or didn't. And if someone had it, how long would they keep it? And if they didn't have zest, how could they genuinely acquire it?

Valentino was asleep in my bed. The early morning sunshine beamed so bright, I started squinting, looking at the leaves on my trees. Leaves, branches, fruit — interdependent. All relying on the roots to provide nutrients. Kind of like a human body needing us to make healthy choices to care for our bodies from the inside out. Unhealthy foods could deteriorate our organs, destroy our arteries. And unhealthy habits, behaviors, could be just as destructive.

My body had weathered many storms and faced another. Unaware of what my test results would reveal, I didn't want to go to the doctor's office this morning. I'd never taken a blood test before where I had to schedule an appointment for the results. Pap smears, had so many I could do my own.

Fear consumed me. What if, out of all the johns I'd fucked, one was infected? Condoms were mandatory but occasionally broke. What if Benito had contracted something and given it to me? What if Grant had an STD? I'd indirectly had sex with all the women my sex partners had fucked. Grant had fucked Red Velvet, Sapphire, probably Jada, and whomever else. I had no idea who Benito had sexed while we were together. I fucked Valentino once, not so long ago. If he had something, I could have it too.

My family history was a mystery. I didn't know if my mother or father or their parents had diabetes, hypertension, or any forms of cancer. Soon I hoped I'd know what caused me to faint.

"Hey, what are you doing out here?" Valentino joined me on the patio, where I sat at the table. "You want coffee? Juice? Water?"

"I'm good, thanks."

"How do you feel?"

"Nervous." I inhaled fresh air, trying to exhale my worries, release them into the universe. Too concerned to pull out that chair in the corner of my mind and sit a spell. "Have you ever taken a blood test?"

He shook his head, became introverted for a moment, then said, "I need to but if they told me something I wasn't ready to hear, that shit would fuck a nigga up."

"That's how I feel."

Valentino extended his hand. "Come here."

I repositioned myself to his lap. His arms embraced my waist.

I laughed, then said, "I'm more afraid of these results than I was when you kidnapped me. I could've shot and killed you. But if I have an incurable or life-threatening disease, it's not that simple."

"Lace, I'll be there for you no matter what," he said. "I promise you."

"Sounds good. Easy to say now."

Valentino slapped my ass. "Go get ready for your appointment."

I cried in the shower. Called myself a big baby. What was I really crying for? Losing Grant? Not loving my parents? How nice Valentino was to me? I brushed my teeth, stared at my naked self in the mirror. I was the picture of what men considered gorgeous. But my exterior was a shell. What if I had breast cancer and had to have a mastectomy? What if I lost my long luscious golden hair to chemo? I put on a pair of emerald slacks — green was the color of faith. A long sleeve blouse in pink, which represented grace and elegance. And my pink and green sling-back shoes.

I peeped my head out the patio window. Valentino was dressed in earth green pants and a matching short-sleeved collared shirt. "I'm ready," I said, dialing on my cell.

Onyx answered, "Hey, how are you feeling?"

"Nervous. We're headed to my appointment. We'll meet you at the office."

"It'll be okay. We're handling all of the clients. Take care of yourself now. We need you," she said.

"Thanks," I said, ending the call.

"I'm driving," Valentino said, following me to the driveway.

"I can drive. I'm not handicapped." Starting the car, I asked him, "When is Benito coming back?"

"That nigga got back with Tyra; she put it on him. He's stuck. No telling when that nigga will leave her house. Women are weak! That nigga was MIA damn near all his son's life, then walked back into her life and she let him stay there?" Valentino shook his head.

"Benito is annoying but he is a good person. And he's smarter than most people assume," I said in his defense. Parking in the hospital's garage, I silently prayed for courage.

CHAPTER 52
HONEY

We entered the office, approached the receptionist. Flatly, I said, "I'm Honey Thomas."

"Yes, Ms. Thomas, I'll let the doctor know you're here. Have a seat," she said, tapping on her keyboard.

I thumbed through the newspaper and read, DECATUR WOMAN RAPED BY A MAN DRESSED LIKE A WOMAN. The headline saddened me. Ken Draper immediately came to mind but the condition I'd left him in, the only way he could rape anyone would be with a dildo.

The doctor's assistant opened a door. "Honey Thomas."

"Yes," I said, putting the paper on the end table. I had my own worries.

Valentino followed me, held my hand.

"Sir, you can wait out here," the assistant said, blocking Valentino's entry into the patients' private area.

"It's okay. I want him to come with me." Whatever the results were, they weren't going to change because Valentino was in the lobby. His hearing at the same time meant I wouldn't have to repeat whatever the doctor said.

"Ms. Thomas, hello. How are you feeling?" the doctor said. "Please, have a seat."

"I'm good," I answered, sitting on the vinyl love seat with Valentino.

"And you are?" the doctor asked Valentino.

"Her friend with benefits, BFF, whateva," Valentino said, bringing a smile to my face. I was relieved he hadn't called the doctor a nigga.

"Okay, let's get to it," the doctor said, flipping through my chart. He looked up at me. Then smiled. "Congratulations, Honey."

I smiled. "You mean I'm fine? I'm healthy? I was just stressed?

The doctor smiled back at me and nodded. "Yes, you are healthy. And you're pregnant."

No way. My smile shrunk. My face and neck tensed, body became numb. I pressed my lips flat together. Frowned. Tucked my hand between my thighs. Covered my mouth with my other hand. I felt the tears forming inside my eyes. Placed my elbow on my knee, my forehead in my hand.

Rested my chin in my palm. Instantly I thought *abortion,* but did I really want to kill my baby? I couldn't make that decision right now.

Valentino placed his arm around my shoulders, took my hand with his other arm. "Baby, it's okay."

"Easy for you to say, knowing it's not yours," I cried.

"It *is* mine. Honey, I promised you I wasn't going anywhere, and I'm not. I want you to marry me."

Chapter 53
Sapphire

Eight months later . . .

I woke up in Charlotte to the sound of young voices laughing. What had I gotten myself into?

Knock. Knock.

"Just a minute," I said, tying my robe. "Come in.

"Ms. Bleu, we're hungry," the boys said in unison, sitting on the bed.

The time on the digital clock displayed 8:00 AM. "Where's your dad?"

"He went to the —" Santonio's older son covered his brother's mouth with his hand.

"Store. He went to the store," the older son said, then spun his brother around, held his shoulders.

These two were so amazing. Happy kids, full of life. Zest. Joy. Love.

Facing me, the younger brother said, "We want to go out for breakfast. Please."

Was I being set up to do something Santonio had told them not to? "What did your father say?"

"Dad doesn't mind," the younger one said.

"Okay. Give me twenty minutes to pull it together."

"Can you pin your hair up? We like your hair pinned up," the older brother said.

"Go," I said, smiling. *Pin my hair up?*

Children certainly added energy to a house. Santonio saved me that day I'd planned on killing Alphonso, provided me with a happier environment. Once a month I went to visit my mother. Last month Santonio and I took the boys to Los Angeles. We went to Universal Studios and Disneyland. My mother went with us.

I showered, slipped into my cerulean silk pants and a matching button-up blouse. Put on my three-inch aqua slip-ons, opened the bedroom door. "Boys, you guys ready?" I asked, walking toward the living room.

As I approached the dining room, I heard the boys yell, "Surprise!"

Blue and silver balloons covered the ceiling. A three-tier cake sat on the dining room table. "Okay, that cake is too small for your dad to pop out of. Where is he?"

"Happy birthday, beautiful."

I turned around. Santonio was suited in a tuxedo. He handed me a bouquet of wild magnolias. My throat tightened. I swallowed hard as I hugged him. "I'm dreaming."

The boys hugged us. The older son stepped back, cleared his throat. The younger positioned his father beside me. They faced us.

The younger one said, "It's kinda like a dream but it's real."

Santonio hunched his shoulders. "I promise you I did not put them up to this."

The older son said, "Dad, we like her."

The younger son chimed in, "And, Dad, we haven't seen you this happy since Mom died."

"Sapphire, you're really nice to us. We like the way you take time to listen to us."

"We like the way you teach us life skills, and thanks for teaching us how to drive."

Santonio's eyes widened.

Speaking without parting my lips, I said, "That was supposed to be our little secret." I smiled at Santonio. "I know they don't have a license but they are teenagers and you trust them to ride with their friends. You never know what might happen, and their knowing how to drive could save their lives."

His older son said, "Yeah, see, Dad? That's one of the many reasons we think she's so cool."

The younger son moved his hands from behind his back. The older son opened a small box, then said, "Sorry, Dad. You were taking too long."

In unison they said, "Sapphire, will you marry our dad?"

I couldn't help but to laugh. The widest smile crossed my face.

Santonio's lips pressed together as he tried not to laugh himself. "That's my boys. Wow." He shook his head. "I guess I'm the only one who hasn't asked then. . . . . Sapphire, will you marry us?" Santonio said, removing the ring from its box. Santonio's thick fingers almost dropped the tiny single chipped diamond in a silver setting.

"If you say yes, I'll get you another ring, beautiful," Santonio said.

"I don't want another ring. The ring is perfect and so are my guys. Yes, I will marry all of you," I said. "Are we going to breakfast?" I asked.

"Can't be gettin' mad! What you mad? Can't handle that! . . ." resonated from the bedroom. "Excuse me. That's probably my mom."

It definitely wasn't my boss, because I'd turned in my badge after I was supposed to kill Alphonso. Every now and then I wondered if I'd done the right thing. I hoped it was my mother so I could share my joy.

I smiled, then answered, "Hey, Red Velvet."

"Red Velvet was my stripper name. Velvet Waters is my stage name. I go by Velvet now. Happy birthday, Sapphire," she said. Her voice was upbeat.

"Thanks, Velvet." I wasn't sure I wanted to tell her about my engagement quite yet. "How are things?"

"I called to invite you to my screening. You, plus one guest," Velvet said.

"My day couldn't possibly get any better. I'd love to come." I gave her my mailing address.

"Charlotte?" she asked.

"I'll explain later." Ending the call, I inhaled deeply, left the bedroom, and walked into the arms of . . . my mother?

"Happy birthday, baby." She wrapped her arms around me, rocked me, then said, "I love you, Sapphire. I'm so glad God gave us, gave *me* a second chance to be a real mother. I promise, this time I won't mess it up."

CHAPTER 54
RED VELVET

"Mommy, Mommy, wake up. It's your big day. It's the screening we've been waiting for." Ronnie tugged my covers, then climbed in my bed and lay on top of me.

I tickled his tummy really good. "You happy? You happy? You happy?"

"Yes! Stop it! Stop it!" he laughed, tickling me.

"You stop it," I said, smothering his face with kisses.

"You two stop it," my mom said, standing in the doorway.

"Grandma, come here," Ronnie said, smiling.

My mother sat on the edge of the bed. "Ronnie sweetheart, go make your bed and straighten up your room for Grandma."

"What about the maid?" he asked. "Isn't she supposed to do that on special occasions?"

My mother gave Ronnie a stern look.

"Okay, I'm going," he said.

"Velvet, sit beside me, baby," my mom said.

"What is it? Everything okay?"

With my mom, I never knew if she was going to take me back to my childhood, if she was going to tell me what to do, or ask a ton of questions to hear what I was thinking.

"Velvet, this is your day. This is the day you'll witness all your hard work and dedication in front of the camera on the big screen. Stay focused. I'm not going to be here forever, so I want you to keep Ronnie grounded, you hear me?"

I nodded. "Yes, Mama."

"Don't get so busy that you forget to be a mother to your son. Do you understand?"

I nodded again. "Yes, Mama."

"Don't just 'yes mama' me. Hear what I'm saying."

I exhaled. This was *my* big day. Why was my mother so serious? "Ma, you okay?"

"I'm fine, baby, but seeing so many things happen like that plane landing in the Hudson, the planes in Denver and San Jose taking off, then returning shortly after takeoff all because of geese and seagulls being sucked into the engines. And that plane that snapped into three pieces on the runway.

The world is changing, sweetheart. People are so busy living with cell phones, the Internet, GPS and tracking systems, and flying around the world. They don't know where their home is anymore."

I hugged my mother. "Ma, you are the best mother. I wouldn't be here without you. And I wouldn't be the woman that I am without your love and support. Thanks."

"I want you to give thanks to the men who really matter."

Men? Okay, now my mom is tripping.

"Before you shower, eat, make or answer a phone call, give thanks to the Lord. Then make sure you call Brennen. That man loves you and your son. He's going to ask you to marry him. I can feel it. And when he does, your family will come before me."

"Aw, no, Mom. That's not so."

Tears flowed from both of us. My mom was worried about us leaving her. Los Angeles wasn't her home. She'd come here for me. And I was so excited, I hadn't thought about her.

"Ma, I'm not sure Brennen will ask me to marry him. But if he does, you're going to live with us. I will not leave you alone."

Mama smiled. "When you stand on stage today, be in the moment, baby. Take in every second. I know you've invited Honey,

408

Grant, and Sapphire and their guests, but do not let anything take you away from your time. This is your day, baby, and Mama is so proud of you. I love you."

"I love you too, Ma."

Mothers were the foundation. Before I thanked the Lord for my success, I'd thank Him for my mother. She'd taken, not good, but excellent, care of me. I was not going to abandon her. If Brennen should happen to ask me to marry him, he'd have to agree to my mother living with us or there'd be no us standing at the altar.

CHAPTER 55
GRANT

Jada taught me a lot about menopause.

Once she started on bioidentical hormone therapy, our life together was amazing. Her mood didn't swing due to a hormone imbalance. Her vaginal dryness was no more. And she initiated sex as much as me.

One year from the day that I had proposed to Jada we'd set our wedding date. With sixteen weeks left, our plans were finalized. The wedding was a million-dollar investment. Jada's son Darius prepaid all expenses, saying, "I haven't seen my mother this happy in a long time. My paying for the wedding and reception is my gift to my mother . . . and you. Do not fuck up."

Fucking up was not part of my plans. I was only getting married once. I'd flown with Jada to Los Angeles. Preseason for basketball was underway. We'd enjoyed watching Darius play the night before at the Staples Center but my excitement tonight was attending Velvet's screening.

"I really don't want to go to the premiere with you," Jada said as we shared a bottle of wine. "You know she's going to be there. I'd rather not attend. Why don't you go without me? I can have dinner with Darius, Fancy, and my grandson."

"Why does Fancy travel everywhere with the baby and Darius?" I asked, hoping to soften Jada's attitude.

"We've been together long enough. You already know the answer to that question," Jada said. She left the bedroom, sat in a chair in the living room.

Fancy was wise for making sure Darius's pussy was always available to him. If more women felt that way, they'd keep their men happy.

The one-bedroom suite was the same room we'd stayed in for the Grammys. The welcome fruit basket filled with oranges, apples, and bananas sat on the coffee table. I peeled a banana, bit a chunk, then said, "Baby, please. Do it for me. You're my fiancée. She's not. I love you. I don't love Honey. It's been eight and a half months since I've seen or heard from Honey. She's moved on. We've moved on. I'm going to show my support for Red Velvet."

Jada snapped. "Red Velvet? You're going

because of her, not Honey? You're sure?"

"Velvet Waters, yes. Baby, please. I don't want to go without you."

What had happened to Jada? It wasn't that serious. She was tripping off Honey when I'd had zero communication with Honey since . . . the last time we'd had unprotected sex. What if Honey was still angry? What if she confronted Jada and told her we had sex that night? I'd already told Jada what happened, but not the whole story, and I didn't want her to hear it from Honey.

"It's okay. I understand. I'ma go get dressed. I'll go alone," I said.

"You're going without me?" she asked.

I bit my bottom lip, then said, "I'm going. You decide whether or not you want to go."

I showered, shaved, put on my black tuxedo, splashed on cologne. Secretly, I did want to see Honey. I knew she'd be there. How would I react when I saw her? Who would be her date? Not having to worry about Jada studying my every move, I stepped out of the bathroom, admired myself in the full-length mirror. How would Honey react?

Jada was seated in the same chair dressed in her long orange gown with purple accents. Her hair was pulled back into a bun, and her lips were a dazzling peach. "I'm ready. You're right. I should go."

"Why'd you change your mind?" I asked.

"The question is, have you changed your mind?"

Women were so complicated. Jada had me questioning if marriage was right for us. I'd noticed we no longer completed one another's sentences after I'd lied about not using protection with Honey. Was that my fault?

Jada stood, opened the door. "Let's go."

Awkward silence filled the limo en route to the theater. When we arrived, the driver opened the door. The first person I saw that I knew was Sapphire.

"Hey, Grant. How are you? This is my husband, Santonio Ferrari."

Ferrari as in the family that owned the cars? I wondered. Probably not. Sapphire wouldn't fit into that circle.

"Please to meet you," he said, extending his hand.

Wow! Sapphire's glow lit up the red carpet. What a difference that Santonio guy had made in her. Sapphire had lost a few pounds in the right places. Her waistline was streamlined. Her face more defined. Her DDD were bangin' and on exhibit.

"Hi, I'm —"

"Jada Diamond Tanner, mother of Darius Jones and my fiancée," I finished for her.

"Fiancée?" Sapphire commented. She looked at me, then Jada, and said, "Pleased to meet you," and walked away with her husband.

After exchanging pleasantries, we walked the red carpet. The ushers escorted us to our front row seats. Perfect. Jada and I were seated on the aisle. Sapphire and her husband were seated in the row behind us.

I was excited and disappointed that Honey was not there.

CHAPTER 56
HONEY

Stomach pains, spotting. The timing was horrible.

Valentino paced from the vanity to the tub. "Lace, I should take you to the hospital. Please let me," he said, standing in front of me.

"I'm not having my babies in Los Angeles. These pains will pass." I'd spent the last hour on and off the toilet. The contractions were sporadic but more than an hour apart. I prayed this was a false labor and that they'd go away. I didn't want some strange doctor delivering my babies.

"Can we weigh on the side of caution? Please, Lace," Valentino pleaded.

"I'm getting up. I'm getting dressed. And we are going to the screening. That's final."

"Lace, we're already late. I think our boys are coming tonight."

Valentino was happier than me when the doctor had said there were two heartbeats.

When the ultrasound showed both were boys, he'd shouted, "Yes!" like they were his seeds.

"Late is relative. I'm sure there are preliminaries. The screening probably won't start for another hour. I can't disappoint Velvet on her big night."

"I understand, baby, but by the time we get dressed and get there, they'll have started."

I stood, washed my face for the tenth time. I reapplied my makeup, removed the band from my ponytail, and slung my hair left, then right. I stepped into my boy shorts, tucked in a sanitary pad. In the bedroom, I took my red spaghetti strap ankle-length dress off the hanger and over my head, then slid on my five-carat engagement ring.

"Fine," Valentino conceded, escorting me out the door.

CHAPTER 57
HONEY

We arrived at the theater just as an usher was preparing to close the doors. My being pregnant gave us an advantage. The usher had refused to seat a couple ahead of us, but she looked at my stomach and said, "Follow me," leading the way.

Holding my hand, Valentino followed her.

The usher said, "Excuse me, sir, these people need to be seated quickly."

Grant looked up at me, down at my stomach, then stared at Valentino. Jada stared at my stomach, then at Grant. I sat in the seat next to Jada; Valentino sat to my right. I decided to sit next to Jada for two reasons. One, to keep Valentino from kicking Grant's ass if Grant got out of line. Two, in case my contractions became too intense, I'd be closer to the aisle.

Sapphire tapped my shoulder. "Hey, Honey. How are you? Hi, Valentino."

I turned around and smiled. She looked

fantastic. "Hey, we have to get together after the screening. A lot has changed," I said, rubbing my stomach.

"For me too," she said, holding up her ring finger. "This is my husband, Santonio Ferrari."

The lights dimmed. I whispered, "Nice to me you, Santonio."

Valentino held my hand throughout the movie. Velvet was remarkable. She played the role of CoCo so well I prayed she'd win a few awards or at least get nominated her first time out. Forty-five minutes into the movie, I moaned, "Owww."

Valentino whispered, "Lace, you okay?"

"I'm good," I lied.

I heard Jada ask Grant, "She changed her name back to Lace?"

He replied, "I don't know. I haven't talked with her. I told you that."

I whispered, "Hush."

Jada spoke to me. "I know you're not hushing me."

"Baby, it's okay," Grant and Valentino said in unison.

I chilled. Another forty-five minutes and the lights came on. Velvet was so wonderful I was glad we'd come.

"Baby, look," Valentino said.

"Oh, my, gosh. I cannot believe my ears."

Tears filled my eyes. I let them fall.

Jada whispered, "Hush."

I ignored her. She was not ruining this special moment. Brennen Mosely was proposing to Velvet. As he concluded with putting the ring on Velvet's finger, the audience gave them a standing ovation.

While everyone stood, I alone remained seated and stunned. My water broke. Not wanting to spoil the moment, I sat in a soaked seat, fluids streaming down my legs to the floor.

"Move, Grant. Let me out," Jada said, tilting her ass in my face.

I hissed, "Inconsiderate bitch," as she slipped on my fluids.

"What the hell?" she yelled.

Grant caught her. Regaining her balance, she pushed him away.

I whispered to Valentino, "Baby, my water bag broke. We've got to go."

"I'm going with you," Sapphire said, then shouted, "We're having a baby!"

People behind us divided their attention between clapping when Velvet said, "Yes, I will marry you," and the mama drama I'd suddenly found myself starring in.

Grant didn't move.

"Nigga, best you get your ass out the way," Valentino said.

Sapphire said, "Grant, what is your problem? Move!"

Grant stepped into the aisle, stared at my stomach again. Tucked his tongue between his teeth and upper lip. Jada stood beside him, then sarcastically said, "Congratulations."

I was cool. Wasn't going there with her insecure behind. I stood in front of her and Grant, then said, "Yes, congratulations are in order."

"Baby, don't talk to him," Valentino said.

"Can we just get to the hospital?" Sapphire said, standing behind Valentino.

Jada sternly said, "Grant, let's go."

"Wait," Grant said, looking at me. I held my stomach as he asked, "Honey, is that my baby?"

"Nigga, if I have to tell you —" Valentino began.

I reached behind me, placed my hand on Valentino's side. "It's okay, baby." I wasn't sure who was listening more closely for my response, Grant or Jada. I said, "Baby, he should know the truth," then told Grant, "No, it's not your baby."

Grant exhaled. Jada answered her cell phone, "Hey, sweetheart. I'm sorry I forgot to call and cancel for dinner. I'm okay . . . no really I am. . . ."

420

Grant nodded to me as if saying, "Get going."

I stood one inch from his face and said, "It's not your child but these babies are your twin boys."

Jada lowered her phone, then said, "Grant, she's lying. You told me you didn't fuck her without a condom," pressing the phone back to her ear. "I'm sorry, Darius. I didn't hear you, baby. . . . Grant, let's go." Jada proceeded to walk off.

"You mind moving out of my way?" I said. "I'm the one in labor."

"Grant," Jada cried. "Fancy was hit by a drunk driver. We've got to go to the hospital."

"Give me a minute," Grant said as if he hadn't heard her. "Honey, why didn't you say something?"

I backed away from him. "Would it have mattered? Say something just so I could hear you tell me how I trapped you? How I planned this? So you could blame me for ruining your chances with Jada? So you'd stay with me because of the kids? What would you have done if I had told you, except call me a liar? Huh?"

"Grant! Did you hear me? Darius's wife was hit by a drunk driver! Let's go."

"I've gotta go," Grant said to me, then

told Valentino, "You're not raising my boys. Those are my twins."

Sapphire hopped over the back of the seat, moved Grant aside. "Come on, Honey. We've got to get you to the hospital."

Grant seemed confused. A part of me was relieved that he knew. The other part wished he'd never known.

EPILOGUE: HONEY

Twelve hours in labor, stitches in my vagina, and seven days in the same hospital with Darius's wife, Fancy. Valentino stayed with me the entire week except short periods of time to go to our hotel room to shower, change clothes, and snag a few hours of sleep.

Valentino kissed me. "Baby, it's time to feed again," he said, holding Luke.

I eased my pinky finger at the tip of my left areola, handed him London.

Luke latched on to my right breast immediately. I could tell Luke was more like me and London was more like Grant. Luke was my firstborn. He fed first and he'd only nurse from my right breast. He slept an hour at a time as though he'd miss something if he slept longer.

London was mellow. As long as he ate he was fine. London didn't fuss. He took his time coming out, an hour after his brother.

He slept peacefully. London ate slower but his reflexes were faster than Luke's. I was happy that they both smiled a lot.

The boys were identical and had my green eyes, slick dark hair, and my skin color. They were long like Grant, both twenty-three inches. Handsome like Grant too.

"What do you think they'll grow up to be?" Valentino asked, rocking Luke.

"London will design spaceships and Luke will be an astronaut," I said, not knowing if that were true, but I believed they'd be street smart and extremely successful.

Valentino was great with the boys. A part of me hoped we'd get his twins and his son Anthony together but Summer had moved and no one knew where she was. The last time Valentino called her, the number belonged to someone else. He feared Summer had gone crazy after Sunny was killed. Perhaps one day he'd see his kids.

"You're a great mom already," he said, kissing my forehead. "You should've seen how wide your pussy opened," Valentino said, stretching his hands apart. "I almost passed out but I refused to give that nigga Grant bragging rights about how he saw the boys first. Still say you should've given them my last names."

"I know, but he is their father," I said.

"And when I recover, you're going to get this good pussy for the second time in your life every which way."

Valentino smiled. I studied his face.

"What?"

"Can't believe you're the same man. You're so gentle with the boys."

He kissed my forehead, took London, who'd fallen asleep in the middle of eating. "I'ma take the boys to the nursery, grab a bite, and I'll be right back. You get some rest."

Valentino walked out. I closed my eyes, trying to find my "reserved" seat in the corner of my mind. A few minutes after sitting down with myself, I heard, "Hey, Mommy. How are you?"

Opening my eyes, I said, "I'm good," then asked Grant, "How's Fancy?"

"Not good. She's in a coma. Darius is freaking out. Jada had to make him go play ball, said there was nothing he could do at the moment. She's staying by Fancy's side and texting Darius every hour on the hour with a report." Grant held my hand. "I still wish you would've told me."

I shook my head. "Stop it. Please. I know I did what was best."

He nodded. "You have no idea how happy you've made me."

"Maybe you can tell me," Jada said, standing in the doorway.

Grant released my hand. "Don't come in here like that. You know I love you."

I smiled, recalling the times Grant and I shared those words. I also remember telling him, "Sometimes love isn't enough." Like musical chairs, I'd gotten up, and Jada had sat in my seat. Better her than me.

"I guess her having your babies could be a good thing," Jada said, standing by the door, inside my room. "You have your sons, we don't have to adopt, and we'll have joint custody," Jada said, as if the decision was hers.

"You will not touch my boys unless I say so," I told her.

"You, my dear, are an unfit mother. You don't deserve those boys. Keep it up and I'll make sure they're taken away," she said, excusing herself from my room.

I pointed at Grant. "You had better put that bitch in check. She does not know who she's fucking with. I don't give a fuck about your marrying her but if either of you fuck with my boys, I will kill you."

"Mommy, calm down. She's not serious," Grant said, holding my hand again.

I told him, "Let me say, you've been put on notice."

"Honey, you and I were never right for one another but . . ." He paused, pressing his fingers into his tears, then continued. "Now that you've had my boys, I will always have a place in my heart for you. Honey, you have given me the greatest gift a woman can give a man."

"Knock, knock," Sapphire said, walking in with Velvet and lots of flowers.

"I did not die. I had two babies," I said, laughing. "Y'all making me hurt my stomach."

"That's why we brought you two bouquets," Velvet said. "We know Luke has to have his own everything."

"And six ballons," Sapphire said. "You should've named one of the boys Bleu. But I do like the names you picked."

I frowned, tilted my ear toward the door. "Do I hear Luke crying?"

"Girl, you need some rest. This is a maternity ward. All babies cry," Sapphire said, sitting on one side of my bed while Velvet sat on the other.

"Grant, please. Go check on the boys," I said to his back. Grant was already on his way out the door.

"Let me see your ring, girl," I told Velvet, reaching for her hand. "You think it's big enough? Sorry about interrupting your proposal. Damn! Congratulations are in order. You are one bad bitch."

Sapphire said, "I second that emotion. I've seen her make a full water bottle disappear in her pussy and come out empty."

Velvet's smile was wide and bright. "Yeah, I guess stripping has its benefits."

Sapphire said, "If anyone would've bet that the three of us . . . each of us, would be in happy meaningful relationships, I would have told them they were crazy. I'm married to a wonderful man and both of you are happy and engaged. Honey, when you get settled back in Atlanta, we have to celebrate."

I held their hands, smiled. "I want both of you to be godmothers to my boys."

"I got Luke. He's a lot like you," Sapphire said.

"I guess that means I've got London. I'm going to teach him how to act."

Grant rushed into the room, interrupting our conversation. "Honey, did Valentino take the boys?"

"Yes, to the nursery." I sat up.

Sapphire and Velvet stood.

Grant shook his head. "The boys are not in the nursery."

"What!" I placed my feet on the floor. My vagina hurt so bad I had to sit down.

"Velvet, you stay here with Honey," Sapphire said. "I'll find them."

Velvet held me. I cried until Grant and Sapphire came back to the room with the nurse. Valentino walked in behind the nurse. "What's going on?"

The nurse said, "A woman came into the nursery after you left." She pointed at Valentino. "Said she was with Child Protective Services. We were obligated to . . ."

Valentino and Sapphire ran out of the room. Grant rushed out too.

"Get out!" I yelled at the nurse.

Velvet sat on the side of my bed facing me. "Luke and London will be back shortly. I'm sure it was a simple mix-up. . . ."

As Velvet continued talking, I got up, gathered my open gown in the back. I held my stomach, dragged my feet two steps from my bed.

Valentino entered my room. "We're on it, baby."

A police officer opened the door, then asked, "Honey Thomas?"

"Yes, I'm Honey Thomas. Where are my boys?"

The officer asked, "Do you have knowledge of the whereabouts of Anthony Valentino James?"

My heart dropped to my stomach. My

body tensed. I closed my eyes.

Valentino said, "I'm Anthony Valentino James."

I looked at him, at my BFF, and wanted to cry but I didn't.

The officer gripped his cuffs, locked Valentino's hands behind his back, and said, "You're under arrest for grand theft auto. Anything you say can and will be held against you."

"Velvet, go find Sapphire!" I cried.

Velvet ran out the door.

I removed Valentino's ring from my finger, placed it in his hand, then said, "Don't worry. Sapphire will have you out in no time."

Valentino dropped the ring on the floor, then asked, "Lace, why?"

Not responding, I watched the officer escort him out, praying Valentino hadn't betrayed me. Did he know where my boys were? If he didn't, was Valentino the kind of man I wanted to raise Luke and London?

We both knew Valentino had stolen that car. What I didn't know was how the police in Los Angeles knew about the car theft in Atlanta. As upset as I was about Valentino, I was furious not knowing where my boys were. Alone in my room, I could not continue to lie in bed doing nothing but worrying. I had to do something. I made it to my door, opened it.

Jada stood in front me, shrugged her shoulders.

The space in front of my eyes faded to black.

Silently I prayed.

Brain? Courage? Heart?

ACKNOWLEDGMENTS

I thank the Creator for blessing me with you, the person who has chosen to read *Unconditionally Single.* I pray your life is filled with self-love, peace, and prosperity. FYI, Mary B. Morrison is the name my parents gave me at birth, HoneyB is my pseudonym. I write under both names.

I am grateful and appreciative for the independent booksellers, chain bookstore staffs, and library employees. I don't know all of you by name but I want to say thanks for supporting me and my career.

My son, Jesse Bernard Byrd Jr., is my pride and joy and he's the journalist for his basketball team at UC Santa Barbara. You can read Jesse's Journal online at: *http:// ucsbgauchos.cstv.com/sports/m-baskbl/ ucsb-m-baskbl-body.html.* I have to admit, at twenty-two, Jesse writes better than his mom. I'm trying to convince him to write a novel. Somewhere between basketball, college, and his personal life. We'll see.

I thank and dedicate this novel to Selena James, who's young, perky, vibrant, wise, and just the best damn editor. My world of writing wouldn't be the same without my scintillating editor, Karen R. Thomas. My wonderful agents, Andrew Stuart and Claudia Menza, I appreciate all you do.

Both of my parents have made their transitions into eternity, my mother when I was nine years old, and my father when I was twenty-four years old. They blessed me with the greatest siblings — Wayne Morrison, Andrea Morrison, Derrick Morrison, Regina Morrison, Margie Rickerson, and Debra Noel.

Much love to my friends Gloria Mallette, Victor McGlothin, E. Lynn Harris, Richard C. Montgomery, Felicia Polk, Marissa Monteilh, Kimberly Kaye Terry, Vera Warren-Williams, Michele Lewis, Kim Mason, Eve Lynne Robinson, Mother Bolton, and Sarah Brown aka Indie Jackson.

Feel free to hit me up with a piece of your world at www.MaryMorrison.com. Peace and prosperity.

MY PUSSY — MY PREROGATIVE

BY MARY B. MORRISON

My pussy
My prerogative

The last time I'd checked
My pussy was attached to me
Not some wanna be lover
Claiming my pussy
Was his pussy
And reciting the same line
To the other
Pussy in his face
After I cum
He's gone without a trace

You see this pussy
That's between my legs
Is attached to a head
With brains
That can drive a man insane

My pussy

My prerogative
To give
Or to keep
To remain celibate

To sale a bit
Or to creep
Or to freak

To snap
Or to rap
Around a man's head
In and out of bed

Unconditionally
My pussy is
My prerogative

Wanna taste
Wanna slide into first base
Second? Seconds?
Third? Thirds?
My pussy has the first and final words
On whether your dick is worthy
Not
If your dick is dirty
Your pockets are dry
You're a selfish lover
Your back hurts
You cum before my pussy gets wet

You leave right after your cum is dry
Don't ask me why
I refuse to let you fuck me
Just take your dick
And let my pussy be
Free to choose
The right stroke
The right man
The right lover
The right dick

Unconditionally
For as long as I live
It's my clit
My pearl
My pussy
My world
My prerogative

Cum correct
Or don't cum at all

DISCUSSION QUESTIONS

1. What's your definition of *unconditionally single?* I ask this question first because there are too many miserably married people and not nearly enough people who understand how to be happily single.

2. I believe couples are better off ending an unhealthy relationship. Have you stayed in a relationship too long? What characters in *Unconditionally Single* do you feel should stay together? Why? What characters should not be together? And which characters should have never developed a relationship?

3. Do you believe some marriages fail because the couple is incompatible? How important is compatibility? Do you believe opposites attract? Explain.

4. Should women bear arms? Do you think

the federal government should permit adult citizens to legally carry weapons? Would our country be safer? Why or why not?

5. Who do you believe is involved in the disappearance of Luke and London Hill? Jada? Grant? Valentino? Sapphire? Child Protective Services? All of them? None of them?

6. Under what circumstances do you believe it's better to be married or single? I believe that marriage is overrated and undervalued. What do you think? Why?

7. After not caring for his son for years, Benito moved in with his baby's mother, Tyra. Do you know women who allow men to come and go as they please? Why do you believe Tyra should have allowed Benito in her home and her son's life?

8. Do you believe people can change their ways? Most of the characters changed during the series. Which ones are believable?

9. Is it possible for one person to satisfy all of your sexual needs and fantasies? Before answering, what are your sexual needs and

fantasies? Do you believe Grant will remain faithful to Jada? Will they marry? Why or why not?

10. Do you think Honey should've given Valentino eighteen million dollars? Do you feel Honey should've allowed Valentino to help her with her business? Do you believe Valentino reformed?

11. Considering how Honey was observant of her surroundings, how important is it for a woman to pay attention to details? Do you feel Honey should've shot Ken Draper? Should she have killed Reynolds? Does Honey deserve to go to jail? Explain.

12. Would you marry a man like Grant? Like Hunter? Valentino? Benito? Why or why not?

13. Which book did you enjoy most in the Honey Diaries series? Do you feel there should be a book 4 in this series? E-mail me at marybmorrison@aol.com with your response.

INSTANT MESSAGE
FROM MARY "HONEYB" MORRISON

I'm asking ALL adults to support me in sharing this very important message.

EDUCATE, DON'T PROCREATE

There is no reason ANY teenage girl should have a baby. None. We have too many teenagers getting pregnant for all the wrong reasons. It's time for adults to stop under-educating young females and start empowering them. I'm most concerned with the females because the majority of males are not accepting responsibility for their actions.

I understand that most African-American women suffer from post-slavery sexual trauma. Whether it was our parents misinforming or undereducating us, our being molested and raped, battered and abused, or our being taught that sex out of wedlock is sinful, it's time for a monumental epiphany in the way women of all nationalities view sex and our bodies. As a woman who is comfortable with my sexuality, I want to spark an empowering sexual movement for other women.

Young girls should be educated about their bodies and their hormones. They need to know safe sex practices. They need to know they are in control, not the guys.

I hope you join me in imparting this very important message to our young girls.

PURPOSE OF BEING UNCONDITIONALLY SINGLE

PART II

SEXUAL KNOWLEDGE IS POWERFUL

I have fun dating whomever I like, knowing that the man I will enter into an open relationship with will show up. I don't have to build him, change him, or create him out of clay. (But if I did build him, I'd use Stephen A. Smith as my model). I don't have to look under the covers or search the corporate boardroom for him. I meet men everywhere I go.

Here are my relationship needs:

- He must be intelligent, highly capable of expressing his views on politics, the youth, the elderly, the recession, religion, sex, and sexuality.
- He must have friends. A man's friends tell you a lot about him. I don't want to be his only best friend.
- He cannot be a minimalist, satisfied with getting by getting over to make

his ends. Minimalists are underachieving, shiftless, lazy leeches looking for handouts. I don't date cheap or selfish men. He can do bad on his own.

- He must be an entrepreneur or realistically striving to become his own boss. I don't mean the men who spit game about what they gon' do all the while they layin' up on a woman burying her under his philosophical bullshit. "Baby let's buy a _____to-ge-ther." Translation, his credit is fucked up. "Next."
- He cannot be envious of my success or my lifestyle. I work extremely hard. Trust me, lots of men are jealous of successful independent women. I'm a full-time writer for two major publishers. I travel extensively. I own Mary B. Morrison, Incorporated, Sweeter than Honey, and Lift Every Voice and Write (my nonprofit for students interested in writing).
- He must have a sense of humor (this ranks at the top of my list). He must know how to laugh and make me laugh. Have fun. And Lord knows he cannot be depressing, dragging around his garbage like he's a sanitation engineer. I'm no comedian, but I can be

silly at times. I love to make people laugh.

- Under no circumstances can he be broke. Hell-to-the-capital-N-O. I do not support men. A broke man should suck his own dick, then tuck his dick between his balls and fuck himself in the ass. Especially if he's sitting on his ass all day waiting for someone else to provide for him. I can't comprehend his mentality.

- He must be great sexually. Open to exploring new sexual territories. It amuses me that the men who are mediocre in bed say to me, "I hope I gave you some material for your book." All I can say is, "Obviously you haven't read my books." The guys who are skilled in bed know it.

- He must agree to an open relationship. Even if I never have sex with anyone except him, I can't commit to exclusivity because I might meet someone else that I decide to have sex with. It's not like I plan to meet a man who excites me. He usually shows up when I least expect him. Ladies, you know the ones that make your pussy pucker instantly. It's like, "Oh, damn. I'm definitely fucking him." No guilty pleasures for me.

- He must understand that he is my partner, not my dictator or dick-ta-tor. I have no need or desire for a second husband. Marriage is wonderful for those who need or want it. I don't. I'm happy and intend to stay this way.

Y'all, I can't stand talking to a man who says, "Call me later." Then when he calls me he says, "I thought you were supposed to call me." To avoid confusion, I say, "No, I'm not calling you later. When you want to talk, call me."

Then there are the ones who say, "Let me know when you want to go out." No, I'm not. If you want to go out, ask me. . . .

"So why didn't you call me when you got home?" Because you don't tell me when to call you, then hold me accountable to your request. Obviously I was busy. I've got things to do. . . .

"I like you but I'm not going to be the one calling all the time." Then we won't be talking. I don't mean to come across harsh but I've learned that men have fragile egos. Men are accustomed to creating situations to make women pursue them.

Black women and men are not taught how

to treat one another. We have inherited generational relationship dysfunctions. Our mothers' mothers' mothers were raped of their virginity, their children, and their men. Our father's father's fathers were used for breeding with no emotional attachment to family. We still deal with post-slavery trauma. We still struggle to genuinely love, appreciate, and respect one another. Black men must stop running away from their paternal obligations. Black women must stop unconsciously opening their legs and their hearts, giving birth to unwanted heartaches and babies. I know it's hard but we seriously have to think about the "what ifs" before we become involved. Our relationships will have a higher survival rate when we learn to respect one another. We have to start someplace. You are the catalyst for change in your life. Your relationship starts with you.

Stop entering into relationships primarily to fill a void of loneliness. Sometimes you're better off being alone. This doesn't mean you have to be lonely. I encourage parents to talk to their children and teenagers about healthy relationships. Take time to embrace and express your needs and desires. Irrespective of your partner's views, your open and honest communication will prove productive in your relationship.

In closing, I'll share with you the wisdom my father shared with me when I was fourteen years old. My daddy said, "Speedy, if you can't put it in your pocket and take it with you, don't worry about it. That goes for your house, your car, your money, and your man."

My dad, may his spirit shine bright throughout the universe, called me Speedy, not because I moved fast. Actually, I've always moved slowly. I eat slowly, I think a lot when I'm writing, and yes, I love slow, seductive, grinding sex. The exception, doggie-style. My dad called me Speedy because even as a child, when I made up my mind to do something, the only thing everyone could do was get out of my way. I was the one who would question him. So if I asked questions of my father, you can imagine that I always ask questions of the men in my life.

ABOUT THE AUTHOR

Mary B. Morrison is the *New York Times* bestselling author of *Who's Loving You, Sweeter Than Honey, When Somebody Loves You Back, Nothing Has Ever Felt Like This, Somebody's Gotta Be On Top, He's Just a Friend, Never Again Once More, Soul Mates Dissipate, Who's Making Love,* and *Justice, Just Us, Just Me.* She's also the co-author of *She Ain't the One* with *New York Times* bestselling author Carl Weber. Mary lives in Oakland, California. Her son, Jesse Byrd, Jr., is pursuing his vision to play in the NBA. Jesse is currently on scholarship with the UC Santa Barbara men's basketball team. Visit Mary and Jesse at www.mary morrison.com

The employees of Thorndike Press hope you have enjoyed this Large Print book. All our Thorndike, Wheeler, and Kennebec Large Print titles are designed for easy reading, and all our books are made to last. Other Thorndike Press Large Print books are available at your library, through selected bookstores, or directly from us.

For information about titles, please call:
(800) 223-1244

or visit our Web site at:
http://gale.cengage.com/thorndike

To share your comments, please write:
Publisher
Thorndike Press
295 Kennedy Memorial Drive
Waterville, ME 04901